CONUNDRUMS & COINCIDENCES

A Pride & Prejudice Variation

J MARIE CROFT

Quills & Quartos
PUBLISHING

Edited by Jo Abbott and Jan Ashton

Cover by Pemberley Darcy

ISBN 978-1-963213-77-5 (ebook) and 978-1-963213-78-2 (paperback)

To Kathy and Glance. They'll understand.

I

THE LETTER OF THE LAW

The guard was clad in livery and armed with a blunderbuss, two pistols, one timepiece, and a yard of tin—a long horn with which he alerted others to yield right of way. Beneath his feet, the letter was secured within a canvas sack in the coach's rear boot.

Sporting the words 'Royal Mail' on its doors, the vehicle was on an exact and demanding mission, stopping only for deliveries and collections at Enfield and Broxbourne before arriving in Meryton at several minutes past midnight. There, the sack was thrown down and landed with a thump at the feet of the waiting postmaster, who tossed an outgoing post-bag up to the guard and bid him Godspeed.

Mr Clark then locked the sack inside a safe in his office at the market town's coaching inn, The Copper Kettle.

Seven and a half hours later on that early-May morning, Mr Clark was back at his employment, opening the post-bag, sorting correspondence by family name, and completing a tedious but necessary written record of each item before placing it in its assigned pigeon-hole on the back wall. Being the inquisitive sort, he lingered over one particular letter addressed to a local girl in care of her father. Holding it up to sunlight streaming through a dingy window, he could distinguish the names on an enclosed card. "Odd. Her own uncle is an attorney. Why would Miss—"

The sound of the bell interrupted him. With a start, he shoved the letter into its slot and turned towards the jarring clangs.

"Good morning, Mr Clark." One of the Longbourn maids, either Patty or her sister Rose, smiled sweetly at him while setting down the heavy hand-bell. "Is there aught for Longbourn today?"

"Aye." The postmaster fetched four items from the Bennets' compartment. "These three look like mercantile invoices from tradespeople wanting accounts settled." He winked while handing them to her. "No doubt the result of Mrs Bennet's shopping on tick for fripperies in London, eh? And"—he paused, holding back the final piece—"this here seems intriguing." Before relinquishing the letter, he extended his other palm and waggled his fingers. "That will be sixpence per item, missy."

The maid hesitated. "Mr Bennet might gripe about paying for post from a stranger."

Leaning in, Mr Clark whispered, "I think it could be of great importance."

She passed him the necessary coins before snatching the letter from his hand.

☙❦❧

THANKFUL THAT COLONEL FORSTER'S MILITIA REGIMENT would be on its merry way to Brighton within a fortnight—taking Mr Wickham with it—Elizabeth hummed while lightly tripping down the stairs on a mid-May day. Upon reaching the bottom, she was met by her father, who had just come out of his library. "Good morning, Papa. You seem puzzled. Is aught amiss?"

"Ah, Lizzy, I was going to look for you. Come into my room."

She followed him thither, and her curiosity to know what he had to say was heightened by the supposition of its being in some manner connected with the sheets of paper in his hand.

Once they were settled across from one another in matching armchairs with faded upholstery, Mr Bennet held up the foremost page. "This letter has astonished me exceedingly. As it principally concerns you, you ought to know its contents."

Upon discerning the close, masculine penmanship, Elizabeth placed a hand over her heart and felt the rhythm of its pulsations quicken. With the writing resembling his, she was convinced the letter was another from Mr Darcy.

Since virtually memorising the missive he had written to her in Kent, and understanding—if not entirely agreeing with—his way of thinking, her animosity towards the gentleman had softened into something like esteem. But what might be his current opinion of her? Did he still wish to make her his bride? Had he the audacity to apply to her father first? With mixed sentiments over such a probability, she prayed the letter instead contained hope for Jane and Mr Bingley.

"Ahem, Lizzy. You have not attended to a word I just said, have you?" Peering over his spectacles, Mr Bennet tut-tutted. "I said that about a fortnight ago I received this letter. Today I opened it, thinking it might require immediate attention—an astute assumption on my part, seeing as it is from a Mr

3

Monroe of Pemberton & Monroe." He showed her a card with words printed in dark type. "You see? Puffed-up London attorneys."

"Town attorneys? Then how could the matter in any way concern me?" Having no limits, Elizabeth's imagination ran wild with drastic possibilities, and her entire face grew warm. Mr Darcy never seemed the vengeful sort. He certainly could not sue for breach of promise; he had made her an offer but was flatly refused.

Setting aside the missive and card, Mr Bennet observed his favourite daughter. "Your colour is exceptionally high. Have you a fever?" Leaning in, he aimed for her forehead with the back of one hand.

Batting away his fingers, Elizabeth said, "I am perfectly well, other than being in a fever of expectation about the letter's contents."

"Burning with curiosity, are you? Here," he said, handing the pages to her. "Mr Monroe may provide a measure of palliative but, sadly, no immediate remedy."

There was a slight tremor in her fingers as she read the attorney's tidings. In essence, she had been named as a beneficiary in the will of Miss Phoebe Armstrong, who had died in February. At their earliest convenience, and no later than the twenty-ninth of the month, she and her father were to meet with Mr Monroe of Pemberton & Monroe on Chancery Lane in London. A timely response, the attorney wrote, would be appreciated.

Elizabeth gave a huff of petty annoyance. "A *timely* response. Good grief, Papa, this letter was penned on the thirtieth of April."

"Yes, yes. But have you any idea who this Miss Armstrong was? Or has Mr Monroe committed some sort of clerical error?"

"It is rather peculiar. I was somewhat acquainted with Miss Armstrong, and I am grieved to learn of her death. She was the dear old lady from Buckinghamshire whom I assisted in Cheapside over a twelvemonth ago. At the time, she enquired where correspondence might be directed to me, and I subsequently received a very nice thank-you letter from her. Remember?"

Casting back her mind, Elizabeth recalled that November day, eighteen months ago.

❧

ON THAT PARTICULAR MORNING, MRS GARDINER HAD requested her visiting niece's assistance in choosing a pair of velvet slippers for Mattie, her eldest daughter.

It had been a pleasure for Elizabeth to accompany her aunt as they strolled through the bustling marketplace. With its hurry-scurry comings and goings of people and conveyances along Cheapside's busy thoroughfare, excursions in that part of the city left her either invigorated or enervated.

As they were about to cross the street, a terrible commotion arose to their left. Shouts of warning rang out. People fled hither and thither. Horses slipped on cobblestones, hoofs clattering. Women screamed. Handcarts overturned, spilling their goods. Out of the melee, a huge, mounted horse —ears back, eyes wild, nostrils flared—bolted in Elizabeth and her aunt's direction.

The panicked rider seemed helpless to control the frenzied creature's headlong course as it galloped straight for a beggarly old woman in the middle of the street. Bystanders hollered at her to move, but she seemed paralysed, staring slack-jawed at the advancing black menace.

Without a thought for her own safety, Elizabeth darted out onto the cobbles and into the horse's path. She grasped the woman's coarse sleeve and, just in the nick of time, gently but forcefully pulled her from harm's way.

Over her shoulder, Elizabeth shouted to the inexperienced rider. "Use your reins!" Although no skilled horsewoman herself, she had learnt to ride under her father's tutelage. Furthermore, she possessed more than her fair share of common sense. "Turn his head to the side! Stop forward movement!"

Leaving the shaken, trembling woman in her aunt's care, Elizabeth approached the horse and rider. "Easy now. Just keep turning him in small circles until he behaves."

"I am so terribly, terribly sorry!" cried the young man while carrying out Elizabeth's instructions. "Bailey has an excess of energy to burn this morning, and I should not have brought him to such an unfamiliar, busy place. All these people, the loud noises, and other horses have frightened him."

Once Bailey had calmed, the young man dismounted, tied his horse to a tethering ring, and joined the three women. His face was an alarming shade of red, and as he doffed his hat, Elizabeth saw a shock of copper-coloured hair and hazel eyes.

He bowed low to the elderly woman. "I most humbly beg your pardon, madam. Are you well? Have Bailey and I caused you any harm?" He fumbled about in a breast pocket. "Ah. Here is my card. My name is David Hadley. May I have the pleasure of knowing all your names?"

Mrs Gardiner provided her information as well as Elizabeth's.

"I am Miss Phoebe Armstrong from Buckinghamshire," said the elderly woman. "And you and that beast of yours, sir, are a danger not only to others but to yourself. However, thanks to this brave young miss"—she patted Elizabeth's arm —"I am unscathed."

After breathing a sigh of relief, Mr Hadley said he was comforted to hear it. "But please tell me how I may make amends for giving you such an awful scare."

Miss Armstrong assured him there was no need for reparation. Still, he insisted on doing her a kindness at the very least, so she gave him her direction. "If ever you find yourself passing through Buckinghamshire, stop and visit me at Oakwood Manor." With a catch in her voice, she added, "I have no one, you see."

Bowing over her hand, Mr Hadley said he was from Eton Wick and had an older brother living there at Eastmeadow Park. He promised to call on her whenever he was in her vicinity. Then, tipping his hat, he took leave of them all.

"Now, dearie," Miss Armstrong said to Elizabeth, "may I please have your direction? Once my hands stop shaking, I should like to convey my gratitude to you in writing."

While providing Longbourn's information, Elizabeth took particular notice of the woman's appearance. Of medium height and thin and sallow, Miss Armstrong was garbed in a black bonnet and a grey woollen cloak held together with rope, both items showing signs of considerable wear. Conversely, above pattens, her shoes sported shiny golden buckles, and she carried a gold-headed cane.

⚜

A YEAR AND A HALF LATER, HER FATHER'S VOICE ROUSED Elizabeth from her thoughts. "You were wool-gathering again, my dear. What would you like me to do about this letter? Shall I reply to the attorney with a polite refusal?"

"No." Elizabeth passed the papers to him. "Let us go to town and hear what Mr Monroe has to say. But please do not wait until the eleventh hour to reply to him."

"Very well. The epistolary debt is on my side, so I forthwith shall reply to this drafter of documents. Never let it be said I am a negligent or dilatory correspondent." Rising, Mr Bennet leant over to kiss the top of Elizabeth's head. "My little Lizzy, a beneficiary."

"Do not excite yourself, Papa. Miss Armstrong was little more than a beggar-woman…albeit one with golden buckles upon her shoes."

"Well, child, with any luck, those buckles might be bequeathed to you. Let us hope the benefaction will, at least, reimburse me the sixpence it cost to receive this letter."

Once seated at his desk, her father flung aside the missive and opened *Critique of Pure Reason*. "For the time being," he said from behind the book, "do not breathe a word of this to my wife. No need to add fuel to the flame. Our own curiosity may burn, but were your mother to learn of the possibility of a windfall, she would go up in smoke."

❧ 2 ❧

ELEVENFOLD

S itting in his carriage on a busy London street, Fitzwilliam Darcy tossed aside the newspaper and, for the second time, consulted his watch. Growing impatient, he drummed his fingers on his thigh. How he despised idleness and being left alone with his thoughts. *Only you, Elizabeth, with so few words, could have caused such agony.*

His appointment was arranged for eleven o'clock that morning, and, coincidentally, eleven minutes remained before he should sally forth. Were he the superstitious sort, eleven might be his unlucky number. Not that he remembered the incident, but at eleven months of age the young master had nearly succumbed to the measles.

When he was but eleven years of age, his beloved mother had breathed her last. Eleven years later, his father had died. In July of the year eleven, Darcy had installed his sister, Georgiana, at No 11 Chapel Place in Ramsgate. He should have known better. Her stay there nearly ended in a scandalous disaster.

Then, just five weeks past, on the eleventh of April—after

the woman Darcy loved had scathingly refused his offer of marriage—he had left Rosings Park a mortified, bitter, and heartbroken man.

He had not been expecting it. He had thought she and he had come to an understanding and that everything had been going swimmingly. Every detail of how their life together would unfold had been carefully planned. But those castles he had built in the air had fallen to the ground and shattered like glass on stone.

Following that disappointment, he had fled to Pemberley and had intended to remain there for most, if not all, of the summer. Curiosity, not avarice, about Miss Armstrong's bequest had lured him away from his estate. Wishing he was in Derbyshire still, Darcy consulted his timepiece for the third time before tucking it back into his fob pocket. Listlessly, he watched passersby on the street without really seeing them until…

"By Jove!" Lurching forwards, he craned his neck for a better view down Chancery Lane. *Is that?* He thought he had seen her and her father entering a carriage farther down the street. But seeing Miss Elizabeth Bennet was nothing extraordinary; he saw her wherever he went.

Easing back against the squabs, Darcy closed his eyes. *Never is it really her. No matter.* He had shifted for himself perfectly well before meeting the young lady, and he would shift well enough again without her in his life. Surely he would. Some day.

Taking up his walking stick, he stepped out of his equipage and stood then on the street, watching the carriage in question—which very much resembled Mr Bennet's—pull away from the kerb. Longing to peer inside, he was disappointed that the only glimpse he could catch was of a gentleman, hat pulled low, sitting on the rear-facing seat. Darcy turned towards the building and, as he climbed them, he counted the steps to the entry.

Eleven. Of course.

At precisely eleven o'clock, he was greeted by Mr Monroe of Pemberton & Monroe and invited into his office. Five minutes or so later, after tea was served by a young clerk named Stevens, Mr Monroe folded his hands atop the desk and dispensed with chit-chat. "Now then, Mr Darcy, as reported in my letter dated the thirtieth of April, Miss Phoebe Armstrong became physically infirm and unable to care for herself in January of last year. God rest her soul, she died this February, and you, sir, have been named as a beneficiary in her will."

"I presume you speak of the Miss Phoebe Armstrong who was born in the Northwest and later came to reside in Buckinghamshire."

The attorney responded in the affirmative and made it known he had served as Miss Armstrong's man of business for just over two years. "She wished to bequeath something to you in thanks for"—he opened a document case—"your kindnesses in the year nine. As I understand it, you learnt of the difficulty she encountered on her southward journey from Carlisle."

"Yes. She had planned to stay two nights in Lambton, but the inn had been damaged by fire. Accommodation was provided at Pemberley for a number of inconvenienced travellers during the closure."

Mr Monroe continued reading the document. "It was not only that, sir. Three years ago, you performed another kindness." Looking up, he smiled. "And each time I visited the ailing Miss Armstrong at Oakwood Manor, I was enthusiastically greeted by her beloved Biscuit."

Darcy was surprised to find himself smiling in return. Of

late, such an expression occurred but rarely. "Ah yes, the Pomeranian pup she grew attached to during her stay at Pemberley. Whatever happened to Biscuit when his mistress died?"

"He was left in the care of the old butler, but the silly creature dashed out onto the lane and was crushed beneath the wheels of a neighbour's recklessly driven carriage. The dog, that is, not the butler who, by the bye, is no longer employed at Oakwood. It is conjecture, of course, but it is assumed poor little Biscuit thought the carriage was bringing his mistress back home, and… Well…" Leather creaked as Mr Monroe shifted in his chair and rather needlessly shuffled papers about on his desk. "At any rate, my client wanted to show her gratitude for your good deeds. Unfortunately, such kind acts were rarities during the lady's life. Her servants were a slovenly lot, and she had few friends. Miss Armstrong once told me that the more she dealt with people, the more she became disenchanted. She much preferred plants and animals. Dogs particularly. Horses not so much."

They both turned at a sound from the office door.

"Ahem, Mr Monroe." Stevens apologised for interrupting. "Your next appointment has arrived, sir."

Glancing at his watch, the attorney gave a brusque nod. "Thank you. I shall fetch him anon. Now, Mr Darcy, back to business. There are conditions attached to your bequest. But first, I have here a token bestowal." Mr Monroe disappeared beneath his desk. When he emerged holding a large parcel, his eyes conveyed something like an apology. "I am afraid Miss Armstrong was rather eccentric."

Darcy wondered whether the man's face was flushed from embarrassment or from the exertion of lifting the bulky bundle from the floor.

Without a word, the attorney advanced and thrust the package at Darcy before sitting behind his desk again. "Go on," he said, gesturing with an upward tilt of his chin. "Open it, if you want. Or perhaps you would prefer to do so at a later time." Mr Monroe appeared most eager for that choice. "I do have my next appointment waiting, and I have not yet informed you of the greater bequest or its conditions."

Setting aside the cumbersome parcel, Darcy was quick to respond. "By all means, let me not detain you any longer than necessary."

Succinctly, Mr Monroe told him that four other beneficiaries had been named in Miss Armstrong's will. Each would receive, or already had received, a small token of her appreciation. "All of you, however, must compete for the lady's legacy—namely, Oakwood Manor in Buckinghamshire and fifty thousand pounds in assets including nine thousand pounds in gold guineas. I am told it took four stout men to lift my client's iron money box."

Darcy could hardly conceal his astonishment, and he knew not what to say until overcome by both inquisitiveness and a measure of caution. Resting both elbows on the chair's arms, he steepled his fingers. "The beneficiaries must compete, you say. How, exactly?"

"As mentioned, Miss Armstrong was an eccentric old dear. Some questioned whether she had full control of her mind towards the end, but I can attest to her *compos mentis*. Weak in body but mentally strong, she spent her last months devising a tournament of sorts. All I am able to impart at this time is that the five of you must spend, at most, a se'nnight together at Oakwood Manor and participate in a game of skill—nothing of the physical sort. The victor will inherit all."

When Darcy enquired what would happen should none

succeed during the seven days, Mr Monroe replied, "In such an event, Oakwood Manor and the fifty thousand pounds will pass to a young man of business whose plan is to undertake—no pun intended—the creation of a pet cemetery within Oakwood's spacious park, complete with headstones for dogs, cats, birds, and such."

Darcy thought that a rather bizarre and unnecessary enterprise. His ancestors had set aside an area of Pemberley for the burial of beloved family pets, of which there had been many. Biscuit's own predecessors were interred there.

Mr Monroe continued. "On the morning of Thursday the eleventh of June, participants are to report to Oakwood Manor between the hours of nine o'clock and twelve midday —no earlier, no later. Barring elimination from the contest or a personal emergency, they are to remain on the premises until someone successfully completes the contest—which will end at the stroke of midnight on Wednesday the seventeenth of June. I assume you never visited Miss Armstrong at Oakwood, sir?"

"No." Shaking his head, Darcy regretted he had not.

"It is a lovely place, and Miss Armstrong insisted the tournament occur while the blooms in her beloved gardens unfold. This being Friday, you have until this coming Monday to inform me of your decision."

Darcy took a sip from his cup, but the tea had grown cold. "I assume my valet will be welcome."

"Sorry, no. But a coachman and one footman per contestant can be comfortably accommodated in a dormitory at a nearby estate. Speaking of servants, for various reasons, we found it necessary to dismiss in March all previous employees of Oakwood Manor. Competent replacements have been installed, and none of them will provide assistance to competitors. Neither conspiracies nor bribes will be tolerated. Such attempts will result in immediate dismissal of the employee, and the guilty beneficiary will be eliminated from further participation."

The attorney continued placing marks beside items listed on a document. "Gentlemen will share the services of two footmen capable of performing the duties of a valet. Likewise, ladies will share two maids. There is, of course, a housekeeper, a butler, a very good cook, et cetera, et cetera. I shall be staying at Oakwood as host, overseeing the proceedings. In any dispute, my impartial judgment will be the final word. Also, we have hired a chaperon for the ladies—a strict spinster who once served as governess for a prominent family."

"Ah," said Darcy. "Ladies. So, at least two. May I be advised of the other beneficiaries' names?"

"You most certainly may not."

"I venture a guess that one of them is your next appointment."

The attorney huffed in annoyance, then, gaining his feet, spoke in a brusque manner. "If there are no further questions, sir, I really must fetch that next appointment. I shall look forward to hearing from you on Monday, if not sooner."

Darcy stood and thanked Mr Monroe for his time. In the outer office, clasping the bulky bundle against his side, Darcy collected his hat, gloves, and walking stick from Stevens.

A nervous young man with a shock of fine coppery hair and a bouncy leg was seated against the wall. Darcy gave him a nod, and the fellow smiled widely at him. *Good grief! He could be Bingley's twin.*

As he walked out of the building, Darcy contemplated whether or not to participate in the competition. He was not one for tomfoolery, but he did enjoy chess. Perhaps that was what Mr Monroe meant by a game of skill.

As for the legacy, if he married and became a father, Oakwood Manor might be a nice inheritance for one of his children. *Marry? Ha. I am too particular to settle for a marriage that is less than I desire or deserve. However, fifty thousand pounds would more than recoup Georgiana's dowry if ever she weds.*

Descending the eleven steps to the kerb, Darcy thought the tournament might, if nothing else, keep his mind off Miss Elizabeth Bennet for a se'nnight. *By Jove, I shall do it.*

Turning on his heel, he marched up the steps and back into the outer office of Pemberton & Monroe. The copper-haired fellow was gone in with the attorney, but Stevens remained and asked whether he could be of assistance.

"Yes. Please be so kind as to inform Mr Monroe that I shall be at Oakwood Manor on the eleventh of June." *Of course it would have to be the eleventh.*

In the carriage, Darcy shed his hat and gloves, untied the twine from round the strangely shaped parcel, and carefully peeled back the brown paper. "Oh, bloody hell," he muttered.

❧ 3 ❧

MISS BENNET!

So that they might arrive at Oakwood in a timely manner on Thursday the eleventh of June, Elizabeth and Mr Bennet had taken rooms the previous night at the Knight's Rest in nearby Slough. The mattresses in their rooms had been terribly lumpy and stale-smelling, and they had slept poorly.

In the morning, Elizabeth watched with commiseration as her tired, slouched father was jostled about on the rear-facing seat. Their carriage was ample in size but not particularly well-sprung, and the roads it traversed were in an atrocious condition.

At Hunsford, Mr Darcy had arrogantly asserted fifty miles was an easy distance by carriage. *Humph. Perhaps where fortune makes travel comfortable and the expense of it unimportant, distance may be no difficulty. But such is not the case here and now.*

As loath as Elizabeth was to admit it, she conceded that Mr Darcy's confident manner was part and parcel of his attractiveness, and she certainly had no objection to the fact that he was in possession of a good fortune. *How entirely agreeable it would be to travel in comfort.* She, too, had grown weary of being jounced about on the hard seat.

When the horses were slowed from a jog to a walk and the carriage was turned onto a tree-lined lane with a sign indicating Oakwood Manor, she felt nothing but relief. Nose almost pressed to the side-glass, she caught her first glimpse of the old house, which spread outwards and upwards in various directions and styles. Its stonework, exposed wood frame, large chimneys, and steeply pitched gable roofs topped by finials suggested parts of the manor had been there for two or three hundred years. Already elevated since leaving Longbourn, the flutter of Elizabeth's spirits heightened. *And of this place I might become mistress.* She patted her drowsing father's arm as they drew to a halt on the gravel sweep. "Papa, we have arrived."

Sitting up, Mr Bennet grinned at her. "Well, Lizzy, if adventure will not befall a young lady in her own village, she must seek it in Buckinghamshire, eh?" When the carriage door was opened, he climbed out first to assist his daughter.

As she stepped down, Elizabeth huffed at the rumpled state of the delicate netted reticule she had been tightly clutching since leaving the inn. Gazing then at the manor's facade, she whispered to her father that she was equal parts eager delight and anxiety. "I shall not know a single soul here."

Mr Bennet linked his arm with hers, and they climbed the steps to the front door. "My poor Lizzy. What a sad state of affairs that strangers never can be introduced at a house party."

Elizabeth remembered having spoken similarly sarcastic words to Mr Darcy at Rosings. *Why, at every turn, must I be reminded of my interactions with that man?* The gentleman was in her thoughts more often than not, and she felt saddened by the notion their paths might never again cross. If nothing else, she owed him an apology.

At the arched entryway—graced by pots of deliciously fragrant pink and cream-coloured sweet peas—they were met by a familiar countenance and received with professions of pleasure. Middle-aged, Mr Monroe had a kind face and shortish dark hair greying at the temples. Although not considered a gentleman, the attorney's manner was courteous and gallant.

Elizabeth assumed he would show no particular favouritism in regard to the competition, but she feared he, in consideration of her gender and age, might become protective of her during the se'nnight. *I require neither coddling nor cosseting, thank you.*

Beckoning them inside, Mr Monroe welcomed the Bennets to Oakwood Manor and presented them to Mrs Vincent and Mr Atwater, the housekeeper and butler. Those introductions were followed by inconsequential conversation until a pendulum clock chimed ten times, and Mrs Vincent hinted the guests might care to see Miss Bennet's room.

Escorting them upstairs, the housekeeper showed Mr Bennet where he might refresh himself. "And," she said, "Mr Monroe will be waiting for you downstairs, sir, whenever you and your daughter are ready. Now, Miss Bennet, please follow me to your bedchamber."

Inside the room a maid curtseyed, then resumed unpacking Elizabeth's small trunk.

"Rachel," scolded Mrs Vincent, "why are the curtains still drawn?" The housekeeper went about opening them and letting in sunlight while speaking to Elizabeth. "Rachel will be at your beck and call during your stay, and another girl, Henrietta, will be Miss Kensett's maid."

Pleased to know she would not be the sole female in the competition, Elizabeth nevertheless took particular note of the solitary bed, the largest piece of furniture in the room. Although she and Jane shared a bedchamber at Longbourn, she dreaded doing so with a stranger. "Am I, then, to be accommodated with another lady?"

"Oh no, Miss Bennet," said the housekeeper. "According to Mr Monroe, Miss Kensett insisted on having her privacy."

Left alone then, Elizabeth took off her gloves, bonnet, spencer, and half-boots and changed into slippers. She wandered about the richly decorated bedchamber, touching furnishings and fabrics. It was not to her taste but spacious and spotless. Three tall, narrow casement windows with diamond-shaped panes looked down upon verdant lawns, lush gardens, and a wooded hill beyond.

When she flung herself upon it, the feather mattress passed her test for freshness and comfort, and she anticipated a better night's rest than was had at the inn. At a sound from the door, followed by her father's voice, Elizabeth sprang to her feet, smoothing her hair and gown.

"Well, well, Lizzy, what do you think of Oakwood Manor? I conducted a bit of an exploration and found eclectic furniture and all manner of whim-wham. Floral-design papers cover every second wall, and there are varying room heights, angled passages, nooks, crannies, and alcoves galore. From what I have seen, there is not much symmetry to be had. Still, it is quite the place you have here. Would it be too much to ask that you not wait until I am put to bed with a shovel to install your mother and silliest sisters here? I could use some peace and quiet at Longbourn before my eternal rest."

Accustomed to her father's ill-natured aspersions about his womenfolk, Elizabeth bit her tongue and remained silent as they made their way downstairs. Full well she knew that certain members of her family left much to be desired, but she loved them all. And, because of that love, she suffered a measure of guilt. Her mother and younger sisters had not been told the true reason for her and her father going to Buckinghamshire. They had been informed only that Elizabeth and four more friends of the late Miss Phoebe Armstrong had been invited to meet, stay awhile at her house, and enjoy her gardens. Only Jane knew the truth.

Little interest, however, had been shown in the whole affair once they had examined Elizabeth's bequest. Considering her daughter had saved the woman's life, Mrs Bennet had declared the gift piddling. Lydia, of course, was in Brighton by then; but Kitty had laughed over Elizabeth owning a cane, and she thought the golden buckles downright garish. Mary, however, had said that one's faith was more important than false ideas about the necessity of riches.

The thought of potentially being able to financially assist her family sent Elizabeth's spirits soaring again as she and her father spotted Mr Monroe awaiting them in the vestibule.

There, with utmost civility, the attorney hinted it was time for Mr Bennet to be on his way. Beneficiaries were not permitted to entertain guests. "I am sure you understand, sir. And, as promised in London, I give you every assurance your daughter will be quite safe here at Oakwood. Miss Rigby, the chaperon, will ensure everyone behaves with propriety, and I shall make certain the proceedings are conducted fairly."

Mr Monroe then turned to Elizabeth. "Take a moment to bid your father farewell before joining us in the grand parlour." He indicated the massive room immediately to their left, excused himself, went through, and spoke to someone within.

"Well, my dear, I have been summarily dismissed." Mr Bennet kissed Elizabeth's forehead. "Enjoy your adventure, and do your utmost to succeed. You have something more of quickness than your sisters, so I trust you to be a good girl and secure this house for them." With a promise to return for her in a se'nnight, if not sooner, her father walked out into the spring sunshine.

Thank you, Papa, for placing that burden—which should have been yours—upon my shoulders. Now here I am, on my own and soon to be amongst strangers, four of whom will be my rivals.

No one observing her would have supposed Elizabeth had any wretchedness about her as she entered the grand parlour. The tumult of her feelings was carefully hidden behind fine eyes and a lovely smile. Within, she spotted Mr Monroe, Mrs Vincent, Rachel, another young maid, a lady of around forty years, a gentleman, and a strapping, liveried footman.

"Ah, there you are, Miss Bennet." Mr Monroe shot to his feet.

The other man—reluctant, it seemed, to set aside a plate heaped with an assortment of cakes—stood more slowly. Elizabeth then was presented to Miss Rigby, the genteel chaperon whom she immediately liked.

Next was the gentleman, Mr Peter Fordham, another beneficiary. He resided with his wife just over two miles distant in Slough. Bowing, he said only, "Miss Bennet, how do you do."

Elizabeth curtseyed. "Pleased to meet you, sir."

"Now, my dear," said their host, "sit and have some tea and cake with us." Consulting his watch, Mr Monroe said,

"The other three participants should arrive directly. I shall wait for them before explaining what will be happening over the course of the se'nnight and what rules will apply."

With her insides in tremulous excitement, Elizabeth chose a chair situated diagonally opposite Mr Fordham, all the better to observe the competition. While her tea was served, the four of them chatted about the bucolic countryside and the deplorable roads. Mr Fordham, though, engaged not so much in the art of conversation but in the fine art of cramming food into his mouth. Elizabeth noticed his beverage of choice sloshed in a wine glass rather than in a teacup, and she hardly could credit it when he rose and piled his plate with more sponge cake. She suspected he was an indolent man with a decided taste for sedentary pursuits, living only to eat and drink. Probably fifteen years her senior and not a handsome man, Mr Fordham was on the short side of tall and about a stone overweight. *He certainly is nothing to the fit— Oh, do stay out of my thoughts, Mr Darcy.*

After a few minutes, over the rim of her cup, she caught Mr Fordham, in an unguarded moment, sitting back and contemplating her with a shrewd, calculating look, measuring her up and, she presumed, forming an assessment of her acuity. Elizabeth lowered the teacup and smiled at him. He simply turned away. *I shall be cautious round that one.*

His appearance and manner might once have established Mr Fordham in her mind as being unworthy of the slightest admiration. However, recently taught a valuable lesson, Elizabeth no longer prided herself on her discernment. First impressions often proved wrong. After all, she once had thought Mr Darcy devoid of every proper feeling and that Mr Wickham—the wolf in sheep's clothing—possessed every virtue.

A commotion in the vestibule roused her from those

thoughts and heralded the arrival of another beneficiary. Mr Monroe excused himself to greet them while those remaining in the room waited in silent anticipation.

Upon the attorney's return to the parlour, he brought in with him a gentleman who stopped short and immediately cried out in surprised delight, "Miss Bennet!"

❧ 4 ❧

WHO IS WHO & WHAT IS WHAT

As his carriage approached Oakwood Manor, Darcy thought he saw his good friend entering the house. But it could not have been Bingley, for he and his sisters were visiting relations in Scarborough. And, it being the eleventh of the month, there was no chance he ever could be fortunate enough to have his friend's cheerful company during the seven-day ordeal. Still, the other young man had seemed so familiar, with the same energy and quick step and tall, slender build as Bingley.

With more dignity and less enthusiasm than his friend might have had, Darcy made his way to the front door and rapped the knocker, dreading the imminent yet necessary chit-chat and thinking it was insufferably tedious to attempt conversation with unfamiliar people. A footman granted him entry, and a stout man who identified himself as Mr Atwater, the butler, received him. While Darcy was being divested of hat, gloves, and walking stick, the host, Mr Monroe, appeared in the vestibule and greeted him with a warm welcome and polite enquiries about his health and his journey.

"Now," said the attorney, "unless you would prefer to be shown directly to your chamber, do come and join us in the parlour. We await only one more beneficiary before we can commence with the proceedings. The two other gentlemen and Miss Bennet are already here." He gestured towards the room he had come from.

At the mere mention of that name, a dagger reopened the wound in Darcy's heart. *Please make the bleeding stop.*

"Sir," said Mr Monroe, "are you unwell? Your face has grown pale. Mr Atwater, fetch Mrs Vincent. Our guest must be taken to his bedchamber."

"No, no. I am perfectly well." *After all, how many Miss Bennets are there in the world?* Many, Darcy supposed. There were five at Longbourn alone, and the surname was common throughout the kingdom.

With attorney and butler hard on his heels, he moved towards the parlour. Upon entering, Darcy came to an abrupt halt. While Mr Monroe managed to dodge round him, the portly Mr Atwater bumped into him from behind. Already caught off balance by surprise, Darcy tottered. *Criminy. It is…* "Miss Bennet!" Her name had sprung unexpectedly from his lips. The eyes of both instantly engaged. On their faces heat bloomed; on Darcy's tongue words withered and died.

The occupants of the room—eleven, if one counted him and Elizabeth—gaped at the two of them. Whispers then circulated round the parlour like wind through willows.

"Well," said Mr Monroe, going to stand beside Darcy. "This is unexpected. I knew Miss Bennet was acquainted with Mr Hadley here." The attorney indicated the blushing, widely smiling young man with coppery hair. "But this association was unforeseen."

Of course! Bingley's double—that nervous chap I saw at Pemberton & Monroe. How the deuce does he know Elizabeth?

"Ahem." Mr Monroe raised his voice. "I had planned on addressing this once Miss Kensett arrived, but I want to make something perfectly clear right now. No matter their prior connexion, there will be no collusion permitted between competitors." He pointedly caught Elizabeth's eye, then Mr Hadley's, then Darcy's. "Is that understood?"

Everyone nodded, including the butler, a liveried footman, two serving girls, and two women Darcy had yet to meet, one in much finer clothing than the other.

And who is that? Darcy watched a gentleman, slightly older than himself, sidle up to Elizabeth. He and Mr Hadley demonstrated a marked interest in her, but whether it was of an adversarial, platonic, or romantic nature—or just Darcy's own imagination—was debatable. *Not that it is any concern of mine, but I shall keep an eye on them nevertheless.*

Cheeks overspread with a rosy glow, Elizabeth said something to both gentlemen, then moved in Darcy's direction, still looking as utterly astonished to see him as he was to see her. Had she read his letter? Would she even acknowledge him?

It immediately became evident her manners were as unaffected and pleasing as ever. She curtseyed and greeted him and smiled so sweetly that Darcy's poor heart ached. Then she turned to Mr Monroe. "I am curious, sir. I realise we beneficiaries will be rivals and that it would be to one's disadvantage to assist another. But why is collaboration strictly forbidden?"

The attorney rubbed his temples. Darcy suspected he had a headache. "Really, I should wait for Miss Kensett before delineating the rules." Consulting his watch, Mr Monroe muttered, "She has less than a quarter of an hour to arrive with any degree of punctuality. But, very well, I shall gratify your curiosity. My client made it indisputable that her house was not to be put up for purchase—which is what Miss Armstrong and I assumed would happen if two or more competitors joined forces and won the tournament."

He contemplated Elizabeth and Darcy for a moment. "Unless... I suppose... If two beneficiaries were engaged to marry... Young lady, do you and Mr Darcy have an understanding?"

Squaring his shoulders, Darcy spoke up. "Miss Bennet and I do *not* have an understanding." As though such a pronouncement was not crystal clear, he added, "We most certainly are not engaged to marry." *She would not have me.*

She regarded him with something like regret—not that she had refused him, of course, but that he had just behaved so poorly, and Darcy felt like the worst sort of boor. *Bad form, you idiot. Bad form.* But what else could he expect on the eleventh?

One of the mature women, the more finely attired one, rushed to Elizabeth's side and spoke softly while patting her arm.

In Kent, Darcy had been certain he, eventually, would be the one to comfort her and offer succour. Alas, it never was to be. Accustomed to obtaining whatever his heart desired, he still could not understand why such a fate had befallen him. Nor could he imagine how he would make it through the se'nnight in one piece.

After what has passed between us, it will ill suit the feelings of either to remain in the same house. One of us will have to politely makes our excuses and depart.

Mr Monroe consulted his watch again and muttered, "Someone is in imminent danger of being eliminated."

Yes, I deserve that. Darcy hoped eliminated simply meant disqualified and not something more dire. Glancing round the room, he noticed the unfamiliar gentleman smirking while watching the goings-on.

"We shall wait exactly eleven more minutes for the late Miss Kensett." Releasing an exasperated sigh, the attorney looked heavenwards. "Late I mean as in tardy." He rubbed a temple again. "Mrs Vincent, more tea, if you please."

While the other mature woman—the one Darcy assumed was the housekeeper—sprang into action, Mr Monroe turned to Darcy. "Since you are already acquainted with Miss Bennet, allow me to make you known to the rest of our party."

Subsequently, Darcy was presented to Miss Grace Rigby, the lady who had comforted Elizabeth and was acting as chaperon for the se'nnight. He surmised she was in her fortieth year. Next he was formally introduced to Mr David Hadley and Mr Peter Fordham. Then he met the household servants— being the housekeeper, two maids, and the footman Christopher, who, in addition to his other duties, would provide, along with his brother Alfred, the services of a valet to the gentlemen.

By that time the ladies had crowded round a table and were pouring out the tea. Thinking it advisable to get his apology over and done with as soon and as quietly as possible, Darcy approached Elizabeth. It took exactly eleven steps.

Blocking his way, Miss Rigby moved closer to her and, in a whisper Darcy could not help overhearing, said, "That man will not come and bother you, Miss Bennet, I am determined. You want nothing to do with him, do you?"

Miss Rigby certainly seems to know who is who and what is

what. Not to be thwarted in his attempt, Darcy leant round the chaperon and, with commendable respect, begged for a moment of Elizabeth's time. Likewise leaning to one side, she nodded her acceptance and moved with him so they might, if they spoke quietly, be out of everyone's earshot.

"Miss Bennet"—*I long to hear your name or see your face and no longer care*—"I beg forgiveness for the harsh manner in which I responded to an enquiry made to you by Mr Monroe moments ago. It was not only rude but unfeeling, and I truly am sorry for my boorish behaviour. There can be no excuse for it. But, to be honest, your presence here shook my equilibrium."

"I rather think the butler's impact did that, Mr Darcy. But, please, think nothing of it. You spoke only the truth." Her words were kind, but the look in her eyes still spoke of disappointment in his conduct.

She assumes I have not taken any of her words to heart. But he had, and he was trying to better understand how the whole affair had gone so wrong. And he was trying to be a better gentleman. He could not afford to repeat the same mistakes when, if ever, he fell in love again.

Between them, silence stretched taut. The strained tension seemed endless to Darcy, but according to the tick of a nearby pendulum, it had lasted mere seconds. *Since Hunsford, days feel like months, weeks like years.*

On both sides then, civil enquiries and responses on common subjects were attempted. All the while, what had happened at Hunsford—his marriage proposal, her vehement refusal—loomed over them like a heavy, friction-filled cloud.

Mr Hadley advanced and gave Darcy a dark, thunderous look. "Miss Bennet," he said, expression gentling and concern evident in his tone, "I could not help noticing... Are you well? May I fetch you another cup of tea? Or a glass of sherry?"

She smiled and thanked him but declined. "Mr Hadley, if it is not meant to remain private, will you tell me about your further association with Miss Armstrong? I assume you visited her here."

Darcy could not subdue his own curiosity. "If you have no objection, I should like to hear about both of your connexions with her." *And about your own acquaintance. Not that I care a jot.*

The three of them were joined by Miss Rigby, and together they sat in a cosy grouping of four leather chairs with Darcy across from the chaperon and Mr Hadley opposite Elizabeth. The younger man then enthusiastically recounted his wild ride through Cheapside and Elizabeth's rescue of Miss Armstrong.

"And so, the dear old lady bequeathed me a curricle and two flashy Cleveland bays. Although curricle accidents are common, I suppose she thought I might be less danger to myself and to others while sitting atop a buggy rather than a horse."

Darcy's features twisted into a reproachful expression. *There is no excuse for such ineptitude...nor for blushing like a missish maiden every time Elizabeth smiles at you.*

Evidently eager for any scrap of her attention, Mr Hadley turned to Elizabeth. "You may be pleased to know Bailey now roams greener pastures at Eastmeadow Park over in Eton Wick and is less skittish than he was in London. Originally, our family was from the North, but my older brother, Owen, inherited our uncle's modest estate. I often stay there with him and Bailey." Pausing, he took a sad look about the parlour. "I am grieved Miss Armstrong is gone. I visited her frequently and chatted with her in this very room, and— I say!" His eyes opened wide. "Do you suppose *that* is why she named me in her will?"

Darcy's heart gave a little lurch when Elizabeth smiled sweetly at the other gentleman. *Yes, madam, the youngster's humility is to be commended. It is a virtue seated between the abominable vices of arrogance and moral weakness.*

"Mr Hadley," he said, "you remind me of a very good friend of mine, not only in appearance but in character, which is a compliment to you." Although speaking to the young man, Darcy's gaze rested upon Elizabeth. "Having given him some ghastly counsel, I have not been such a good friend as he has been to me."

"Oh well, if he is anything at all like me," said Mr Hadley, "he will forgive you. But only after you are honest with him and apologise for whatever ghastly guidance you gave."

"Excellent advice," said Elizabeth. "Do you not think so, Mr Darcy?" Her silent challenge spoke volumes.

"Indeed. And that is why, upon leaving Kent, I put pen to paper and did what is morally correct, as advocated by this clever young man here."

Head bowed, Mr Hadley denied being clever. Sitting up straighter, he said, "Speaking of counsel and of advocation, though, I hope to plead cases in a court of justice one day."

"Studying to be a barrister, are you?" enquired Miss Rigby.

"Yes, madam, and during my stay here I hope Mr Monroe will answer some questions about *his* occupation."

"I rather expect," said Darcy, "we shall be too busy trying to win the forthcoming tournament, whatever it might entail, to think about much else."

"Oh, I have no expectation of winning a contest of mental acuity. The chaps at the Inns of Court say my wit is as thick as Tewkesbury mustard."

"Spread no malicious slander upon your knowledge, Mr Hadley," said Elizabeth, eyes twinkling. "I cannot abide false-spoken statements."

Turning red, he thanked her. "Now I am all anticipation to hear about your more well-deserved bequest from Miss Armstrong. Will you speak of it, please, Miss Bennet?"

"Certainly." Raising her feet and a bit of her hems clear of the floor, she exposed not only dainty brocade slippers with shiny buckles but, unintentionally, a pair of nicely turned ankles.

As it would have been ungentlemanly to ogle them, Darcy averted his eyes. *Besides, I already glimpsed those ankles at Netherfield during Bingley's ball when she danced a lively reel with some unworthy partner.*

"I was given Miss Armstrong's gold-headed cane and these pretty little golden buckles from her shoes. Are they not lovely?" Elizabeth waggled her feet back and forth, and Mr Hadley followed the movement with undue interest until Miss Rigby cleared her throat and gave the young man a stern look.

Crossing one leg over the other, Darcy silently scoffed. *A rather meagre legacy, considering you saved the woman from harm.*

When he was asked about his own experience with Miss Armstrong, Darcy recounted the woman's brief stay at his estate, his gift of a Pomeranian pup, and his being given a strangely shaped parcel during his appointment with Mr Monroe. "I had an inkling what might be inside. Still, when I unwrapped the unwieldy bundle, it was disturbing to have the preserved Biscuit the dog land feet up upon my carriage floor."

"By George!" cried Mr Hadley. "Good old Biscuit! I knew

the dear dog well. Miss Bennet, if you like, in the galleried hall I can show you several portraits of Biscuit."

When she indicated she would like that, Darcy told himself he cared not a groat about the two of them spending time together. That was before eleven foolish words spilled forth from his tongue. "I can do better than that. I, essentially, have Biscuit himself." *Of course, you would have to go to my town house to see him, and that will not be happening in either of our lifetimes.*

Miss Rigby broke a prolonged and awkward interval of silence. "I have heard of upholsterers using rags to stuff the cured skins of trophy animals but not of family pets."

Regaining a modicum of his considerable dignity, Darcy said, "Cotton-wrapped wire was used, I believe, to support Biscuit's form."

"My word! What a peculiar bequest! Some might consider it *stuff* and nonsense." Mr Hadley grinned with pride when Elizabeth uttered a delightful little giggle.

Darcy cared nought for wordplay. Nor did he care for the pleasure the two younger people seemed to find in one another's company. Witnessing it hurt his wounded pride.

A crunch of carriage wheels from the gravel sweep sent the attorney and housekeeper scampering from the room.

At that point, Mr Fordham—holding a wine glass with his left hand and a plate of fruit and nuts in his right—hooked a foot round the leg of a Hepplewhite chair. Dragging it, with a screech, inch by inch across the oak floor, he manoeuvred it into place beside Miss Rigby and apologised when a walnut fell upon her lap.

Shortly thereafter, a female voice cried out, "Here I am! At last!"

5

THREE MISSES

With seconds to spare, the last beneficiary had arrived on time.

Thank goodness. I shall not be the sole female in this tournament after all.

From out in the vestibule, Miss Kensett's voice reached the parlour where Elizabeth sat with Miss Rigby and the three male beneficiaries. "You there! Yes, you, footman. My inept servant, not disposed for exertion of any sort and soon to be dismissed without reference, struggles with the baggage out there. Go and fetch my large trunk and portmanteau. He should be able to manage the smaller one as well as my three bandboxes and a valise. For what are you waiting? Move!"

Christopher, the footman who had remained in the parlour, stiffened at the newcomer's tone of voice as she addressed his brother Alfred in the vestibule.

And I thought Lady Catherine was a dictatorial and insolent woman. Elizabeth had hoped the only other female beneficiary would be an agreeable addition to the party; however,

Miss Kensett's brusque and impatient manner was not an immediate recommendation. But, after all, the two of them were destined to be opponents rather than bosom-friends.

The woman's voice yet carried. "Ah, there you are, Mr Monroe. But where is everyone else?"

Did Miss Kensett expect everyone in the manor to line up and welcome her? Scolding herself for once again being hasty in making a judgment, Elizabeth bit her bottom lip and fretted over having brought only one small trunk, one valise, and no bandboxes at all. Fashion, she knew, was a trifling distinction, and excessive solicitude about it often destroyed its own aim. Still, she wondered whether her attire would be found wanting. Too plain? Too informal? Too lacking in quantity or quality? *Oh, stop it.* There was nought to be done about it and no sense in worry.

If there was anything for Elizabeth to fret over, it was Mr Darcy's presence. To be forced into one another's proximity just two months following their contretemps at Hunsford was a dreadful circumstance. It certainly added another aspect to her apprehension about the forthcoming tournament. And she would have to find an opportunity to discreetly apologise to him.

As for Miss Kensett, she still could be heard making a fuss while approaching the parlour. "No, no. I shall endure for the nonce, although I am terribly fatigued from my five-mile journey from Maidenhead. I thought of stopping at an inn for a brief respite, but you would not believe the sort of riffraff places like that attract."

The unflattering mental picture Elizabeth had painted of the harridan in the vestibule in no way resembled its subject when the lushly rounded woman—whose age she estimated as being at least four-and-twenty, and that was being generous—swept into the parlour on their host's arm. As one, the three gentlemen jumped to their feet and set about adjusting cravats, pulling on cuffs, and tugging down waistcoats.

With flawless complexion, brunette hair, and sapphire eyes, Miss Kensett was even more handsome than Jane—truly a diamond of the first water. A floral perfume wafted in her wake, and her skirts softly rustled as she passed in front of Elizabeth, who by then was feeling decidedly under-dressed in a sprigged muslin.

Furthermore, the beautiful Miss Kensett possessed that which Miss Bingley had extolled at Netherfield, being a certain something in her air and manner of walking. And, as the newcomer glided towards them in her clinging silk gown, something about her drew the eyes of Messrs Darcy, Fordham, and Hadley.

"Mr Monroe, I am already acquainted with Mr Fordham, but please make me known to these two gentlemen." Sparing Elizabeth and Miss Rigby the barest of glances, Miss Kensett added, "And those ladies, of course."

Their host performed the honours; and when Miss Kensett acknowledged Elizabeth and Miss Rigby by only the slightest of curtseys, it was easily perceived that Mr Monroe was embarrassed by her ungraciousness.

Mr Hadley whispered to Elizabeth, "Miss Kensett actually met me once before. Apparently, I am entirely forgettable."

"One's memory sometimes is weak. But for my part, sir, you will never be easily forgotten."

When Mr Hadley blushed bright red at her compliment, Mr Darcy shot him an irritated look. Elizabeth was surprised he paid them any attention at all; she had thought he only had eyes for Miss Sophia Kensett.

After the introductions, the newcomer bestowed a partic-ularly winsome smile upon Mr Darcy and said, "It will give me immense pleasure over the course of this se'nnight to improve my acquaintance with you…all."

Somewhat amused, albeit in a dissatisfied manner, by the lady's behaviour, Elizabeth realised she once again was obliged to spend days trapped in a house with a supercilious woman. *And Mr Darcy.* Superimposing Mr Bingley's face over Mr Hadley's first and then Mr Hurst's over Mr Fordham's, she silently sighed. *Just as I feared. Netherfield Park, all over again.*

While Miss Kensett was across the room being presented to the household servants, the chaperon leant in and spoke to Elizabeth in a near whisper and a tone filled with scorn. "That woman's intentions are those of utter coquetry as well as an insatiable desire for universal admiration."

"I believe," said Elizabeth, "that one is apt to wrongly interpret assurance of manner as coquetry." That was, she suspected, what had happened between Mr Darcy and herself. She had been brimming with confidence while pitting her wits against his, and, of all things, he had mistaken her playfulness for flirtation.

Furthermore, she suspected people like Miss Kensett were all pretence and, perhaps, fragility. Thinking of Miss Bingley, who constantly craved recognition, Elizabeth wondered what cruelties a tradesman's descendant might have been subjected to at that exclusive seminary she had attended in town. *She always was so desperate for Mr Darcy's approval.*

Stealing a look at that gentleman, Elizabeth suppressed a sigh. *Who could blame either Miss Bingley or Miss Kensett for wanting the regard of such a man?* Noticing his frown as their eyes met, she feared it was distasteful for Mr Darcy to be in her company. *How he despises me!*

There came then a bustle, an exodus of servants as Mrs

Vincent herded her two maids—and Mr Atwater and his two footmen—from the room.

In company with Miss Kensett, Mr Monroe approached the other beneficiaries and brought over a chair for her. To that lady's evident satisfaction, it was placed beside Mr Darcy.

Standing then in front of a tall settle chair beside the stone fireplace, the attorney requested everyone's attention. "As you know, I shall be your host for this event, and, in addition to her other duties, Miss Rigby"—he indicated the chaperon—"will be your hostess. I should also say that, although I was Miss Armstrong's man of business for two years, my partner, Mr Pemberton, is the actual executor of her will."

"I have a question, Monroe," said Mr Fordham. His arms and ankles were crossed, and he was somewhat slouched in his chair, legs stretched out before him. "Considering how solicitous you were towards Miss Armstrong, one would assume you would have been named in her will. So, why are you not a participant in this competition?"

"Your benefactress, indeed, had set her heart on leaving me a munificent legacy," said the attorney, "but it would have been unethical of me to accept a testamentary bequest from a client. There would have been not only a conflict of interest but suspicion of undue influence, and I have a duty to not undermine public trust in the integrity of the legal profession. Be assured, sir, that I was well compensated for my services during my years as Miss Armstrong's attorney."

Mr Monroe sat then upon the centuries-old box chair, which, in Elizabeth's opinion, looked terribly uncomfortable. "I thought we might take a few moments now to speak of Miss Phoebe Armstrong," said the attorney. "Some of you may not be aware of all that occurred between her birth in

Carlisle and this past February when, at the age of ninety, she died here in Buckinghamshire."

He withdrew something from a pocket and handed it to Mr Fordham. "Have a look at that miniature of her as a young woman, then pass it round for others to see. Miss Armstrong's maternal ancestors included no less personages than a bishop, a viscount, a chaplain to Queen Elizabeth, and various Members of Parliament. Her father was a wealthy cloth merchant, draper, moneylender, and mayor of Carlisle. He owned extensive personal property, including Oakwood Manor, and was landlord of numerous other houses and farms. Ergo, his daughter lived in the manner of the moneyed merchant class and never was involved in the family drapery business. Miss Armstrong was educated. She had dance masters and all manner of powder, pins, ruffles, ribbons, et cetera."

"Oh, indeed," said Miss Kensett. "Years ago, she showed me the blue silk court mantua created for her when she was a young woman. The silver lace on the gown was *hugely* expensive, and I had hoped… Well, my bequest was her pearl parure." She looked pointedly at Elizabeth and Miss Rigby and, apparently for their edification, added, "A parure— French for 'set'—is jewellery designed *en suite*. The parure bequeathed to me has matching necklace, earrings, brooch, and bracelet."

Mr Fordham shifted in his chair, which creaked beneath his weight.

Miss Kensett gave that gentleman a curious look and a sniff that, to Elizabeth, smacked of contempt. "Although it was awfully trite of her, Miss Armstrong also left me what she called 'pearls of wisdom.'"

"Will you share with us one of those pearls?" enquired the chaperon.

Looking more displeased by the second, Miss Kensett withdrew a slip of paper from her reticule. Rather than reading it herself, she gave it to Miss Rigby, who spoke the words aloud. "Whoso walketh uprightly shall be saved: but he that is perverse in his ways shall fall at once." As she passed the paper back, she said, "Proverbs 28 is not to be sniffed at, madam."

Elizabeth could almost feel enmity radiating between the two women, and she was grateful when Mr Monroe stepped in.

"Thank you for sharing that with us, ladies, but let us return to Miss Armstrong. I shall make this a short and compendious history. When their father's death was followed by that of their mother, the eldest son inherited all and held back the stipulated provisions for his two brothers and one sister. After the deaths of all her older brothers, Miss Armstrong—with a lively intelligence and ready insight into the process of litigation—spent fifteen years in a legal dispute at the Court of Chancery trying to reclaim her own and her brothers' legacies from grasping cousins. At the age of sixty-nine, she finally gained possession of the family fortune and became an independent woman. Victorious, she left London and returned to Carlisle, where she was landlady of all her late father's properties and insisted the rents be paid in gold or silver. You appear astonished, Miss Bennet. Do you have a question?"

"I do. With so much wealth, why, when I met Miss Armstrong in town, was she dressed like a pauper?"

The attorney nodded in understanding. "After such a long court battle, my client hoarded her hard-won wealth and spent as little as possible on herself, particularly on her attire." With a smile, he added, "I do know, however, that she drank not only sherry but brandy and port wine. And, as you can see, she spared no expense when it came to refurbishing this house. But, back to my story. In Carlisle, Miss Armstrong's neighbours called her a miser and treated her poorly. That is why, in the year nine, she moved here to Oakwood and became something of a recluse."

Mr Hadley spoke up. "Miss Armstrong once told me she dressed poorly in London so she would not attract pickpockets. In Carlisle, and later here in Buckinghamshire, she kept loaded pistols to deter robbers."

Frissons of excitement coursed through Elizabeth's veins. *What a singular woman. Might I, like Miss Armstrong, become wealthy and independent? But I very much would like to be a wife and mother some day.* Her eyes strayed to Mr Darcy.

He looked at her just as he used to do in Hertfordshire and Kent. *His current expression cannot mean what it had back then.*

Since his proposal, and more often than Elizabeth cared to admit, his words at Hunsford—'*you must allow me to tell you how ardently I admire and love you*'—occupied her mind like an appealing and memorable piece of cheerful music.

At the thought of ending up a spinster like Miss Armstrong, Elizabeth was dismayed to find 'Old Maid in the Garret' had taken up residence within her brain. The song, however, was soon intruded upon when their host struck together his palms, startling her and demanding everyone's attention.

6

A BATTLE OF WILLS

"After my long-winded preamble about your benefactress," said Mr Monroe, "it is time to discuss the tournament. All the information I am about to impart has been printed on broadsheets, which I shall hand out in a moment." He held up a sheaf of printed papers. "Afterwards, I shall answer your questions with, I hope, insight and meticulousness."

Almost three-quarters of an hour later, after the attorney's speech and numerous clarifications and the distribution of printed matter, the five beneficiaries glanced at one another in shared puzzlement. In Darcy's opinion, puzzlement was an apropos description, considering it was to be not a chess match, as he had hoped, but a tournament of wit and whimsy.

Seated next to Darcy, Miss Kensett leant close and spoke in a complaining tone of voice. "I am at sixes and sevens. Please make this intelligible to me, sir."

Darcy shifted away from her as subtly as possible so as

not to offend, and he tapped his sheet of instructions. "Everything is printed here."

"Yes, but if you will read it to me or explain it in your own words rather than an attorney's, I surely shall under-stand it better." She fluttered long, dark eyelashes at him and pursed pouty lips.

Darcy looked away and, in doing so, caught a pair of fine eyes observing the two of them. At once inattentive to Miss Kensett, he responded, "Yes, of course, Miss Bennet." Whip-ping his head back to the lady beside him, he felt the tips of his ears grow red hot. "Forgive me. I have made an egregious blunder. I meant to say Miss Kensett, not..." *Dash it!* He remembered the day's date and prayed he was not doomed to make endless mistakes.

The lady's expression made it clear she was not appeased by his apology, but before Darcy could make amends by clearly communicating the tournament's details to Miss Kensett, Mr Monroe again demanded their attention.

"I have in here"—he shook an upside-down grey felt hat —"five folded pieces of paper. Each of you, alphabetically by surname, will select one. Do not show whatever is printed on your page to anyone other than me." He walked over to Elizabeth and presented the hat.

With dainty fingers she withdrew and opened a piece of foolscap. After briefly studying its content, she refolded the paper and placed it upon her lap with the other document. Elizabeth's features, customarily so expressive, revealed nothing.

It was his turn next, and Darcy dithered between reading his chosen paper straight away or doing so after being shown to his room. Deciding on the latter due to Miss Kensett's proximity, he further folded the page and placed it inside a breast pocket.

Mr Fordham chose his, but finishing his Madeira seemed more important than anything.

Mr Hadley's leg bounced while he awaited his turn. After perusing the paper he had plucked out, he glanced across at Elizabeth, whereupon his face reddened.

"Well! This is terribly unfair," cried Miss Kensett. "I really have no choice, do I? I must take the only remaining paper. If I do not like it, may I exchange mine for someone else's?"

"You most certainly may not." The attorney passed the hat to her.

"How unjust it is that the others have a surname closer to the beginning of the alphabet than mine." Rather sulkily, she grabbed the last piece of paper and unfolded it. From the corner of his eye, Darcy noticed her moving it back and forth in front of her face. *Has she—in addition to vacancy of mind and incapacity for thinking—poor eyesight?*

Meanwhile, the housekeeper had discreetly drawn close to Mr Monroe and whispered a few words before going to stand by the parlour door.

"May I have your attention again, everyone," said the host. "Mr Darcy, whenever you are ready, Mrs Vincent will show you to your bedchamber. Miss Bennet has settled in already, and, because they have stayed here before, the others have been assigned their customary rooms. Also, Mrs Vincent has reminded me that, for those who desire it, a midday repast soon will be placed on the sideboard here in the parlour. Dinner will be served at six o'clock in the formal dining room, so please return here a quarter of an hour prior. Other than that, the five of you are at liberty to enjoy the manor and its demesne and, hopefully, move forwards in the tournament. Remember, whenever you believe you have achieved success with a problem, bring it to me for verification. At that point, you may proceed with your next one. As you set off to achieve your goal, I wish you all the best of luck." Mr Monroe collected his belongings, bowed, and left the room.

Mr Fordham stretched and sauntered to the far side of the parlour, where he took up residence, supine, upon a plush pink sofa.

"Well, ladies," said Miss Rigby, "may I persuade you both to take a turn about the gardens? The flora is delightful, and a walk will be refreshing after sitting here for such a duration." She glanced at Mr Fordham, but he appeared fast asleep. "Mr Darcy and Mr Hadley, would you care to join us?" The latter agreed with alacrity.

Darcy recalled an evening at Netherfield when Miss Bingley had invited Miss Eliza Bennet—as she called her—to take a turn about the room. He truly had believed the more enticing lady had been flirting with him, and he had reciprocated. Or so he had thought. *Utter idiot.* He startled when he heard his name being spoken.

"Mr Darcy and I shall be unable to join you, Miss Rigby. He has agreed to help me with this." Miss Kensett waved her set of instructions at the chaperon.

When the other two ladies stood, Darcy and Mr Hadley jumped to their feet.

"I shall be delighted to see the gardens and enjoy some exercise," said Elizabeth. "Sweet vernal freshness has given way to the summery scents of newly mown grass, lilacs, mint, and Shakespeare's 'luscious woodbine'. Physical activity out of doors often helps one arrive at a solution to a problem, and I do have quite a perplexing one now." Gathering her papers, she turned to Miss Rigby and Mr Hadley. "Shall we?"

The chaperon frowned at Miss Kensett before going to speak to the housekeeper, who still stood by the door. Mrs

Vincent then occupied the chair vacated by Miss Rigby. "I shall just wait here until you are ready to be shown to your room, Mr Darcy." The housekeeper gave him a pointed look while withdrawing some sort of fabric and a needle from a pocket in the folds of her skirt. Lowering her eyes, she set about her work.

Darcy's gaze lingered on the doorway even after Elizabeth, arm in arm with Mr Hadley, had gone from sight.

"Now then," said Miss Kensett, demanding his attention, "make this silly little game comprehensible to me."

"As you wish, madam. Simply put, there will be a series of enigmas, riddles, and such for you to ponder and solve. Doing so is only part of the task. When you solve a puzzle, you must then use information gleaned from it to locate your next puzzle. Each is unique. So there is no point in spying on another participant because they will be seeking something completely different from you...at least until the end. The ultimate conundrum will be the same for all remaining contestants. And that final answer will lead to the prize—the deed to Oakwood Manor and the key to Miss Armstrong's money box."

"So, whoever finds that final hiding spot will inherit all, correct?" When Darcy answered in the affirmative, Miss Kensett heaved a gusty sigh. "Far too much work! This competition is utterly ridiculous and quite beneath me. I should just be given the deed without further nonsense. My grandmother, may God rest her soul, was Miss Armstrong's dearest friend."

"Nevertheless, this was Miss Armstrong's scheme, as specified in her will, and we must persevere. With any luck, someone will solve all the puzzles in one day and locate the deed. In which case, the tournament will end, and we each may go our own merry way."

Miss Kensett scowled at her creased paper. "But what does this mean?" She turned the puzzle towards Darcy, who looked away. "I require assistance," she whinged. "Will you not help me?" She moved closer and, when he glanced over, fluttered her lashes at him again.

He held back from enquiring whether she had some sort of irritant in her eye. As handsome as she was, the lady was becoming an annoyance. *I wager Elizabeth is out there using her incomparable ingenuity to find the answer to her poser.* At the mere thought of her, another wave of heartbreak crashed into him.

Maids and footmen entered the room and unobtrusively set out the repast, but food had held little interest for Darcy since Elizabeth's refusal of his offer.

Miss Kensett awaited an answer, so he patiently said, "You must work through that riddle yourself. Mr Monroe said the puzzles have been tailored so all contestants have a fair chance of winning."

"But if you read it aloud to me"—she placed her hand upon his sleeve—"I might better grasp the phrasing."

Grasp, indeed. Darcy freed his arm from her restraint. "According to the rules, madam, there can be no collaboration. Nor can a beneficiary impede another."

"Is that not what you are doing at this very moment— impeding me?" Pressing her lips together, she shifted her body away from his. "Very well. I shall ask that darling Mr Hadley to help me. Or...I simply shall search this entire house, top to bottom, and find the deed without all the fuss and bother of working on foolish riddles."

Darcy shook his head. "I very much doubt Mr Hadley will violate the rules. And if it is proved that a beneficiary has been cheating, they will be eliminated from the tournament. Also, there is little point in searching without solving puzzles. According to Mr Monroe, the prize is extremely well hidden and its whereabouts known by only him."

Despite being ever the gentleman, Darcy was losing his patience with Miss Kensett. Her belief that she was inherently deserving of privileges and special treatment was beyond the pale. Furthermore, he was eager to begin working on his own conundrums—the one in his breast pocket and Elizabeth's presence.

"I know what I shall do." Miss Kensett held her head high. "My brother is fascinated by word games. He absolutely adores them beyond expression."

"May I remind you that, barring an emergency or a disqualification, beneficiaries are to remain at Oakwood with no external communication until this time next week. Writing to your brother is not permitted."

"Yes, but books have been published on the subject." She gave him a superior smile. "And there is a library just across the vestibule."

Keeping his countenance extremely well, Darcy asked whether she had been listening when Mr Monroe told them they would find no collections there by Peregrine Puzzle-brains, Peter Puzzlewit, or their ilk. "All such material has been temporarily removed. Now, Miss Kensett, if you will excuse me, I shall remove myself."

He stood and bowed to her. "Oh, by the bye, in case you have not remembered, there are certain rooms beneficiaries are forbidden to enter during the tournament." He consulted his set of instructions. "The wine cellar, the servants' quarters and their hall, the larder, scullery, kitchens, butler's pantry, housekeeper's office, and all bedchambers other than one's own."

Turning then to the housekeeper, he said, "Please be so

kind as to show me to my room now, Mrs Vincent. And I apologise for keeping you waiting."

AT THE WRITING TABLE IN HIS ASSIGNED BEDCHAMBER, DARCY contemplated the words written upon the piece of paper he had unfolded the instant he entered the room.

Three-fourths of a cross and a circle complete,
Two semicircles and a perpendicular meet,
A triangle standing on two feet,
Two semicircles and a circle complete.

Crossing out his initial attempt at a solution, he put pencil to paper and tried again. *In which direction are the blasted semicircles supposed to face? Where, exactly, should the vertical line be placed? And how should all this be arranged on the page?*

His mind was preoccupied by that other conundrum, the one with intelligence, sparkling wit, incomparable mettle, fine eyes, pretty smile, and a strong sense of right and wrong.

The tip of the pencil snapped when, from an open window, her sweet voice floated on the breeze, all the way into his soul.

He rose to close the window. Instead, he lingered there watching Miss Rigby and Mr Hadley smiling at something Elizabeth said while they strolled, arm in arm, through the gardens.

Darcy turned away from the sight and sound of her. He vowed he would be polite, and he would show her that he had changed for the better. But he would not allow himself to be ruled again by anything other than rationality—not by his heart and certainly not by physics. *Elizabeth may have all the pull of gravity, but I shall not fall for her again.*

In an attempt to expunge the woman from his thoughts, he went for a brisk walk along woodland paths beyond the park. An hour or so later, while returning to the house, he noticed the occasional small cloud of smoke rising from the shrubbery. Concerned about fire, he investigated and discovered Peter Fordham sitting on a bench and puffing contentedly on a meerschaum pipe. Darcy nodded and greeted the man as he passed.

Although Darcy neither smoked a pipe nor used snuff, he found the wafting aroma rather pleasing, with its components of sweet honey, fresh orange, and smooth vanilla. The fragrance teased his nose and prodded his brain. *Eureka!*

❧

AT DINNER, MR MONROE CALLED FOR EVERYONE'S ATTENTION. "I congratulate one of you for having solved, in a trice, their first puzzle."

"Oh, well done, I say!" cried Mr Hadley. Almost immediately upon that utterance, his face grew red, and he gave a little laugh. "Well, obviously, the clever person is not me."

Mr Monroe rolled his eyes before continuing. "The solution has been verified by me, and the beneficiary is already working on their second. I trust that I shall not be divulging any secrets when I say that the poser they solved was an anagram."

The puzzle Darcy had solved was not one of that sort, and he had not yet gone looking for a place where 'tobacco' might be found. The butler's pantry was forbidden and Mr Fordham's bedchamber not a possibility either.

Miss Armstrong enjoyed spirits. Might she also have indulged in sot weed? Darcy had heard that snuff cured headaches and that Queen Charlotte was fond of it. As soon as possible, he would search for snuff boxes.

But which of the beneficiaries had solved, in a trice, their first poser and was working on their second? A glance round the table gave Darcy no clue as to which of his rivals was in the lead, but he knew it was not Mr Hadley and assumed it was not Miss Kensett.

So, either Mr Fordham or she of formidable intelligence and quick understanding.

7

RIDDLE ME THIS

On Friday, bathed in mellow morning sunshine, Elizabeth strode across Oakwood's lawns, the dewy grass dampening her hems and darkening her half-boots.

Now and then she caught snatches of male voices floating upon the breeze, and she spotted gardeners clipping the hedges. She paid them little notice, for her mind was otherwise engaged.

After solving her first conundrum—an anagram—the previous day, Elizabeth had been in a sanguine turn of mind. The letters in 'moon starer' quite readily had been rearranged to read 'astronomer'. Following that success, it had taken but a moment for her to find a book by Galileo Galilei upon a shelf in the library. Thumbing through its pages, she had discovered her next poser tucked between copper-engravings of lunar phases.

That next morning, though, as she walked farther away from the house, she was a little less confident in her ability. Frowning at the paper in her hand, she muttered, "The leaves of an oak tree are green in summer." Elizabeth peered about the grounds at the many deciduous trees in full leaf. *Oakwood has more oaks than Miss Kensett has waspish aspersions to utter.*

The night before, while the three ladies had sat chatting in the parlour waiting for the gentlemen to finish their ports and whatnot, Miss Kensett had turned to her and said, "You remind me of someone, Miss Bennet. There is something terribly familiar about your looks, your attire, and those country manners of yours." Tapping her fan upon her chin, she had paused as though in deep rumination. Finally, she had cried out, "Oh, I have it now! You put me in mind of dear Edith, my poor little maid whom I had to leave behind in Maidenhead. I believe she, too, comes from Herefordshire."

Before Elizabeth could make any sort of rejoinder, Miss Rigby had spoken. "Then you are most fortunate, Miss Kensett, to have in your service such a comely, well-dressed, genteel lady. But I must correct you, dear. Despite the two counties being only one letter removed from one another, Herefordshire and Hertfordshire actually are two separate places, and Miss Bennet is from the latter." The chaperon had then set aside her embroidery and clasped her hands together upon her lap. "Now, madam, I understand from Mr Monroe that your father is a prosperous bellows maker…"

Smiling in remembrance, Elizabeth thought it rather convenient to have a chaperon who also happened to be one's champion. At Longbourn, the only person who ever spoke up on her behalf or acted in support of her was her dearest sister, Jane.

Stopping near the shrubbery, she inhaled the sweet fragrance of pale pink dog-roses. On the other side of the hedge, gravel crunched beneath heavy footsteps.

"It most certainly is not."

"By gad, sir, how can you not see it? Here"—a paper

rustled—"look again. See? It is meant to be, I am quite sure of it."

About to quietly slip away before being caught eavesdropping on a private conversation, Elizabeth stopped in her tracks when the other gentleman was heard again.

"Your supposition, Hadley, is not only barmy but most improper." That deeper, more cultured voice belonged to none other than Mr Darcy. "Furthermore, as you must know, showing your puzzle to me and consulting my opinion is strictly forbidden. More importantly, how could you possibly think that leg in any way resembles Miss Bennet's lower limb?"

Rooted to the spot mid-stride, Elizabeth felt both her colour and her choler rise. *How dare they!*

Mr Darcy was still speaking. "Your visual puzzle plainly depicts part of the dining room's epergne. I expect you will find your next poser in one of its hollow legs." There was an interval of silence, then a huff. "Blast. I should not have revealed what I believe to be your solution. Forget I mentioned it."

"The dining room's what?" asked Mr Hadley.

"Epergne. Did you not notice the ornamental display in the middle of the table during dinner last night? No? Too busy gazing elsewhere, like a mooncalf, were you?" A sigh was heaved. "I speak of the ormolu centrepiece and its four cranberry-glass dishes overflowing with pyramids of fruit and nuts. Our host mentioned the Egyptian-influenced epergne was created for the Fifth Earl of Carlisle. As you know, Carlisle is where Miss Armstrong was born and raised, but Mr Monroe did not know how the ornate piece ended up in his client's possession. At any rate, its supporting legs are those of lions, Hadley. Lions, not Miss Bennet's shapely—"

Rounding the hedgerow and bristling with indignation, Elizabeth cleared her throat and was more than a little appeased by the looks of surprise, guilt, and mortification upon the gentlemen's faces. Mr Hadley quickly hid a piece of paper behind his back and hung his head. Mr Darcy consulted his watch and muttered something that sounded like, "Eleven o'clock. Of course."

Two grown men resembling naughty schoolboys caught in the midst of wrongdoing threatened to ruin Elizabeth's solemnity. Embarrassment and pique quickly converted to amusement.

First to regain his voice, Mr Darcy bowed to her. "Miss Bennet, please forgive us for speaking out of turn. It was badly done, and I apologise."

Red-faced, Mr Hadley nodded his agreement. "It was my fault, and I am duly ashamed and terribly, terribly sorry."

She gave the gentlemen as stern a look as could be managed under the circumstances. "Upon hearing myself discussed in such a way, I had considered reporting the two of you to Mr Monroe for collusion. But I shall not let the cat out of the bag. Such collaboration, it seems, was unintentional."

One of the gardeners earlier seen working along the hedgerow stepped up and doffed his cap. "Begging your pardon, madam, sirs. Is there some dishonest behaviour afoot here? Ought Mr Monroe to be fetched?"

The three beneficiaries looked guiltily at one another.

Elizabeth told the man there was no need. He gave each of them suspicious looks but lumbered away, shaking his head and mumbling to himself.

Once he had gone, she faced the gentlemen and said, "As Mr Darcy is aware, I delight in the ridiculous. Your remarks concerning lower limbs—mine and not mine—qualify as absurd. You are, therefore, forgiven."

She turned to go but swung back. "The creatures on the epergne are sphinxes, by the bye. They have the legs, paws, and claws of lions. I, on the other hand, am clawless...until provoked." She curtseyed then walked away, head held high.

Rounding the hedge, she heard Mr Hadley exclaim, "Upon my soul! Remind me to never again provoke such a lion-hearted lady."

Elizabeth grinned. *Lion-hearted. I like that. Much better than being sphinx-like.*

Upon first acquaintance, she had thought Mr Darcy and The Sphinx had a similar inscrutability. But at Hunsford she had witnessed the gentleman's agitated manner and heard his passionate declaration. Furthermore, since arriving at Oakwood, he had apologised to her not once but twice, and each time his feelings had been completely transparent. He was, after all, capable of passion, of making self-deprecating apologies, and of accepting humiliation. Her esteem for him flourished.

But what of his temper? At Netherfield he had suggested it might be resentful. Once his good opinion was gone, was it, indeed, gone for evermore?

She certainly had lost Mr Darcy's good opinion in Kent, but might it be regained in Buckinghamshire?

At present I cannot indulge any expectation of it. But she seriously turned her thoughts towards achieving such an accomplishment.

❧

FOR NO OTHER REASON THAN TO AVOID A SECOND ENCOUNTER with the gentlemen, Elizabeth retreated to the house.

Peeking inside the parlour, she found it occupied by Miss Kensett and Mr Fordham, both under the watchful eye of Miss Rigby, who was silently engaged in needlework. The other lady's work—a turban, it seemed—sat upon her lap, untouched; and the gentleman was seen wandering about the room, picking up and carefully inspecting each piece of knick-knackery.

Why are those two not working on their puzzles?

The chaperon's company would have been welcomed but not that of the other two. So Elizabeth wandered into the great hall with its massive but unlit hearth, its screens, coloured flagstones, dais, gallery, and what she had been told was a 'squint'—a peep-hole for spying or eavesdropping. The large cavity in the stone wall of the dais was concealed behind one of the room's seventeenth-century tapestries. The small peep-hole in the textile could only be seen if one knew it was there, for it was well disguised.

Earlier that morning, Mrs Vincent had taken Elizabeth and Mr Darcy, the only beneficiaries unfamiliar with the manor, on a tour of its public rooms. To the new housekeeper's understanding, the great hall had once been used for large-scale entertaining such as dancing or performances by a touring company of actors. Miss Armstrong, it seemed, had not offered any such diversions during the few years of her residency.

Feeling very small, Elizabeth thought such an immense, cold, draughty room ought not to be so long deprived of a merry crowd. *Oh, the private balls one could host here!* Imagining minstrels playing in the gallery, Elizabeth held her arms in a rounded formation, gently grasped her skirts, and performed a number of quadrille sequences. Even the exertion of dancing could not dispel the chill, and she shivered. Glancing suspiciously at the suits of armour and at the peep-hole, she felt as though someone was watching her.

Too uncomfortable to remain any longer, she crossed the vestibule and entered the manor's newest addition, built during the last century. Therein was an elaborate billiards table and other surfaces appropriate for playing games. Fresh packs of cards were scattered about, and three tables already were set up for backgammon, draughts, and chess.

Mr Monroe had told his guests they were responsible for their own entertainment between breakfast and dinner. "I invite you," he had said, "to enjoy your empty hours in the gardens, on walking paths, playing pall-mall or lawn bowls, or trying your hand at archery. There is fishing tackle to be had and a stocked fish pond. Indoors, Oakwood's library has a plentiful supply of old and new publications. And just off the parlour there is a chamber complete with pianoforte, a small organ, a harp, guitar, and popular books of music."

Elizabeth noticed that each room seemed to have an endless supply of new candles and writing materials. Nothing was lacking, as far as she could see. *There can be no excuse for ennui here.* Again, she wondered at some people's idleness.

Settling herself near the unlit fireplace on one of the room's many sofas, she again contemplated her puzzle. *The leaves of an oak tree are green in summer.* Was there some sort of hidden message within the sentence? *The 'eaves' in leaves, perhaps?* Was she to search under the eaves? Or had it something to do with eavesdropping through the peep-hole in the great hall?

So intently was Elizabeth studying the page that Miss Rigby gave her a start by speaking her name. She had neither heard the woman's approach nor detected her familiar rose-water perfume.

"Miss Bennet, may I join you? Miss Kensett has retired to her room for a well-deserved rest. I fear the rigours of incessant bleating, carping, and grumbling have quite fatigued the creature. And what are you working on there, dear?"

"Needlework…as in looking for the proverbial needle in a haystack." Elizabeth waved her piece of foolscap. "There must be something hidden within this rather simple sentence. Oh, fiddlesticks!" She folded the paper and tucked it inside the hidden pocket of her skirt. "I was not supposed to show that to anyone other than Mr Monroe."

"Indeed. And as much as I should like to assist you, I cannot." Miss Rigby settled beside her. "Gracious, this sofa is rather unyielding, is it not?"

Elizabeth had been staring at her puzzle for such a duration that the sentence, each word of it, each letter of it, was permanently, she feared, fixed behind her eyes. *The leaves of an oak tree are green in summer. Leaves of a... s of a...* "Yes!"

Gaining her feet, she curtseyed. "Miss Rigby, I beg your pardon, but I must leave you. There is something I must do that cannot be delayed." *For I very much wish to be the victor in this contest.*

The chaperon graciously excused her, and Elizabeth fled. With Miss Rigby occupying the games room and Mr Fordham in the parlour, she could not search those places. *But there are sofas in other roo—* "Oh!"

At that moment, Elizabeth discovered what happens when an unstoppable force, namely herself, meets an immovable object—namely the stolid, and very solid, Mr Darcy.

8

A SPECTACULAR DISPLAY

"Good God!" cried Darcy with more passion than politeness. "Are you well?" So great was his astonishment that it overcame the bounds of propriety, and he put his arms round her. While grateful to finally have her there, concern over her welfare overrode any other emotion.

Recollecting himself, he apologised for the collision, although it had been she who had rammed into him with great force. Soft curves remained obligingly crushed against his chest until he strengthened his resolve and slowly backed away. "Whatever is the matter?" From the corner of one eye, Darcy saw Miss Kensett descending the staircase, but he paid her no mind.

Miss Bennet stammered, "Forgive me. I was just... I..." Regaining her composure although her cheeks were ablaze, she drew herself up and said she was perfectly well. But when she touched her nose, she winced.

Her eyes are watery. The impact with my sternum must have been painful. "Shall I summon Mrs Vincent or one of the maids? Do you require a cold cloth or some ice?"

Darcy's earlier outburst must have alerted Miss Rigby, for suddenly she was before them, asking what had occurred and casting suspicion upon him. Placing her arm across Elizabeth's slender shoulders, the chaperon gently guided her towards the staircase, all the while murmuring to her as they left Darcy standing alone.

Before gaining the first stair, Elizabeth looked back over her shoulder at him. The soft expression upon her face crossed the distance separating them and laid claim to his heart—the heart he had tried with all his might to harden against her very presence. The struggle had been futile. He still was as much in her power as he ever had been.

He watched until his heart's desire, in her simple jonquil gown, retreated from sight. Her fragrance's sillage lingered in the air and on his clothing. Sniffing his sleeve, he caught a whiff of powdery sweetness, vanilla or honey, and fresh, crisp fruitiness. Fresh, pure, and—heaven help him—romantic.

Rousing himself, Darcy went hunting for tobacco. The most probable places were forbidden—the butler's pantry, bedchambers, and the ground-floor boudoir Miss Armstrong had used while still ambulant but unable to manage stairs. *Where else might blasted sot weed be kept?*

There was no one he could question about whether the elderly lady had even used tobacco. Neither Mr Monroe, the other beneficiaries, nor the servants would be of assistance. *If asked, the youngster, no doubt, would inadvertently give the game away.* Darcy shook his head at Mr Hadley's naiveté but could not help but like him. The younger man's little fever of admiration for Elizabeth proved he possessed good judgment, at least regarding the ladies.

Turning his musings towards his other conundrum, Darcy remembered there was in the library a cabinet, which

Mrs Vincent described as containing family heirlooms and knick-knackery from Miss Armstrong's formative years in Carlisle. He supposed its shelves might house a snuff box or two that once had belonged to her father or brothers.

Upon reaching his destination, Darcy greeted one of the footman brothers who was stationed beside the door.

"Miss Kensett is within, sir." Alfred's tone revealed nothing; his eyes conveyed a warning.

Darcy considered retreating and returning another time but chastised himself for cowardice. Shoulders back, he strode into the room. At first glance, the place seemed unoccupied until, above the back of a rose-coloured armchair, he glimpsed the tip of a brunette head. So as not to startle her, he softly cleared his throat before rounding the seat. Leant over a piece of foolscap, Miss Kensett seemed not to have heard him.

Averting his eyes from the puzzle resting upon the lady's lap, Darcy softly said, "Good day, madam. I hope I am not disturbing you."

The lady jumped and gave such a shriek of alarm that Alfred dashed into the room.

By the time Darcy had looked from the footman back to the woman, Miss Kensett had gained her feet, and her puzzle had slid to the floor. Her next action occurred so swiftly that Darcy might have missed it. But he did not. The thick spectacles that had rested upon the lady's blushing face were quickly torn off and concealed within the folds of her gown.

"Mr Darcy!" Her hand flew to her throat. "I… I…rarely wear those dreadful things. Truly! I require them only for reading, you see, and…" She seemed absolutely horrified that he had caught her wearing spectacles.

Heaven and Earth! Such vanity! Giving Miss Kensett a chance to regain her dignity, Darcy, without reading it, fetched the fallen paper from the Axminster carpet. The footman, he noticed, had left the room but loitered just beyond the door.

"Perhaps now, Mr Darcy," said the lady, snatching the puzzle from his hand, "you can comprehend why I required your assistance with yesterday's instructions. To make amends for refusing me that kindness, you may help decipher this." She waved the paper beneath his nose. When he refused to even look at it, she smiled a mirthless smile. "Or shall I apprise Mr Monroe of what I witnessed earlier? I distinctly remember you telling me that, according to the rules, there can be no collaboration between beneficiaries. Yet I saw you and Miss Bennet in an ardent embrace."

Darcy bristled. "That, madam, was not"—*as much as I might wish it*—"an embrace, ardent or otherwise. It was more of a...a clutch as the result of a collision." *One with quite an impact on me.*

Mr Monroe advanced towards them. "Alfred informed me there might be some sort of problem or misconduct here. Is that so, Miss Kensett? Mr Darcy?"

"No, sir," said Darcy, looking the attorney in the eye. "Neither problem nor wrongdoing has occurred. I am afraid I startled poor Miss Kensett. She dropped something, and I retrieved it for her."

"Yes." The lady nodded in agreement. "The gentleman caught me quite unawares."

Mr Monroe looked as though he did not believe either of them.

Sidling up to the older man, Miss Kensett said, "Now, sir, I wonder whether I might have a moment of your time." She hooked her arm through his. "I am having a spot of bother with this silly little puzzle, you see, and..." They strolled from the room.

Darcy wondered what Miss Kensett actually might say to Mr Monroe, but it mattered not. *Elizabeth and I did nothing wrong.*

Left blessedly alone, he walked about the library, marvelling at its furnishings and decorations. He had been there the previous day in the company of the housekeeper and Elizabeth but had been too distracted by the latter's disturbing presence to take note of much anything else.

With cosy corner nooks on either side of the fireplace and its floral this and its delicate that, never before had Darcy been in such a book-room. Two walls were pink, two covered with flowery papers, and the paintings gracing them featured plants or dishes of fruit. Cream-coloured paint coated the furniture, bookcases, shelves, and windowsills. Fabrics of various designs and in every shade of light green had been chosen for curtains, upholstery, tablecloths, and cushions. Delights fresh from the garden burst forth from eight delicate vases, and three elegant Axminster carpets in soft shades and leafy patterns were scattered across the oaken floor. With several pretty shawls flung over the backs of sofas and chairs, the room was decidedly feminine.

In contrast, the hundreds of periodicals and leather-bound volumes covered a multitude of topics such as astronomy, history, gardening, war, and, predominantly, law. There were atlases, travel guides, dictionaries, and a few works by poets. Notably missing were conduct books, novels, and periodicals of *La Belle Assemblée's* ilk.

The lady truly was something of an enigma.

Darcy had his own enigma to solve, and situated between two windows was the cabinet he sought. Inside its glass doors, shelves displayed an eclectic assortment of fripperies and curiosities—fragrant sachets, pomanders, perfume bottles, cockle shells, a pair of homemade shoes, old fairings, a couple of pocket watches, and a collection of rather hideous statuettes.

When he opened one of the cabinet drawers, Darcy discovered, to his great satisfaction, a variety of snuff boxes —eleven, to be exact—nestled amongst bunches of dried herbs and flowers. *Similar to Elizabeth, Miss Armstrong undoubtedly had an appreciation for nature.*

Glancing through one of the windows overlooking Oakwood's rose garden, he remembered the day in Kent when he had caught the independent Miss Elizabeth Bennet picking wildflowers while humming and wandering alone through a meadow.

Only then, standing there at that window, did he realise how akin to wildflowers she was—blooming, fragrant, bright, natural. She thrived without much assistance. She was delicate yet hardy and, to a degree, uncultivated.

His traitorous mind then imagined Mr Hadley obtaining a pretty posy of wildflowers from an obliging field and presenting them to her. *Why did I not think of doing something similar in Kent?* To his chagrin, Darcy realised that, even in his imagination, the younger man knew how to please Elizabeth far better than he, himself, ever had. *Should I offer Elizabeth a bouquet from the gardens here? What would be her response to such a gift from me?*

Enough! He could not, would not, risk having either his heart or his pride injured by her a second time. With steely determination, he set about opening and examining each snuff box, hoping to find his next puzzle.

Most likely never used for its intended purpose, the pristine interior of an ivory box held a scrap of red silk. Nestled within was a single jade earring.

Nothing but a tortoiseshell lining and a piece of fluff was found inside the gold box.

Sporting a magnificent dragon on its lid, an enamel box was filled with what Darcy assumed was desiccated tobacco. He sniffed. *Not snuff!* He sneezed. *Pepper!*

The pair of matching boxes crafted from malachite each held a pencil stub but no puzzle.

A silver bracelet, its inscription tarnished beyond legibility, rested within the *papier-mâché* box, the flower and butterfly design on its lid barely discernible beneath a layer of grime. Darcy wiped his palms on his handkerchief and continued.

The most unusual snuff boxes were the five carved from a variety of exotic woods. The odd-shaped fish surrendered nothing but a musty smell, and the comical frog had captured an insect.

A teak monkey with eyes of glass looked promising but proved disappointing. When its hinged neck was tipped back, the creature's stomach revealed a mouldy bit of something that once might have been edible. The lid was quickly snapped shut on that one.

Two boxes remained.

Engraved with the words 'to warm the heart', the box carved to resemble a bellows probably had been given as a love token. It held a tiny, torn scrap of vellum. *Could it be?* When unfolded, the fine parchment cracked, and its edges crumbled. Barely legible in faded ink were the words 'Your Servant, EK'. *Not a puzzle, then, just the closing of an archaic love letter.*

Rather than acrimony, I should have written words of love to Elizabeth. Better yet, I should have spoken them to her.

Since that evening at Hunsford, Darcy had spent far too much time reliving unfulfilled dreams. Sleep had been lost, as had much of his appetite. Thankfully, he had a large, prosperous estate to oversee, and he was bound and determined to do his duty and do it well. But those two long, lonely months had been difficult.

Now, seeing again those fine eyes, basking in her smiles, inhaling her unique fragrance, and hearing her voice...but knowing she never will be mine is nothing less than torment.

Chastising himself for still pining for that which he never had, Darcy opened the final box.

Well, well! As is always the case, whatever one is looking for is found in the last place one looks.

In retrospect, a miniature wooden shoe, symbolising luck, should have been the first snuff box he opened, not the eleventh.

But that eleventh box would lead him one step closer to winning the tournament. And, just as eleven steps had led him up to the offices of Pemberton & Monroe, that meeting had led him—for better or for worse—back to Elizabeth Bennet.

Settling into the same armchair Miss Kensett had vacated, Darcy unfolded the prized paper. The penmanship inscribed upon it had long, thin, angular lines like a spider's legs. Reading what he assumed had been the elderly Miss Armstrong's handwriting, he smiled because he had learnt both the puzzle and its solution as a child.

To places where ships are safe from a storm
Add that which makes part of your face;
And when these two are together, they'll form
The name of a very brave place.

How and where would one find a place in Hampshire at Oakwood Manor? During his tour of the public rooms, Darcy had noticed no framed paintings of the naval base. But, in the very room in which he sat, there were globes and, more importantly, atlases. Choosing the volume featuring a collection of maps of England, he thumbed through its pages and found not only Portsmouth but a piece of foolscap with his next poser.

He congratulated himself and sought Mr Monroe and verification.

⁂

AT DINNER, THE TABLE'S EPERGNE CAPTURED MR HADLEY'S fulsome notice. Apparently, neither the vivacious Elizabeth nor the handsome Miss Kensett could hold a candle to the reappearance of that ormolu and cranberry-glass wonder. The young gentleman's hazel eyes virtually bored holes into the leonine legs supporting the ornate centrepiece.

Try as he might, Darcy could barely conceal his amusement. Seated opposite him, Elizabeth frequently held a linen table napkin against her lips, and he suspected she did so to conceal her own smiles.

During the dessert course, Mr Monroe called for attention. "I congratulate two of you for having correctly solved a second puzzle."

While the attorney had the other diners' ears and eyes, Darcy watched Mr Hadley surreptitiously tilt the epergne—nearly toppling fruit from its glass dishes in the process—and insert a probing finger inside one of its hollow legs.

Mr Monroe asked for a round of applause for the tournament's leaders, and everyone complied, although Sophia Kensett and Peter Fordham seemed to do so reluctantly.

The youngest beneficiary took that opportunity to swivel the centrepiece and try again. With altruistic gladness, Darcy witnessed the moment Mr Hadley removed a slender strip of paper from one of the sphinx's limbs.

"Upon my soul! I have it!" Mr Hadley held up his prize, then pushed back his chair. Fetching another piece of paper from a breast pocket, he rushed to the rather annoyed-looking attorney's side. "Mr Monroe," he said, almost gasping, "please verify that I have correctly solved my first puzzle and found my second."

"Young man, you might have waited until after dinner and spared me, and perhaps others, from a bout of dyspepsia." Their host scrutinised the two pages before announcing that, with two solved puzzles apiece, Elizabeth and Darcy were in a draw for first place. Mr Fordham and Mr Hadley, each having achieved success with one puzzle, held second place.

Miss Kensett's lip curled so sardonically that Darcy wondered whether the woman suffered from a bad case of the aforementioned impaired digestion.

❦ 9 ❧

GAMES PEOPLE PLAY

On Saturday, in as desultory a manner as can be imagined, the seven of them sat round the dim parlour, drinking tea or coffee, eating cake, and listening to rain patter against windowpanes. Amongst them, there seemed little in the way of plan, purpose, or enthusiasm. Few bothered to give even a vague impression of employment.

On the laps of Elizabeth and the other two ladies, embroidery needles sat idle, pushed into fabric held taut within tambour frames.

Although Mr Darcy held a newspaper, he either fixedly looked upon her or stared vacantly into space. It was impossible for Elizabeth to determine his focus with any degree of accuracy. As for the others…

"Faith! I have it!"

Fiddlesticks. Has Mr Hadley solved yet another puzzle and already found his next? For her own part, Elizabeth was having difficulty with her third poser, the one she had found tucked up beneath the cushions of a sofa. Her puzzles were increasingly difficult, and in addition to that inconvenience, she was in a draw for first place with none other than Mr Darcy.

Given the importance of winning Miss Armstrong's legacy for the sake of her family, she had mixed feelings about Mr Hadley gaining on her slight advantage. She liked him well enough and, under different circumstances, might have wanted him to succeed. *Just not at my own expense and that of my mother and sisters.*

Turning his back to the watery window, Mr Hadley exclaimed, "Games! If we are to be confined to the house because of this ghastly wet, I propose we play parlour games here in the parlour. Or perhaps, more appropriately, we might play them in the games room. What do you say?"

"I say," Miss Kensett said rather drily, "that parlour games should be played only in the parlour."

Elizabeth thought the note of sarcasm in the lady's voice and the sneer on her face most unbecoming. "I think," said she, "that parlour games are a splendid idea whether played here in the parlour or in the games room." She leant forwards, waiting with eager anticipation for the others to agree.

A groan emanated from the vicinity of the plush pink sofa. Mr Fordham might even have muttered an oath. "I shall decline. It has been years since I participated in that sort of frivolity. Most likely never, come to think of it."

The chaperon and the attorney declared they were too advanced in years to engage in parlour games; and seated on opposite ends of a striped sofa, Miss Kensett and Mr Darcy remained, respectively, sullen and silent and as dull as the day. Glancing at all the sour, uninspired faces, Elizabeth suspected Mr Hadley and she were the only light-hearted people in the room. By then, though, even he had donned a woebegone expression.

One glance at that young man's disappointed face must have given Miss Rigby second thoughts because, after quietly consulting with Mr Monroe, she addressed the room. "Tut-tut. Such dreadful indifference! Come, come, everyone. We must not curb the vivacity of our two youngest companions."

"Hear, hear!" Mr Monroe injected a dose of enthusiasm into his voice. "Let us not add to the gloom of this dreary day. We all shall be delighted to play parlour games, Mr Hadley."

Miss Kensett yawned behind her fan before speaking in a listless manner. "Oh goody. I am in utter ecstasy at the very thought." Languidly, she turned to Mr Darcy and placed bejewelled fingers upon his sleeve. "What say you, sir? Shall we plunge our faces in flour and our fingers in flames?"

Elizabeth wanted to roll her eyes but would not. *In such cases as these, one must be gracious and easy-going. However, I could neither speak listlessly nor move languidly, even if my life depended upon it. And, Miss Kensett, do stop pawing at Mr Darcy.*

"No, no, Miss Kensett," Mr Hadley was saying, "nothing so hazardous as Bullet Pudding or Snapdragon. I suggest Buffy Gruffy, Musical Magic, or Short Answers. Or all three!"

Another groan emanated from the plush pink sofa. Its disapprobation, having been expressed, was immediately disregarded.

Mr Darcy flung aside his newspaper. "Buffy Gruffy? Surely you jest."

"Up!" Mr Monroe shot to his feet. "Everyone, up! We are for the games room. Miss Rigby and I shall brook no disappointment." He offered his arm to the chaperon, and they led the mostly grumbling parade out of the parlour.

THERE WAS SOME MANOEUVRING FOR POSITION IN THE GAMES room once Christopher had been ordered to arrange seven chairs in a circle.

Miss Kensett had insisted Mr Darcy sit beside her, but both he and Mr Hadley had scrambled for seats on either side of Elizabeth.

Seeking a favourable position had been for nought. Once the first player was blindfolded—Mr Hadley since Buffy Gruffy had been his idea—the others silently rose from their chairs and swapped places. "Now remember," said the ring-leader from the centre of the circle, "you must respond honestly or risk a forfeit. And do try your best to disguise your voice."

To initiate the game, Mr Monroe clapped, and with an enthusiastic step, Mr Hadley walked round in front of the others several times, bumping into knees. Finally stopping at a particular chair, he said, "Are you a man or a woman?"

In a prim falsetto that suspiciously sounded like Miss Kensett's voice, Mr Darcy said, "How dare you question my sex, sir!"

Someone snickered. Someone else gasped. Elizabeth's jaw dropped. *Good heavens. The staid gentleman is actually cooperating and performing.*

"Well, madam," said Mr Hadley, "if you have to pay a forfeit in this parlour game, which of the men here will you kiss?"

Someone, being Mr Fordham, snickered again.

The tips of Mr Darcy's ears reddened. "I suppose"—his falsetto had risen higher—"I would choose...Mr Darcy. But I—"

"Ha! I do not even need to ask a final question. You are Mr Darcy!"

"Was I not convincing?"

"No." Smiling, Mr Hadley removed the blindfold and handed it to him.

With more good humour than Elizabeth anticipated, Mr Darcy went to the centre, donned the blindfold, and waited while seats were exchanged and until someone clapped. He then took his time walking inside the circle, seemingly listening for telltale signs and trying to distinguish each person's scent.

Elizabeth's eyes widened when, on his second pass, he stopped directly in front of her. She had not made a sound. Had he detected the essences she distilled? The unique fragrance she created for herself in Longbourn's still room featured clover, apple, violet, and cucumber.

"Have you ever visited the Hunsford parsonage in Kent?" His shins were but a hairbreadth from Elizabeth's knees.

What can he mean by introducing such a weighty subject in the company of others?

His fine, tall form, his deep voice, his very proximity produced within her such vibrations that it was difficult to breathe let alone answer. Modulating her tone, Elizabeth spoke gently, like Miss Rigby. "Why yes, young man, I have."

His firm jaw clenched, and he seemed to hold himself with a rigidity beyond his customary good posture. "I see. And did anything of significance occur there?"

"Yes," she whispered, forgetting to disguise her voice. "I was cruel to someone that evening, and I long to be forgiven by them." *How can I possibly continue playing this game?* With pensive admiration, Elizabeth regarded the gentleman's handsome face. She could not see his eyes because of the blindfold, but his features had seemed to soften at her whispered apology.

"I am certain you have their forgiveness, madam."

Glancing round the circle, Elizabeth saw an assemblage

of confusion, and she wondered what the others thought about such odd questions and answers.

Mr Darcy cleared his throat. "Last question. During Mr Hadley's interrogation, did I, perhaps, make a cake of myself?" There was a fleeting quirk at the corners of his mouth.

Elizabeth's heart went pit-a-pat. *I do like this good-humoured Mr Darcy. I like him very much indeed.* In an approximation again of the chaperon's voice, she replied, "Yes, young man, I am afraid you did make a cake of yourself, but it was very sweet."

"I thank you, Miss Rigby."

"I am not Miss Rigby."

To all appearances, he had guessed incorrectly, so Mr Darcy then had to move on and ask three questions of another player.

For an interval following their public tête-à-tête, Elizabeth spared Buffy Gruffy scant heed. She was too busy listening to her heart. *I truly feel I could learn to love him. Such perfect timing, Lizzy, now, when all is in vain.*

◈

BY MID-AFTERNOON, THE SKY HAD CLEARED, WHICH WAS MORE than could be said of Elizabeth's muddled thoughts. Pacing in her bedchamber, she fretted and she pondered and she suppressed rising hope.

Had Mr Darcy truly forgiven her? Was it possible he still felt an attachment? *Preposterous!* Such a likelihood was contrary to reason and common sense. It went against the gentleman's very nature. He had made it abundantly clear his temper could be resentful and that his good opinion once lost was lost for evermore.

He is such an enigma! And just when I need to give all my attention to solving this other perplexing one. Frowning at the words upon a piece of foolscap in her hand, Elizabeth stopped at the window but soon walked away. No light had been shed on the puzzle she needed to solve.

Had she been struggling with a problem at Longbourn, she would have set out for a nice long ramble, and her pace would have gradually increased until she was running at full tilt. While such indecorousness could not be attempted at Oakwood, the situation definitely called for a brisk walk. Her decision to go had nothing at all to do with the fact that she had just spotted Mr Darcy striding towards the hilly, wooded paths.

Minutes later, while passing the hedgerows, Elizabeth heard rustling just beyond the dog-roses. *Leaves moving in the breeze?* There was no breeze. She tried peering through the shrubbery.

Without further warning, something green and misshapen rounded the bushes and rushed at her. She screamed.

"Miss Ben—" Bent almost double, holding one hand against her heaving chest and the other at her waist, Miss Kensett panted and wheezed. "Miss Bennet...I have been up and down...those nasty, prickly brambles...all afternoon in the hope of...encountering you. Must you walk with such haste? I had to run to catch up with you. Now I cannot catch my breath...and I have this...dreadful stitch in my side."

"Up and down prickly brambles! All afternoon? Good heavens, 'tis little wonder you are winded."

But otherwise unscathed, it seems. Had I been climbing thorn bushes for hours on end, I might have incurred a scratch or two.

Elizabeth guided Miss Kensett to the nearest bench and ensured it was dry after the morning's rain. She thought the lady might have looked resplendent in that Pomona green gown and emerald-coloured turban had she not been in such a state of inelegance.

Once they both had settled themselves and arranged their skirts just so, Elizabeth said, "You could have sought me in the house, you know. I was there this past hour trying to solve my current puzzle. You need not have enfeebled yourself."

The rasp in the lady's chest by then was a disconcerting whistle. "No, no. I need to speak to you in privacy. Thanks to Mr Monroe's uncouth announcement at dinner last night, everyone is now aware I am in last place. Through no fault of my own, I might add."

Elizabeth simply stared at her.

"Well, it is not my fault that I do not possess the ability to decipher complex rhyming vocabulary. I tried, on two separate occasions, to solicit assistance. Both that handsome Mr Darcy and young Mr Hadley were terribly sorry they could not help me. As for that unscrupulous Mr Fordham... Well! The very sight of him is odious to me. I cannot bear the thought of being outdone by someone so mean and deceitful." She leant in and whispered, "I am sorry to say it of anyone, but he thinks of himself before anybody else and is intent on snatching—yes, snatching!—everything he possibly can."

Miss Kensett placed a gloved hand upon Elizabeth's. "As the sole females in this silly competition, I say we should work together, you and I. What do you think?"

She seemed earnest in her application, but Elizabeth could not risk disqualification. "You know perfectly well such collusion is strictly forbidden. I am sorry, but I am unable to help you."

"Unable or unwilling?" Leaning away, Miss Kensett

uttered an inarticulate sound, making her dissatisfaction known. "How terribly disappointing it is to discover one's friends can be so terribly, terribly selfish." Standing, she spoke in high agitation. "You have provoked me, but I shall know how to exact revenge."

We never were friends, madam. Elizabeth had made an enemy, but she would not relent. "I, too, am acquainted with a woman whose own ease and gratification seem to be her ruling principles, and yes, it is disappointing." Standing, she faced her rival. "Now, if you are fully recovered, I shall leave you." Before striding away, she added, "With any luck, I shall find ease and happiness in yonder woods."

ABOUT A QUARTER OF THE WAY UP THE SHADED BRIDLEWAY, Elizabeth encountered Mr Darcy returning from his walk. He was not alone, and he did not appear best pleased with his companion. Both gentlemen seemed inordinately glad to see her, but it was Mr Fordham who offered his arm and steered her back the way she had come.

"You and I have not had an opportunity to improve our acquaintance, Miss Bennet," said he, "and it would give me particular pleasure to have the chance to do so now. By the bye, I understand you are from Hertfordshire, and I was wondering whether you are at all familiar with…"

🌿 10 🌿
AFFRONT & ABACK

As Mr Fordham walked ahead with Elizabeth, Darcy's steely-eyed glare was focused—not unlike he was aiming a pistol—on the back of the gentleman's skull. *His disingenuous manoeuvres disgust me.*

Not ten minutes prior, Mr Fordham had enquired whether Darcy had ever visited Hertfordshire. Upon receiving a positive reply and proclaiming a fascination with stately houses, he questioned him about his knowledge of Ashridge House and the ruins at Berkhamsted Castle, less than forty miles from Oakwood. Darcy suspected the man's intrigue, in some manner, was connected to a puzzle he could not solve.

While Darcy followed the others, narrow rays of sunlight filtered through overhead leaves and dappled the forest floor. The melodic, fluting songs of blackcaps sounded from nearby trees, and he resented the fact that his peaceful ramble through the old hunting forest had been interrupted by the intrusive gentleman and his prying enquiries. He could not, however, regret the arrival of Elizabeth.

No longer able to hold himself back, Darcy hastened his step, pleased the bridleway was wide enough to accommodate three people walking abreast. "Mr Fordham, if it is your intention to inveigle information from Miss Bennet and me in a bid to advance your standing in the tournament, I advise you to think again. You risk disqualification for not only yourself but us as well, and I will not have it."

"Come, come, old chap. As rivals in this contest, one must do what one must to win." The shorter man held his ground, but Darcy's intense stare was more efficient when applied face-to-face, forcing Mr Fordham to look away. "Humph! I shall not remain here being affronted and listening to more of your sanctimoniousness." A curt bow was offered, and he was gone, down the path, out of sight.

Stepping closer, Darcy offered Elizabeth his arm, and they walked some time in easy silence.

"One must speak a little, you know," said she. "You might say something about that man's deviousness, then I might tell you about Miss Kensett's tactics." She looked up at him, fine eyes twinkling, pretty mouth smiling.

He had an unsettling impulse to dip his head and kiss her. *To indulge one's appetites without restraint is not the action of a gentleman.* The desire lasted precisely eleven seconds. Darcy knew that because he had been counting to ten, battling temptation, but the allure of her lips had heated his blood and distracted him for an additional second.

Tearing his gaze from her mouth, he forced a smile upon his own. "I am unwilling to speak, you know, unless I can say something utterly notable. Shall I quote Shakespeare? 'It is the bright day that brings forth the adder, and that craves wary walking'. Oh, fear not, Miss Bennet. Mr Fordham has gone, and I have seen no actual snakes hereabouts."

There was so much Darcy wanted to say and so much he

needed to say, but the moment was not right. They were almost out of the woods.

And there is that other matter.

The information Mr Hadley had imparted was partly conjecture, and Darcy would spread no rumours. Still, it was his responsibility to protect the interests of those close to him, and that included the precious creature by his side.

"You appear deep in thought, sir. Are you pondering your current puzzle?"

"Indeed, I am." *You are the greatest puzzle of all, Elizabeth. And I could not bear another rejection from you. But if I paid my addresses properly this time and asked again, would your answer be the same as in April?*

Her sweet face was tilted towards him still, and he wondered how and when the sun had reached beneath her bonnet's brim and sprinkled freckles across her button nose.

Placing a gloved hand over the dainty one resting upon his sleeve, Darcy came to a halt. "I am not one for gossip. I dislike hearing it, and I avoid speaking it. But there is something afoot at the manor, and you soon will learn of it at any rate." Glancing ahead, he pointed to a bench embraced on three sides by sprawling junipers. "Come, let us sit there, and I shall tell you what I know as fact."

Seated then amongst spiny evergreens, Elizabeth inhaled deeply and made an 'mmm' sort of sound. "Juniper is such a powerful, intoxicating aroma. Fresh, sharp, sappy. I quite like it."

I am glad to hear it. Darcy, too, liked the scent—so much so that juniper was a base component in his bespoke fragrance. *So, she thinks I smell powerful and intoxicating. And sappy. I trust she does not mean green and juvenile, like a sapling. Still, I do remember the hot, heady days of youth when the sap was rising and...*

"What was it you wanted to tell me, Mr Darcy?"

That I love you still. "When we arrived on Thursday, there was a large vase in front of the parlour's fireplace, and it was still there this morning. Did you happen to notice it?"

"Do you mean the exotic white and blue one with depictions of chrysanthemums, peonies, and dianthus? I recall it being somewhat egg-shaped and absolutely exquisite."

You, madam, are exquisite...and definitely not egg-shaped. "Yes, that one. According to Mr Hadley, Mrs Vincent intended to replace the flowers in it a few hours ago, but it has, apparently, disappeared. While housekeeper, maids, and footmen were searching for it, Mr Hadley arrived in the parlour fully expecting to find a piece of foolscap inside that very same vase. I believe he presently is with Mr Monroe, confirming his solution and asking how to secure his next puzzle. Furthermore, the vase—seventeenth-century Japan— probably is irreplaceable."

Darcy wanted to share with her all Mr Hadley had told him, but he would not malign Mr Fordham without irrefutable evidence.

"There you are!" The chaperon stormed towards them, or, more accurately, towards Darcy.

He sprang to his feet. Never before had he seen Miss Rigby looking so displeased.

"You know better than to abscond with a young lady without informing her chaperon of your intention." The fierce look she gave him would have made a lesser man wilt.

From beyond the bench, another voice, a male one, spoke up. "All is well, Miss Rigby. I've been doing a bit of pruning back here and keeping an eye on the two young lovers for you."

Young lovers? Darcy chanced a glance at Elizabeth. She was blushing, and her lips had puckered into a perfect little heart shape. When he forced himself to look away from her mouth, he espied a worker emerging from the junipers and recognised him as one of the gardeners from the previous day in the shrubbery.

Miss Rigby nodded her thanks to the man, then addressed Elizabeth. "You should not be alone out here with"—she scowled again at Darcy—"him."

Why does she dislike me so? Whatever the reason, he was thankful Miss Rigby had not the supervision of Elizabeth during the young lady's stay in Kent. Had such a strict chaperon been there, she and he would not have been able to meet for their private rambles within the park. *At least I thought Elizabeth and I had an arrangement to meet alone there. The more fool I!*

"Mr Darcy," said the chaperon, "you have been summoned by Mr Monroe. He presently is holding court in the library." With efficient brusqueness, she bid the gardener a good day, turned on her heel, and spoke over her shoulder. "Come along quickly now, both of you."

As the three strode towards the manor, the somewhat less spry Miss Rigby gradually lagged behind, out of earshot.

"That woman makes me feel like a lad being summoned for reprimand."

"I am all astonishment, sir. Do you actually know how it feels to be rebuked?"

Darcy gave her a pointed look. "Yes, I do. And you, of all people, should know that." He feared he had offended her when she turned her head away and was silent. The only sound was wood being chopped somewhere in the distance. To his relief, several beats of his heart later, her eyes met his with a teasing glint.

"Surely Mr Darcy of Pemberley never did anything naughty."

His ears reddened, and he was glad his hair was in need of a cut and that his hat sat low. Inspired by her gentle tease, he waggled his eyebrows at her and was rewarded with a delighted smile. Darcy's heart then soared like a long-winged, forked-tailed red kite aloft on a summery breeze.

"Speaking of things that astonish me, sir, I was equally surprised this morning when you played Buffy Gruffy. I had not thought you would so willingly expose yourself to ridicule. But, with such commendable thespian talent, you could have had a career on stage. How did I not know that about you?"

"There are many things you do not know about me. And, since we parted in Kent, I have tried to change for the better. You may be pleased to know that any improvement you might perceive was wrought entirely thanks to you." He cast a quick look over his shoulder at the chaperon. "But that is all I shall say on the subject for the nonce. As for acting... At age eleven, shortly after my mother died, I was sent to school. There, amongst other things—some more unpleasant than others—we learnt elocution, and we performed scenes from the books we had to read." He further lowered his voice. "In fact, I have been acting my entire life. Acting superior. Acting the fool. Acting—"

Miss Rigby caught up with them, for they had arrived by then at the house.

Subsequent events happened with a swiftness that left Darcy standing alone until Alfred, at his customary post in the vestibule, came and received his hat, gloves, and walking stick. All the while Darcy's eyes remained fixed on Elizabeth as the chaperon swept her away, up the wide staircase.

Next, Alfred opened the library door and announced him. There Darcy was greeted by a distracted Mr Monroe and invited to join him at a Sheraton writing table. Behind them, the footman silently left and closed the door.

Settled into a low chair, Darcy could not help but ask, "Are you well, sir?" The attorney was pale and appeared bone-weary.

"Well enough, I thank you." Mr Monroe rubbed his temples, casting doubt on his assertion of health. "This has been quite the day, though. A valuable vase has gone missing. And the sequence of Mr Hadley's search has been disrupted, but that is the least of my troubles. I have a master list and shall have the young man's difficulty resolved in no time. However, I have had two—no, three—complaints concerning you, sir."

"Complaints? About me?" Taken aback, Darcy uncrossed his legs and sat straighter.

"I am afraid so. The first report concerns a tender moment witnessed yesterday, near the games room, between you and another beneficiary. You cannot doubt to what I allude, yet on Thursday you informed me there was no attachment there." He pinched the bridge of his nose. "Which is it, sir? Do you have an understanding, or are you a scoundrel?"

Darcy opened his mouth to protest, but the attorney held up a hand. "A moment, please. I must emphasise that the young lady in question is under my and Miss Rigby's protection here, and I promised her father she would be perfectly safe. Now, what do you have to say for yourself?"

"I give my solemn word as a gentleman that Miss Elizabeth Bennet is, unequivocally, in no danger from me. What occurred yesterday was the result of an impact. It seems that at the time of the collision neither of us was watching where we were going. If there is any menace here at Oakwood, it is not from me. I cannot speak for the others, but I am fairly certain Mr Hadley also presents no danger to Miss Bennet."

Mr Monroe nodded thoughtfully. "I have heard such differing accounts of you that I am exceedingly puzzled. One detractor says you are disobliging. Cruel even. Another critic asserts you purposely are hampering their progress in the tournament. Yet another fault-finder fears you may be a rake. On the other hand, there is at least one beneficiary who told me they recently changed their mind about you and now believe you hang the moon. As for Miss Bennet, I do not know her opinion."

I would not care for you to know what Elizabeth thought of me two months ago, but I would give the world to know what she thinks of me now.

"You should know, Mr Darcy, that everyone employed here at Oakwood has been tasked with keeping an eye on you and the other beneficiaries during this competition. Several of them, when asked, reported seeing you secretly meeting with others."

"I was not aware that simply being in company with them constitutes collusion."

"Not at all, not at all." The attorney cleared his throat. "But then there was that curious exchange you had with Miss Bennet during Gruffy Buffy or whatever it is called. I could not hear her soft response to your second question. Still, those first two enquiries seemed rather odd and not at all in keeping with a silly game. My concern, of course, is Miss Armstrong's insistence that this property not be sold. However, I am willing to give you the benefit of the doubt. Just be aware you are, almost always, under observation and that I am sure to receive intelligence of any wrongdoing."

Standing, Mr Monroe extended an arm towards the library door. "Oh, before you go... I have not received a request for verification from you today. Do you have something for me?"

Between the morning's parlour games and the afternoon's walk, Darcy had forgotten about his solved puzzle. Standing and reaching into a breast pocket, he withdrew two items. The first, a piece of foolscap, was unfolded and placed upon the table.

I cut my first with my second and put my whole in my pocket.

"That," said Darcy, "required little thought. And this"—he added a penknife with a slip of paper wound round it to the foolscap—"was readily found in the drawer right there beside you."

"Well done, sir." Mr Monroe unfurled the paper from the knife, gave it a glance, nodded, and returned it to Darcy. "Be assured that casting aspersions upon you did not come easily to me, and I wish you continued good fortune in the days ahead."

Pocketing his newest puzzle, Darcy gave the man a stiff bow before striding away. It had not been his first time on the carpet, but it had been many, many years, and he did not appreciate having his integrity questioned.

Upon opening the library door, he came face-to-face with Peter Fordham, who must have been lurking about and, perhaps, eavesdropping.

❧ 11 ❧
JUNIPER, JIMMY, & A ROSE

Elizabeth was about halfway down the staircase when she heard the library door being wrenched open.

Stopping on the stair, she spotted Alfred stationed in the corner between the parlour and the front door. Below, to her right, Mr Fordham had just drawn himself up, his height insignificant in the face of the other gentleman's admirable tallness.

"I suppose you reported me to Monroe for trying to inveigle information about Berkhamsted Castle," snarled Mr Fordham.

"Against my better judgment, I did not." Mr Darcy's temper, in Elizabeth's estimation, was commendable in its forbearance.

"As it happens, your assistance was completely unnecessary." Mr Fordham shook some papers in Mr Darcy's face. "Now stand aside so I may obtain our host's verification."

To spy on their altercation had not been Elizabeth's intention, so she acknowledged Alfred and sneaked down and rounded the staircase. Hearing what sounded like a cry of either anguish or outrage from the vicinity of the parlour, she pushed open its door, which had stood ajar. Stopping short in the doorway, she espied Miss Kensett within and asked, "What on earth are you doing?"

There was a shriek and a crash as the vase from which Miss Kensett had been pulling flowers slipped from her hand and shattered on hardwood. Both ladies gaped at the damage —a spreading pool of water and the jagged remnants of what had been a lovely porcelain vase in soft shades of pink and green. A spray of mignonettes, emitting a delicate, musky fragrance, lay splayed across the wet floor.

"Look what you made me do! What do you mean by sneaking up on me in such a boorish manner? This is your fault, Miss Bennet!"

In the face of adversity, Elizabeth exerted herself to emulate Mr Darcy's commendable forbearance. "I hardly—"

"Begging your pardon, Miss Bennet." Christopher had come from behind. As he slipped past, he was accosted by Miss Kensett.

"You there! Yes, you, footman. Clean this up at once!"

"Mrs Vincent has already been summoned, miss," replied the harried servant. "She and Henrietta will be here directly."

Still standing at the parlour entrance, Elizabeth did a further survey of the room and noticed several other vases had been stripped of their floral arrangements. Bouquets had been carelessly tossed aside and lay wilting on wet, lacy tablecloths.

"Pardon me, please, Miss Bennet." Followed by the maid assigned to Miss Kensett, the housekeeper swept past Elizabeth. "I was informed there might be an issue here." Lifting her hems, Mrs Vincent carefully stepped over the shards of porcelain and spoke in a thinly veiled tone of disapproval. "I see matters have deteriorated significantly."

Wiping wet hands on a handkerchief, Miss Kensett stopped what she was doing long enough to point a finger. "It was her fault. She startled me."

"Yes, I did," said Elizabeth from the doorway, "and I apologise for that. Otherwise, I am not blameworthy. The room already was in disarray when I arrived."

Mrs Vincent then looked askance at the guilty party.

"I was just…um…" Miss Kensett tossed her head, failing to even acknowledge Henrietta, the burly maid who was on hands and knees busily sopping up the spillage. "I was… ensuring the stems had been cut properly." Even she winced at the folly of her own utterance.

At such a heap of absurdity, Elizabeth had to subdue laughter. "How very thorough you were to examine stems of dried flowers." She indicated a green glass vase, tipped on its side. "And then there are those two urns with pastoral scenes now facing backwards on the mantel, their necks too narrow to ever have held a bunch of flowers. Yes, I would say you have been very thorough indeed."

"Oh, very well," snapped Miss Kensett. "Someone mentioned a puzzle was hidden inside a vase here in the parlour, and I thought—"

"I beg your pardon, Miss Bennet." Mr Hadley—red-faced, evidently from rushing—had come to a halt beside Elizabeth. Addressing the room at large, he said, "Does anyone happen to know where Mr Monroe might be found? I am happy to report I have solved yet another puzzle!"

Elizabeth missed any more of Miss Kensett's inanity, not because of Mr Hadley's enquiry but because of a whiff of juniper's fresh, sharp, sappy aroma. Without turning, she sensed Mr Darcy's powerful and comforting presence directly behind her. *Comforting?* Feeling at ease in that gentleman's company was a new and unexpected sensation.

"Miss Bennet"—his voice was alarmingly close to her ear —"this doorway is not wide enough for the three of us. We had much better go out to the avenue, you and I."

When she turned to face him, Elizabeth caught the corners of his mouth forming a heart-warming and, if she were to be honest, captivating smile. Not only had the teasing man made reference to a certain exchange in Netherfield's shrubbery, but, if she was not mistaken, he was flirting rather outrageously with her. Was it an indication of a renewed wish to secure her affection, or was he toying with her? *Surely not the latter!* She turned away from him and caught Mr Hadley's rather shocked expression.

Still leaning in, Mr Darcy must have been heedless of the quizzing looks the younger gentleman was giving the two of them. "And where, pray tell, is that charming chaperon of yours? We must not use Miss Rigby so abominably ill as to run away without telling her we intend to do so."

The proximity of his lips to her ear produced shivers and vibrations and frissons and such. "Alas, I must decline your shocking but tempting invitation."

When she faced him again, Elizabeth was disappointed that his teasing smile had vanished, replaced by a frown. If he, too, was disappointed, an explanation was in order. "Not a quarter of an hour ago, I was on an errand but was diverted by the goings-on here in the parlour. I have, you see, an enigma to investigate and must do so on my own. But," she added with a sugar-sweet smile, "I do wish you and Miss Rigby a most pleasant promenade along the avenue."

She could not be sure, but as she walked away, she thought she heard Mr Darcy mutter, "Imp."

Elizabeth had solved her enigma earlier that day, and thereafter the answer seemed glaringly obvious. Although confident of her solution, she reviewed the rhyme once more while nearing the stable.

> *Tho' mean and humble is my birth,*
> *I sit enthroned on high,*
> *My footsteps far above the earth,*
> *My canopy the sky:*
> *O'er labouring subjects thus in state*
> *I bear despotic sway,*
> *Yet on them condescend to wait,*
> *At break and close of day.*

A stable-boy, when asked, said he knew exactly where Mr Bolton might be found. He gestured for Elizabeth to follow, and it took them but a moment to reach the coach house, attached as it was to the stable.

"Wait here, miss, and I'll fetch him for you." The boy then nimbly wove round several carriages and climbed a set of stairs at the rear of the huge building.

Elizabeth wandered about, trying to determine which conveyance belonged to which beneficiary. From above, she heard footsteps and men's voices. From the adjoining stable came shouts and laughter, neighing and nickering, pails clanging and shovels scraping.

The boy returned some minutes later, followed more slowly by a middle-aged man who limped past the vehicles and over to Elizabeth.

"Begging your pardon for keeping you waiting, miss." The lean, swarthy man doffed his cap and bowed. "I've been thrown from the box more times than I care to admit." He patted his thigh. "So I'm a bit slow getting about on foot."

Belatedly, he added, "I'm Mr Bolton, miss. How can I be of assistance?"

Oakwood's coachman was better clothed than Longbourn's counterpart, but he wore no livery, and Elizabeth hoped she was not interrupting the man's precious leisure time. Oakwood servants, she had learnt, enjoyed one full day off per month and worked reduced hours every Sunday to allow them to attend services and have at least a half day of rest.

"Forgive me for disturbing you, but I was hoping you might have something for me. I am Miss Bennet, one of the beneficiaries staying here, and I have solved a puzzle for which I am fairly certain the answer is 'coachman.'"

When shown the rhyme, Mr Bolton gave a laugh both loud and vigorous. "Ha! I've heard this one before. What think you, Jimmy? Am I despotic?"

The stable-boy shrugged. "I don't know what that means."

"Never mind, son. Well, Miss Bennet, I was told by Mr Monroe to expect someone. And when Jimmy said there was a fine lady down here asking for me, I fetched this." From a coat pocket he withdrew a creased and greasy piece of paper and passed it to her.

Elizabeth accepted it gingerly.

Mr Bolton grimaced and apologised. "Obviously," he said, wiping his fingers on a sullied handkerchief, "I should have done this before touching that. I was oiling the tack, you see. The harness, not the reins, mind. Never the reins! Can't have them slipping through my hands now, can I?"

He rattled on awhile longer about beef tallow, neatsfoot oil, and lampblack. Some of his blather was nonsensical, but his hearty good humour had Elizabeth smiling and engaging in a bit of banter. As soon as seemed civil, she thanked him for his time and then offered both coachman and stable-boy the sweet pistachio comfits she had wrapped in paper and secreted away in her pocket. Jimmy's eyes lit up, and Elizabeth thought she might have made a friend for life.

On her way to the manor, the sun was so warm on her face that Elizabeth adjusted her bonnet. *Mama never will forgive me if I arrive home with more freckles than I already have.* Unfolding and reading the grease-stained puzzle, she thought the rhyme atrocious but had a vague feeling she should know the answer.

Having reached the house, she greeted Alfred and was informed that Mr Monroe could be found in the library. There, she sought and received the attorney's verification and his congratulations, although he, too, had hesitated in handling the paper with oily marks upon it. Slowly ascending the staircase, fingers trailing along the handrail as she went, Elizabeth reread her new poser.

> *The good man who reads me is oft part of a crew;*
> *A mighty ship, the sea, stars, and wind his venue.*
> *My upmost point in life shows that which is true.*
> *Zephyrus! Boreas! My points reckon thirty-two.*
> *Thus, on parchment I am what skilled artists drew.*
> *Yet in gardens, where they were born, then grew,*
> *A different variety has a pricklier, thornier purview.*

In giddy anticipation, Elizabeth changed direction and lightly tripped down the stairs. At the bottom she turned right and hurried along the vestibule. Decorum restricted her from breaking into a run but just barely.

I have it! I have it! Good grief, I sound like Mr Hadley. But she knew the answer and remembered seeing such an engraving on the flagstones in the great hall.

How many more puzzles must she solve? How close was

she to winning? *Please let this next conundrum be the penultimate one.*

She entered the chamber and rushed straight for the very heart of the hall. The closer she drew to the central point, the slower her steps became and the faster her heart pounded.

Yes! Amidst myriad red and buff-coloured flagstones, the circular engraving was just as Elizabeth remembered.

But she simply stood there staring at the compass rose. *Now what am I to do? Where is the puzzle? Must I lift the entire flagstone to find it?*

Kneeling, she tried prying free the slab. *Fiddlesticks!* All she had managed to do was break two fingernails. Sitting back on her heels, Elizabeth studied the graduated circle with its thirty-two directional points. *Aha!* The engraving's circumference had a sizeable groove, large enough for the tip of a finger.

With the compass rose successfully lifted from its flagstone bed and set aside, Elizabeth peered into the cavity. *Hurrah!* The hoped-for, twice-folded foolscap was snatched from its hiding place and the piece of art put back where it belonged.

Cheerful and full of energy thanks to her triumph, Elizabeth was about to leave the great hall when she heard echoing voices.

"And if you do not cooperate, believe me, I shall know how to exact revenge."

That is Miss Kensett. Where is she? Elizabeth explored the screens at the back of the room but saw no one. *The voices must be coming from the peep-hole. What was the word Mrs Vincent used? Squint.*

As she walked towards the dais, she dithered between leaving directly or staying and listening. *I shall remain only long enough to identify the male voice.*

The argument became more heated and the voices louder and clearer the closer Elizabeth came to the peep-hole.

"Do you dare threaten me, madam? You do not want me as your enemy."

That is Mr Fordham's voice. He and Miss Kensett must be in the library.

"Pshaw!" said the lady. "We, all five of us, already are adversaries. And if you will not assist me with my first puzzle and every subsequent one, I shall tell Mr Monroe how you have been—"

"Hush, harridan, or I shall silence you myself!"

Elizabeth had heard enough. Miss Kensett was threatening Mr Fordham with extortion. And Mr Fordham was threatening the lady with… *What exactly?*

12

CALL IT HOPE...AND COMFITS

The day having dawned clear and the church being little more than three-quarters of a mile distant, the tree-lined road beckoned, and the five of them agreed to walk to Sunday services. Their number, however, included neither Miss Kensett nor Mr Fordham.

During the donning of hats and bonnets and such in the vestibule, Elizabeth enquired after the well-being of the absent lady and gentleman.

"Your concern is admirable, dear." Miss Rigby tugged her gloves with more force than seemed necessary. "Miss Kensett declared she had a headache and requested a breakfast tray be delivered to her bedchamber. Henrietta is tending to that with some laudanum and will remain with her until I return. Other than a severe bout of griping, there appeared to be nothing at all wrong with the lady when I paid her a brief visit half an hour ago." The chaperon's expression clearly conveyed her disapproval of both sloth-fulness and religious indifference. "Of Mr Fordham's where-abouts, I have no knowledge."

Displeasure evident in his tone, Mr Monroe said, "On this day of rest, the gentleman apparently has important business to attend to this morning." Alfred passed him a walking stick, and there followed a quiet exchange between employer and footman. All Darcy heard was, "Mr Atwater will be keeping an eye on him."

The information provided by chaperon and attorney seemed to cause Elizabeth more anxiety than relief. Knowing her poor opinion of Miss Kensett and Mr Fordham, Darcy wondered about her sudden interest in them. *Elizabeth has such a kind heart. I should not question her concern.* There would be ample opportunity for them to converse during their walk, and then the subject might be broached.

As they set off towards the quaint country church, its bells summoning the faithful to worship, Darcy had little opportunity to address the matter or to even address Elizabeth at all. Consequently, his steely eyes took aim at the back of another gentleman's head—Mr Hadley's.

The younger man had offered the lady his arm before Darcy had a chance to do so. And, because Mr Monroe was performing the same service for Miss Rigby, Darcy walked alone, feeling superfluous.

For two hours Darcy sat in a pew between Miss Rigby on his left and Mr Hadley on his right. He attentively listened to prayers, Bible readings, a sermon from the pulpit, the soft whispers of Elizabeth and Mr Hadley, and a jealous voice in his head urging him to tell the two of them to hush.

Darcy also prayed. He prayed he would have Elizabeth on his arm for the return walk, and he prayed she and Mr Hadley had not formed an attachment.

After the service, the congregation lingered in the churchyard, smiling and creating a happy hubbub of chatter and laughter. Adding to the morning's idyll, male birds in nearby trees provided bursts of musical vocalisation. Darcy knew they sang not to entertain humans but rather for territorial purposes. *Perhaps I should serenade Elizabeth. What folly that would be.*

Meanwhile, under the watchful eye of Mr Monroe, and with that innate ease of his, Mr Hadley mingled amongst people with whom he was unacquainted. *Ah yes, but how well does the youngster warble?*

Darcy wandered over to where Miss Rigby and Elizabeth chatted with the vicar's wife and joined their discussion about her husband's inspiring sermon. "I appreciated," said he, "that Mr Smith's message about hope arose naturally from biblical text."

Mrs Smith smiled and thanked him on her husband's behalf. Then she leant in and whispered as though she was about to impart a great secret. "I suspect my dear Mr Smith was also inspired, at least a little, by a novel we recently took turns reading aloud to one another. *Sense and Sensibility.* In the story, the Mrs Dashwood character says, 'Know your own happiness. You want nothing but patience—or give it a more fascinating name, call it hope.'"

"I read that story several times and know some favourite bits by heart," said Elizabeth. "Elinor knew that whatever her sister and mother conjectured one moment, they believed the next. 'With them, to wish was to hope, and to hope was to expect.'"

Miss Rigby admitted she had not read the novel. "Nevertheless, there is much to be said on the subject of hope. We treasure and anticipate our wish for fulfilment, even in the midst of disappointment. One should remain expectant." Darcy thought the chaperon, a spinster, looked rather wistful as she added, "Without wishes, we forget to have hope."

"Oh yes," agreed Mrs Smith, "and we must lean on, and trust in, our faith."

"And we must have faith that our wishes and hopes will be fulfilled." Darcy's eyes strayed to Elizabeth. "At least in some measure or manner." There had been no ulterior motive for his joining the three ladies, but it was to his advantage that he was there to offer Elizabeth his arm once everyone in their party agreed it was time to set off for Oakwood.

It also was advantageous that, somewhere along the way, he and she outstripped Miss Rigby, who was walking arm in arm with both Mr Monroe and Mr Hadley. They were not too far behind, just conveniently out of earshot.

As it had been on the hilly, wooded path the day prior, Darcy and Elizabeth walked awhile without speaking. She seemed pensive, and he observed her in compassionate silence, wishing he knew what she was thinking.

"Are you well, Miss Bennet?"

"Indeed I am, thank you. I am only distressed by some dreadful words I heard spoken yesterday." Releasing his arm, she fidgeted with a button on one of her kid gloves, and he was bereft of her touch.

She had seemed so light-hearted mere minutes ago. Wondering whose dreadful words had caused her distress, Darcy glanced behind, assuming it had been one of those three. In wretched suspense and commiseration, he waited.

Silently he wished he had the privilege to enfold her in his arms, to let her pour out her heart to him, to wipe away her tears, and, yes, to kiss away her troubles and take them upon himself. Would that day ever come? *Ah, but without wishes, one forgets to have hope.*

"Mr Darcy, this is going to sound exceedingly brazen of

me, but I desperately need to speak to someone. And that someone is you, but we must do so in private."

Wishes and hopes were all well and good, but he would not let his heart run away with expectation. He leant in a bit, gentling his tone. "I shall arrange something." How that was to be accomplished, he did not know. Mr Monroe had made it clear the beneficiaries were constantly watched.

"Thank you. I fear I am being utterly shameless in my impudence and presumptuousness this morning, but may I enquire about your..." She leant away from him and shook her head. "No, I cannot. Perhaps I am not as shameless as I thought."

Slowing his pace, he turned to her. "Must I frighten you?"

"Frighten me? I do not understand."

She had given him such an appalled look that he almost laughed. "Perhaps it is I who misunderstood...at Rosings. I thought you said you had an obstinacy that never allowed you to be frightened by, or of, others and that your fearsome intrepidity invariably reared its head at intimidation. Ergo, I thought that if I were to frighten you, your stubbornness and courage would surge to such a degree that you would become outrageously impudent."

"Outrageously impudent?"

"What I meant to say is that you would become brave enough to enquire about my... What, exactly?"

Smiling at him, Elizabeth shook her head. "After all that, how can I not ask?" Her smile faded. "It is just that I am concerned on your behalf and wonder at your, um, attentions to"—she winced—"Miss Kensett." Blushing, she bit her bottom lip.

His brow furrowed. "Would you have me behave otherwise? Shall I openly display my selfish disdain of her for everyone to witness? I am trying to behave in a more gentle-manlike manner than that, madam."

"I have noticed, sir, and I appreciate and commend your efforts." She spoke her next words in a near whisper. "It is just that Miss Kensett is… She is…"

"She is…the subject you wish to speak of privately?"

"Partially, yes."

"And if I enquired about Mr Hadley's attentions to you?"

"I would tell you that I like him very much and that we are mutually attached."

Darcy pressed his lips together so firmly they must have formed a straight line.

Slender fingers pressed lightly upon his forearm. "But he and I have no stronger an attachment than friendship."

Darcy muttered, "Perhaps you might inform him of that. He seems utterly ignorant."

"Do you think so? I confess that, due to a lack of eligible gentlemen in my neighbourhood, I have not the necessary experience to properly determine the extent of a gentleman's interest in me. I knew nought of yours until that evening at Hunsford."

Genteel laughter burst forth from Miss Rigby and Mr Monroe, evidently over something Mr Hadley had said. Elizabeth looked over her shoulder and sent them a smile. Then, she looked Darcy in the eye and apologised again for her ill-treatment of him at Hunsford and for believing Mr Wickham's tale. "I made one of the biggest mistakes of my life that evening. I do not mean that I regret my refusal of your offer, for I could not have accepted you at the time. I did not know you well enough. Nor did you know me. But for two long months, I wished for your forgiveness."

"Your admonishments were well-deserved. But, because you wish it, you have my forgiveness." *And more. Much more.*

They had, by then, turned onto the lane leading to the manor, and a neighbour riding a bay cob wished them a 'good day' before passing by.

"Since we are mending fences, there is something I have been meaning to tell you for days now. Before I left London, I received a reply from Bingley. He plans to reopen Netherfield as soon as he returns from Scarborough. I can give you no further assurance of how matters thereafter may unfold for your sister, but we can always hope."

And you, Elizabeth—inadvertently or not—have given me hope by saying you did not regret your refusal of my offer because you could not have accepted me at the time. So, does that mean you would accept me now...or soon?

All his suffering was quickly turning to dogged perseverance. Perseverance, he knew, built character, and character produced hope. With a spring in his step, instead of continuing on to the house, Darcy took leave of Elizabeth and the others and strode towards the stables.

His purpose was twofold—to ensure his team was well tended and to examine his and, if necessary, other carriages in the coach house. He was unsure where his next puzzle might be hidden, but Darcy was certain of the solution to the one in his pocket.

The first is to supply with what you need.
With the second cheese and wine are better.
Put together, like the wind you may speed.
Horses, alas, know restraint and fetter.

While he inspected the stalls housing his team, a helpful stable-boy named Jimmy followed him, asking and answering questions and treating his horses to pieces of carrot.

"Do you ken Miss Bennet, sir?"

"I do. Do *you?*"

"Oh yes!" The expression on Jimmy's face gave Darcy the impression the boy was lost to a daydream. "Miss Bennet is the kindest, prettiest lady I ever met! She gave me comforts!"

Darcy's fingers stilled behind the horse's ear he had been scratching. "Did she?" *I wish Elizabeth would give me comforts.*

"The comforts had pistachios!"

The innocence and cheerfulness of children always added relish to Darcy's existence, and he wished for a family of his own.

A quarter of an hour later, he walked away from the coach house with not only a new puzzle in his breast pocket —the solution, indeed, had been 'equipage'—but a huge grin upon his face as he remembered the rest of his conversation with the boy.

"I think you mean Miss Bennet gave you com*fits*, Jimmy, not com*forts*."

"Oh? Well... I don't know, sir. Those sweet pistachios gave me comforts, no doubt about that." The boy had paused for a moment. "Of course, that was afore I got the toothache."

❧ 13 ❧

THE PLOT THICKENS

On Monday, lost in a brown study and oppressed by a crowd of widely differing emotions, Elizabeth made her way down the grand staircase, her steps slower than was customary.

A worrisome dark cloud overshadowed her elation at having made amends with Mr Darcy. The foreboding gloom was due to the threats she had overheard between Miss Kensett and Mr Fordham.

At least those two are still alive...or were as of last night. Who knows what this day will bring. Elizabeth scolded herself for treating a serious matter with unbecoming levity.

Earlier that morning, Rachel had brought her a steaming cup of chocolate flavoured with cinnamon. "To begin your day in a positive way, Miss Bennet." The maid had come also with a summons from Mr Monroe, and she emphasised that it was not to be taken lightly. "Each and every beneficiary is to arrive in the breakfast room at precisely a quarter to ten this morning. No exceptions, Mr Monroe said. Even if one is indisposed or has important business to attend. Those were his exact words, miss."

At the foot of the stairs, Elizabeth noticed Alfred was not at his usual post in the corner between the front door and the parlour. His brother was there instead. Glancing at the vestibule's tall pendulum clock, she saw it was yet early and decided to go for a short stroll in the gardens. She knew from their days together at Netherfield that, like her, Mr Darcy was an early riser.

"Miss Bennet, good morning to you!" It was not Mr Darcy but Mr Hadley. "I have just come from wandering in the great hall. Seeing you now, I remember my promise to show you the portraits of Biscuit on display in the gallery. Would you care to do so while we await breakfast?" He crooked his elbow.

Beyond the windows, a clear sky beckoned. Turning her back on sunshine, verdure, and the possibility of encountering Mr Darcy, Elizabeth nodded her agreement.

They spent half an hour viewing oil paintings in a gallery rich in specimens of plant life, floral arrangements, fruit, and Biscuits. *Lots and lots of Biscuits!* Elizabeth admitted the Pomeranian had an agreeable face. To be polite, she enquired about the dog's temperament.

"Good old Biscuit. Thereby hangs a tale, no pun intended," said Mr Hadley, pointing to a painting. He then addressed the subject with his usual enthusiasm, telling of the dog's misdeeds and ending with, "He was playful, intelligent, sociable, and affectionate. Most of all he just wanted attention, pats, and belly rubs. Miss Armstrong doted on the rapscallion and spoilt him terribly. He was her only family, you see. She had no one else."

Elizabeth's eyes welled up at such a melancholy thought.

"But she had you…as well as Miss Kensett and Mr Fordham, did she not?"

The question seemed to have made Mr Hadley uncomfortable. As they walked on, his countenance took on an unusual solemnity. "I came here frequently and often saw Mr Fordham lurking about the place. I was told he had offered to have Miss Armstrong's belongings—particularly the heirlooms—inventoried and valued for her. Apparently, he is an antiques collector himself and somewhat of an expert in the field."

If Mr Fordham is spying on us through the peep-hole, so be it. These walls have eyes and ears, and listeners never hear any good of themselves.

"And what of Miss Kensett?"

"In all the many visits I made here since that day in Cheapside, I encountered Miss Kensett only the once. Other than that, Miss Armstrong never even mentioned her—though she did speak of the lady's grandmother a couple of times."

The gross duplicity of that woman! Leading us to believe she was such a good friend to the elderly lady. "I am very glad Miss Armstrong had *your* pleasant and frequent company, Mr Hadley."

A lingering feeling of melancholy left Elizabeth no peace, and she belittled her own contribution to the late Miss Armstrong's well-being. "I am undeserving of inclusion in this competition, sir. I spent but minutes in her presence."

"But it was you who saved her from injury or worse! You are the most deserving of us all."

"You are too kind, sir."

They spent awhile longer in the great hall, admiring the old tapestries and sharing their thoughts about the revelries that might have been held there in olden times.

Standing then in the vestibule, Elizabeth said, "I understand your progress in this tournament was hindered by the disappearance of a certain vase. I hope that impediment has been rectified."

"It has, indeed! Mr Monroe keeps a master list of all our puzzles, and he was able to duplicate the missing one for me." Lowering his voice, he added, "I probably should not disclose this, but I have made remarkable headway since that setback."

"You should not have mentioned that to one of your opponents, and you would do well to remember that in future. Now, I shall have to double my own efforts." Elizabeth smiled fondly at him.

But what am I to do with a poser that says only 'Hearts shall weave'? There is no loom here at Oakwood. Is there?

Christopher cleared his throat. "Begging your pardon, Miss Bennet, Mr Hadley, but the others are gathering in the breakfast room now."

<hr />

As it had been each day, a large table laden with food had been placed in front of the breakfast room's crackling fire, and Christoper stood at the ready to toast muffins over the grate. In pretty pots, honey and preserves sat waiting to be spread upon warm, freshly baked bread or rolls. Guests helped themselves to a selection of fruit, eggs, meat, fowl, and fish; and on the set table there was tea, coffee, chocolate, and even a pitcher of ale.

It was, however, the first occasion since their arrival that everyone was gathered for breakfast at the same time. With one exception. Mr Darcy had not come down.

Mr Monroe waited for him, rather impatiently in Eliza-

'Tis little wonder she wanted to capture Mr Darcy's attention. I pray that one day she will either marry a good man or gain her independence and escape her family's tyranny.

"Shall I help with your gown now, Miss Bennet?"

"My apologies, Rachel. I had not realised you were waiting." Rising from the stool and holding her hair aside, Elizabeth remained still while the back of her gown was unbuttoned. Then, rather distractedly, she thanked and dismissed the maid for the night.

Once abed and with feelings in every way agitated, Elizabeth found repose only with great difficulty. The inquietude of her mind caused so much tossing and turning that she finally exhausted herself and slept.

❦

IN A HEAVY MIST, TUESDAY DAWNED HALF-HEARTEDLY, AND Elizabeth was awake to witness it. Following her morning toilette, she sat in her bedchamber, longing to be out there, enwrapped in the silvery-grey veil.

Equally desirous of solving her puzzle, she stared at the foolscap on the table in front of her. The paper already bore numerous failed attempts to rearrange the letters in *'Hearts shall weave'*. Unsure whether such a method would even prove to be the solution, she flung down her pencil in vexation.

For her mother and younger sisters' sake, she had to win. They were dependent on her providing for them should Mr Bennet die before at least one of his daughters wed a gentleman in possession of a good fortune. And, despite Sunday's talks on hope, followed by Mr Darcy's marked attentions, Elizabeth would not allow herself to hope for more than Jane to marry Mr Bingley.

beth's opinion, until ten o'clock. "This is most irregular and unacceptable."

Elizabeth silently agreed it was irregular. Mr Darcy was never late. Anything like a breach of punctuality was, to him, a great offence. At Netherfield, at Rosings, and there at Oakwood, he had always arrived at least fifteen minutes prior to dinner being served.

"Christopher, go and find your brother. He was assigned to act as Mr Darcy's valet this morning." As the footman hied from the room, the attorney frowned. "I trust everyone here is capable of toasting their own muffins in the interim."

In less than a quarter of an hour, Christopher returned. "Alfred reports that the gentleman is unwell, sir. My brother tried to rouse him hours ago in order to deliver your summons, but Mr Darcy mumbled something incoherent and went back to sleep. Earlier than that, one of the chambermaids went in to light the fire in his room. She said he was drowsy then and stirring restlessly."

Mr Monroe rang for the housekeeper and charged Mrs Vincent with ensuring Mr Darcy received the very best care. "Do not hesitate to summon a physician if such is deemed necessary."

Although not prone to irrational fear, Elizabeth could not but be concerned. Mr Darcy always seemed so robust.

"I shall proceed as planned," said Mr Monroe. "First, the latest tournament results. At present, Miss Bennet, Mr Darcy, and Mr Hadley are in a three-way draw for first place. Mr Fordham is in second, and Miss Kensett trails behind. I remind you that, today included, three days remain for you to succeed. This is not only a race against each other now but also a race against time. The competition ends on Wednesday at midnight."

He paused for a sip of tea. "Now, on to an extremely

vexatious matter...the missing Japanese vase. A search is still underway in the public rooms, and it is hoped the item simply has been misplaced. However, if its whereabouts have not been discovered by midday—an hour and a half from now—a search of the servants' quarters will be conducted under the supervision of Mrs Vincent and Mr Atwater. If that is unsuccessful, your rooms and carriages will be searched on the morrow. It goes without saying that if the article is found in the possession of either a servant or a beneficiary, the local magistrate will be summoned."

Missing Mr Darcy's presence, Elizabeth picked at her food and surreptitiously observed the others. Miss Rigby and Mr Hadley seemed horrified by the notion of a thief in their midst. Miss Kensett kept touching her pearl necklace, and Elizabeth imagined she was concerned that her precious parure might be a thief's next target.

Mr Fordham, on the other hand, gave an impression of studied disinterest in anything other than the generous portions of ham, bacon, and kippered salmon he had heaped upon his plate.

While Elizabeth had been wondering whether Mr Monroe knew Mr Fordham was a collector of antiques, the attorney himself had been speaking.

"...and those of us who attended church yesterday had the pleasure of listening to Mr Smith's sermon regarding hope. Similarly, I remind each of you to not give up, even in the midst of disappointment." He gave Miss Kensett a look that spoke more of pity than sympathy.

"Oh yes," said the chaperon, "do remain hopeful and expectant. Have faith. Your hope will be fulfilled according to plan...but not necessarily your plan."

"Well put, madam." Mr Monroe set aside his knife and fork. "In conclusion, I shall say this. Only one beneficiary will win Miss Armstrong's considerable wealth and the deed to this lovely property. However, none of you will—or, at least, should—leave here worse off than when you arrived." The attorney's pointed look was directed at Mr Fordham.

Head bent over his plate as it was, the recipient of that look seemed unaware of it. Elizabeth, however, knew a measure of relief that Mr Monroe might, after all, be aware of Mr Fordham's pastime.

⚜

AT A TABLE IN THE LIBRARY SEVERAL HOURS LATER, ELIZABETH finished writing a letter to Lydia in Brighton, wishing her a very happy sixteenth birthday. She longed to tell her youngest, silliest sister to behave but knew Lydia would neither appreciate the sentiment nor heed the warning.

Setting the letter aside for the nonce, she tried to occupy her worried mind by rearranging the letters in her latest puzzle: hearts shall weave. All she could think of, however, was Mr Darcy, and she prayed he would be well. Her heart had become irrevocably *woven* with his.

Lounging on a window seat, Miss Kensett did nothing more than sigh and complain about the unjustness of a tournament of wit and whimsy. Elizabeth listened with half an ear and smothered each of the reproofs she could have given. She startled when the chaperon, looking uncommonly distraught, rushed in and sat beside her.

When Miss Rigby spoke, her voice was barely raised above a whisper. "I waited in the garden, as arranged. Why did neither of you present yourselves? Oh gracious! Has Mr Darcy still not come down?"

Elizabeth turned over her puzzle and matched the chaperon's hushed tone. "No, sadly, he has not, and I am beside myself with worry. But I do not have the pleasure of under-standing you. Were you expecting Mr Darcy and me in the garden? If so, I was unaware of any such arrangement."

"Indeed, I was. He arranged for the two of you to have a private conversation there at half past twelve today. Mr Darcy was supposed to mention it to you last evening. But, now that I think of it, he retired rather suddenly and quite early, did he not? Oh dear! He must have been unwell even then."

Elizabeth nodded and encouraged her to continue.

"Mr Darcy reiterated there was no understanding between you but admitted that he hoped... Rather, the gentleman said you had important matters to discuss and solemnly promised the competition would not be part of that discussion. As agreed, I was to keep an eye on you from a respectable distance and—"

"Of what are the two of you so secretly talking?" Miss Kensett trailed a finger round their table as she circled it. "Whispering in company is indecorous, is it not, Miss Rigby?"

"Quite right." The chaperon pursed her lips into a prim expression. Then she smiled, but it was in a manner not reflected in her eyes. "While I think of it, dear, I have been meaning to enquire about the unusual, dare I say unique, appearance of those pearls of yours."

The lady caressed her necklace. "Whatever do you mean? What is unusual about them?"

"Ladies," said Mr Fordham as he strolled in. "Where are the others? Has that slugabed Darcy still not shown his face? I was hoping he and Hadley might join me at the pond and try our luck at a spot of angling. They are jumping out there."

Upon hearing that Mr Darcy had not come down and

that Mr Hadley's whereabouts were unknown, Mr Fordham merely shrugged and eyed Elizabeth's papers for a moment. Apparently seeing nothing of interest there, he sauntered over to a sideboard.

"Fermented fruit cordial! Is that all that is on offer? Pah!" Nevertheless, the gentleman filled a glass from the pitcher, then sat within reach of a table displaying a pyramid of seasonal strawberries, cherries, and melon.

Paying him no further heed, the chaperon gestured at Miss Kensett's necklace. "To me, those pearls appear rather lacklustre. One would expect more of an iridescent shine. May I take a closer look?"

Miss Kensett hesitated but unclasped the necklace and passed it to her.

"Natural pearls are not perfectly round and have tiny irregularities. When rubbed together," said Miss Rigby, doing just that and holding the necklace to her ear, "they would make a gritty sound."

Seated next to the chaperon, Elizabeth clearly heard her whisper, "Paste."

"I beg your pardon?" Miss Kensett's eyes narrowed. "What did you say?"

"Paste, dear. Your precious parure is paste, with a pearly coating."

Mr Fordham choked on his cordial.

"You!" Miss Kensett pointed at him. "You did this!"

He shot to his feet. "Madam, you go too far! I will have you know that Miss Armstrong asked me to have her jewellery valued, which I did last year. That devious jeweller must have kept her real pearls and replaced them with paste. I then unknowingly returned fakes to Miss Armstrong, and she unwittingly gifted them to you. 'Tis unfortunate. But the fault is not mine!"

Their raised voices summoned Mr Monroe; and when the situation was explained to the attorney, he asked Mr Fordham for the name of the jeweller and said he would investigate. The gentleman, however, could not remember to which jeweller he had taken the pearls.

In being so awkwardly circumstanced, the attorney secured Elizabeth's compassion. The poor man had yet another quandary to resolve.

Returning the imitation pearl necklace to its owner, Miss Rigby said that the cost or quality of a bequest should be irrelevant. "What matters, dear, is that Miss Armstrong thought of you and wanted you to have a keepsake."

Glancing at the others and evidently thinking it best to disguise her pique, Miss Kensett sat, smoothed her skirts, and patted her hair. "Well, of course, that is all that truly matters. And, certainly, I am touched by the sentiment." She sniffed and dabbed her eyes with a lacy handkerchief but shed no tears.

Perhaps, thought Elizabeth, Miss Kensett did not feel the need to truly weep because it was said that pearls represented teardrops.

At the sideboard, Miss Rigby held up the pitcher of sweet, blackcurrant-flavoured drink. "Cordial, anyone?"

14

BITTER & BETTER

Looking neat and trim, Darcy stood in front of the large pier-glass that filled the wall space between his bedchamber's two windows. Alfred—the prodigiously capable footman-valet—had ordered a hot bath for him, shaved him without a nick, and performed wonders with his hair and cravat. Nothing could be done, though, about the dark smudges beneath his eyes. Alfred had offered to obtain some sort of cosmetic preparation from the housekeeper, but Darcy had flatly refused to even consider such madness.

"And you say no one else suffered any ill effects whatsoever from the wine?"

Alfred brushed non-existent lint from the gentleman's shoulder. "Not that anyone has admitted, sir."

"Humph." Truth be told, Darcy was more than a little offended that one little glass of wine had kicked him like a Suffolk punch—though, to be fair, those thick-set, short-legged sorrels were incredibly calm and gentle creatures. One thing was certain: he was thankful no one else, particularly Miss Bennet, had suffered a similarly horrific episode.

In the parlour the previous evening, Darcy's vision had blurred, and he had been overcome by a relaxed but dazed feeling. At that point, he had bid the others a good night and walked for eleven outlandish miles to reach his bedchamber and fling himself upon the mattress. All he remembered after that were bizarre, vivid dreams. As far as he could recall, each time he had tried to sit up, he had become nauseous and lightheaded.

When he finally had been able to bestir himself in the early afternoon, Darcy had felt and looked like he had been dragged arsy-versy, thrice, through a hedgerow. His head had ached, and he had been ravenous. Bless his soul, Alfred had brought headache powders, barley water, a dish of broth, and toasted muffins.

"Thanks to you, my good man, I do believe I am ready to face the world again." *And discover what, exactly, was in that wine. Opium? Wormwood?*

When Darcy arrived at the foot of the stairs, Christopher informed him that all the others were gathered in the parlour; and, upon entering that room, Darcy was met with exclamations of relief and enquiries of an intrusive nature. As politely as possible under the circumstances, he returned everyone's greeting but brushed aside their questions.

"Mr Monroe, may I have a private conference with you in ten minutes or so?"

"Of course, of course. Whenever you are ready. And may I say how pleased I am to see you up and about, sir."

Darcy bowed to the attorney and approached the cosy grouping of four leather chairs where Elizabeth, Miss Rigby, and Mr Hadley sat together. Following a silent communication with the chaperon, he said, "Miss Bennet, if the others will pardon us, may I have a private word with you?" With a tilt of his head, he indicated the plush pink sofa customarily occupied by Mr Fordham.

Once she was seated there, Elizabeth expressed with tenderness and solicitude her fear for his health.

"There is no need. I am quite recovered. And you? You are well?" He was about to sit but stilled in expectation.

"Yes, now that you are here with me." She blushed.

Darcy's first smile of that day began slowly and built. He flipped his coattails and sat as close to her as he dared.

She glanced away briefly. "I meant with us. *All* of us."

There was subdued laughter from somewhere across the room, but nothing could distract Darcy from the loveliness of her. Only decorum and the need for information kept him from more pleasurable and provocative behaviour that might attract more than just her attention. They were, after all, in the company of others.

"What, if anything, can you tell me about last evening? I began feeling peculiar after drinking a glass of wine here in the parlour, though at dinner, during the service of fruit and sweets, I had one glass of Constantia wine. And there was the port after you and the other ladies withdrew."

She tilted her head and thought for a moment. "I remember Mr Fordham inviting you and Mr Hadley to join him in a low-stakes game of Brag, but neither of you would play cards on a Sunday. You also said you needed to work on your current puzzle. Then you looked at me as though you were going to approach. At the sideboard, Mr Fordham poured himself a glass of wine and asked whether either of you wanted one. Mr Hadley declined, but you accepted."

It was a serious matter they were discussing, but he could not resist a gentle tease. "So, Miss Bennet, would it be fair to say you spent a great deal of time observing me?" He tried and failed miserably at preventing his lips from twitching.

Never before had he flirted so outrageously, or even moderately, or at all. Then again, never before had a woman been so loveworthy.

"You, sir, were standing directly beneath that painting of lilacs." She gestured towards the sideboard and above it the floral depiction on the wall. "And since I am uncommonly fond of a syringa, I could not help but notice you there." She looked him in the eye. Hers were warm and merry and mischievous.

Simply being in her presence was causing Darcy to feel better and better by the minute. He inched closer.

"To be honest," she said, having grown serious, "I mostly was watching Mr Fordham last evening. Unfortunately, he had his back to me while pouring your wine." Leaning in, she whispered, "I do not entirely trust him."

Darcy rubbed his forehead, trying to remember the previous night and striving to resist her gravitational pull. "I have this vague memory of a remark I made to someone about the wine's unusual flavour. It was bitter and spicy."

"You made that comment to Mr Monroe. He said his glass, poured from the same bottle as yours, was neither pungent nor piquant."

Tearing his eyes from Elizabeth's, Darcy sought the attorney's whereabouts before reluctantly saying, "I really must confer with him." He made to rise, but she stayed him with a gentle touch to his ungloved hand—a touch that sent a lightning bolt of warmth throughout his body.

"Before you go and before I forget, I would like your permission to tell my father about Mr Wickham. Lydia left for Brighton about a fortnight ago with Colonel and Mrs Forster"—she gave him a significant look—"and in the company of the militia."

Darcy immediately understood, and he agreed that her

father should know. He apologised again and again for not warning people in her neighbourhood about Wickham. "Now, if you will excuse me, I really must speak to our host."

In the library with the attorney, Darcy paced, and he let his vexation be known while a mixture of anger and indignation overspread his countenance.

"Such ill-usage! It was bad enough that I suffered through such an ordeal, but I shudder to think how much worse it could have been had one of the ladies ingested whatever was in that wine. I cannot conceive of a more deplorable situation. Did someone incapacitate me merely to give them an advantage in the tournament?"

The previous evening, Darcy had intended to put extra effort into solving his latest enigma, for it had been putting heavy demands on his perspicacity.

"Currently, Miss Bennet and Mr Hadley are in a three-way draw with you for first place." The attorney's tone seemed to be asking him whether he trusted that lady and gentleman.

"Good heavens! Neither of them would commit such a heinous act—and heinous it was. I might have died." Darcy sat then, trying to calm his breathing and subdue his indignation. "When I was thrown from my horse the summer I turned twelve, I suffered a broken arm and was given laudanum, but I baulked at taking a second dose. Since that day, I have refused to swallow or smoke anything containing opium."

Realising he was tapping his fingers on his thigh, Darcy forced them to still; but what he really wanted to do was pound his fist on something. "I suspect that whatever was in my wine contained more than the ten-percent solution customarily found in laudanum." He looked the attorney in the eye. "Do you suppose that whoever drugged my drink realises such a potency can accidentally—or deliberately—cause death?" He kept back his suspicions about Mr Fordham. Without proof, he would not malign the man.

Resting his elbows on the desk, Mr Monroe held his head in his hands. "I am terribly sorry you were so uncomfortably circumstanced while under this roof." Palms flat on the writing surface then, he spoke with grim determination. "Be assured that I shall get to the bottom of this trespass against your person."

"I appreciate your diligence." The angry emotions, which at first had marked Darcy's every feature, were partially subdued by the attorney's assurance.

"And I should inform you, Mr Darcy, if no one else has done so by now, that despite a search of all public rooms and servants' quarters, the missing vase has not been found. As you quite understandably were not at this morning's breakfast gathering, you may be unaware that all guest bedchambers will be searched thoroughly on the morrow. I regret that such an intrusion on your privacy has become necessary, and I apologise in advance for any inconvenience it may cause. For my part, I shall be grief-stricken if the vase or a vial of whatever ended up in your wine is found in a beneficiary's room. To think that someone Miss Armstrong trusted might be implicated in a crime!"

"If one of us is the perpetrator, Mr Monroe, I imagine they somehow have disposed of the evidence by now."

❦

INTO THE AFTERNOON, FOUR OF THE FIVE BENEFICIARIES HAD their proverbial noses to the grindstone as they slaved away at solving posers or rushed about trying to find their next. No one seemed to know the whereabouts of Miss Kensett.

As for Darcy, he finally had found the answer to his enigma:

A riddle of riddles, it dances and skips.
It is seen thro' the eyes, tho' it cheats by the lips.
It never is seen, but often is read.
It is sometimes a feather, and sometimes 'tis lead.
If it meets with its fellow, it's happily caught.
But if money can buy it, it's not worth a groat.

He had a spot of bother, however, understanding where to find 'heart'. As far as Darcy could determine, there was nothing heart-shaped at Oakwood. The pond was an oblong. *What else is heart-shaped? A strawberry or the leaf of a lime tree? Surely not.*

Elizabeth's mouth when she purses her full lips? Good heavens, I have gone mad.

The footprint of a hart? Yes, by Jove! There is a statue of a stag in the shrubbery.

No foolscap was found there. *The only fool's cap is the one I should be wearing. Think, man! What other meaning is there for 'heart'?*

Assuming he was rather clever, he spent a quarter of an hour in the games room searching through packs of playing cards, but there was no folded piece of paper amongst those hearts either.

One particular line of the enigma repeatedly leapt out at him. *If it meets with its fellow, it's happily caught.* His heart had been caught in Hertfordshire. *Now it races just thinking about her.* With a strong awareness of the increased rhythm of his heart, Darcy placed a hand over that part of his chest. *Hah!*

He strode to the little music room just beyond the

parlour, and there he found both an organ and his next puzzle.

Minutes later, Darcy was halfway up the staircase on his way to his room to dress for dinner when his breath caught. At the top of the stairs, his heart's desire, looking happy and healthy in a salmon-coloured gown and with her hair arranged differently, greeted him with a smile. In his eyes, she was perfection, and he longed to tell her so. "Miss Bennet, you—"

A frightful clatter, followed by an outcry, came from the vicinity of the late Miss Armstrong's boudoir.

With Elizabeth following fast on his heels, Darcy trotted down the stairs and joined Mr Monroe, Mrs Vincent, Miss Rigby, and Alfred as they all rushed to investigate.

✖ 15 ✖

THEN THERE WERE FOUR

Without a sound, Mr Monroe lifted the latch of the door and pushed. Those crowded in the doorway, all half a dozen of them, caught sight of Miss Kensett inside. Bent almost double, she held in one hand a wooden trinket box, from which small alabaster balls were still falling and scattering across the wooden floor. With her other hand, she tried to capture the escaped ones, but her dainty palm was unable to hold them all. The more marbles she picked up, the more she dropped.

The attorney cleared his throat. The lady glanced up from her occupation and froze. Wide-eyed, she gaped at them, seemingly overpowered by the suddenness and unexpectedness of people standing there. Brushing past the others, Elizabeth helped Miss Kensett pick up errant marbles.

Meanwhile, closely followed by the chaperon, Mr Monroe stepped inside and folded his arms. "Miss Kensett, you are hereby disqualified from this tournament."

"What do you mean?" Between the lady's eyebrows, a pucker formed. "Whatever for?"

"For being in a forbidden room, madam. This boudoir served as Miss Armstrong's bedchamber during her infirmity. Your set of instructions and rules clearly states that entry to bedchambers other than one's own is prohibited."

"But I was merely searching for...something. And I assumed the rules would not apply to *me*. I have been in Miss Armstrong's boudoir before."

Elizabeth thought the lady's petulant pout was humorously apt. *I may not be fluent in French, but I do know 'boudoir' literally means sulking-place.*

Looking every bit the prim and proper chaperon, Miss Rigby asked, "For what were you looking just now, Miss Kensett?"

Another marble fell, and all eyes watched it slowly roll across the floor.

"I...I was..." Miss Kensett snapped shut the trinket box's lid, revealing a porcelain top embellished with birds, butterflies, and red poppies. By then the colour of her face almost matched that of the fiery flowers.

"Rather like closing the stable door after the horse has bolted, is it not?" said Mrs Vincent.

Aiming an exasperated sigh at both the housekeeper and the chaperon, Miss Kensett said, "I was hoping to find items to replace my imitation pearl parure. Despite what *you* think, Miss Rigby, I am certain Miss Armstrong would have wanted me to have a suitable keepsake." She looked down at the trinket box with great disappointment. "Why would she have kept marbles in this? I expected rings or earrings."

"As intimate as you supposedly were with her, Miss Kensett," said the attorney, "you must realise that Miss Armstrong was a bit of an oddity."

The chaperon swept past Mr Monroe, nearly losing her balance when she trod upon a marble. Righting herself, she attempted to take the box from Miss Kensett's hands. Each of them held fast to an end, and Elizabeth feared the two women were going to end up in a tussle.

"Ladies!" roared the attorney.

At the same instant, they both released their hold on the box, which fell to the floor amidst alabaster balls.

Rather calmly under the circumstances, the housekeeper said to Miss Kensett, "I shall instruct Henrietta to pack your baggage, madam."

"And I," said Miss Rigby, "shall keep Miss Kensett company while that is underway."

To Elizabeth's ear, the chaperon's tone implied that, otherwise, the banished beneficiary might abscond with more than she had in her possession when she arrived.

"Alfred," said Mr Monroe, "have Miss Kensett's coachman and footman fetched from the estate, and notify Mr Bolton that he and Jimmy are to prepare her equipage for immediate departure."

"It will be my pleasure, sir."

About an hour later, in disgrace and showing no little measure of bitterness about being in such a state, Miss Kensett departed Oakwood Manor.

Everyone waved her a fond farewell except for Mr Fordham. He was there, but his pleased expression spoke more of good riddance than good wishes.

***

In her bedchamber that night, waiting for Rachel to come and unbutton her gown and unpin her hair, Elizabeth ended her day in much the same manner as she had begun it

—lost in a brown study and oppressed by a multitude of widely differing emotions.

Miss Kensett's departure meant she then was the competition's sole female participant. Had it not been for complications with her latest puzzle, Elizabeth would have been confident she could hold her own against the three gentlemen. The engaging qualities of her mind were a matter of pride, and they had placed her first in her father's esteem. But what she really needed was to be first in the tournament.

Focusing on problem solving and winning should have been her constant priority, but several diverting occurrences —Mr Darcy's ailment, his recovery, his amorous behaviour, and Miss Kensett's incidents with pearls and marbles and disqualification—had distracted Elizabeth from her purpose. Only two days remained, and she wondered where the time had gone.

Rachel hurried in and apologised for being tardy. "Etta— Henrietta, that is—and a chambermaid were cleaning Miss Kensett's room, and they discovered this."

Elizabeth accepted a folded, sealed single sheet of writing paper addressed to her. Seated at the dressing table while her hair was being unpinned and brushed, she broke the wafer and read the message.

Dear Miss Bennet,
To write long sentences about unpleasant subjects is both tedious and odious, so I shall not.
I only write at all because, of all the others at Oakwood, you were the only one to show me any degree of kindness, though cool and paltry a degree it was. But I begin to understand now, when it is too late, that tournament rules were not meant to be broken.

Nevertheless, despite your uncompromisingness, I hope you will be victorious. Why? Because you are a woman; and if you win, you may become an independent one, and at a much younger age than Miss Armstrong was when she gained control of all that wealth.

Of course, I would have preferred to be the vanquisher. I then might have escaped the influence and control of my father and brother. Alas, it seems I am not quite as clever as you.

Therefore, I am counting on you to outwit Mr Hadley, Mr Darcy, and—most of all—Mr Fordham. Do not trust that man! He is nothing but a weasel and a—

My carriage is ready, and Miss Rigby is giving me that gimlet-eyed glare of hers.

Perhaps, Miss Bennet, when you are mistress of Oakwood Manor, you will remember me and invite me for a visit. My direction, I fear, will still be thus: Under my father's or brother's thumb, Maidenhead, Berkshire.

In the meantime, I remain not your friend but a well-wishing acquaintance,
Sophia Kensett

Elizabeth knew the woman possessed neither quickness nor strong understanding. *But why did she not complete her warning about Mr Fordham?*

Upon giving the letter a second reading, she felt utterly ashamed of herself.

Poor Miss Kensett! To be in such a predicament! Within minutes of becoming acquainted with her, I suspected she was all pretence and fragility. Why did I not try harder to befriend her?

She surrendered to disheartenment for but a moment while her eyes filled with tears of frustration. Angrily, she wiped them away before they could fall, and she flatly refused to work herself into a state of further distress. At that juncture, the honour of victory was doubtful; but she had come too far and was too close to winning to admit defeat.

Resolute, she knew what must be done. The puzzle could wait. A walk amongst misty verdure and dew-kissed blooms would soon set her right. Wearing half-boots and an unlined cloak with attached hood, Elizabeth reached the bottom of the staircase and noticed Alfred was back at his customary post.

Reaching behind himself, the footman produced an umbrella. "In case the mist turns to drizzle or rain, miss." He then opened the door, stepped out, and unfolded the oiled and waxed green silk canopy for her. There even was an acorn attached to its handle to protect her from lightning.

Elizabeth smiled and thanked him. *He and his brother are exceedingly helpful...and handsome, which one's footmen ought to be, if they possibly can. If I am so fortunate as to win Oakwood Manor, I hope it comes complete with Alfred and Christopher.*

With the brume gentle upon her face, she set off southwards and closed the umbrella, the better to admire the scenery. The surrounding countryside was laid out before her in every shade of green—verdant grasses in meadows and fields, lush foliage of trees and shrubs. The colours reminded her of Saturday past when Miss Kensett's Pomona green gown and vivid emerald-coloured turban had harmonised with the variegated shrubbery. *How she had frightened me! And what stories I shall enjoy sharing with Papa during our homeward journey!*

Upon reaching the wet garden and discovering her

ramble might not be a solitary one, Elizabeth's entire being flooded with warmth and expectancy.

For a moment, Mr Darcy looked at her with what she liked to think was unfeigned pleasure. "Miss Bennet, I have been walking hereabouts for some time in the hope of chancing upon you. I remembered that you wanted to speak to me and that I had arranged for Miss Rigby and us to meet yesterday. Please forgive me for not being here at the appointed time." He exuded a strong sense of regret over something that was not at all his fault.

"You have nothing for which to be sorry, sir, for I did not present myself here either. Please put aside your disappointment over that missed assignation and—"

"*Assignation?*" He virtually choked on the word.

"Yes." Elizabeth was all innocence. "An assignation is nothing more than a meeting by arrangement, is it not?"

"Well, no...or rather yes, but..."

Observing his shocked and confused countenance, she could no longer suppress a grin.

He returned her smile. "You know, you really are irresistible." He offered to carry her umbrella, hooked its handle over one arm, proffered his other, and they strolled along winding gravel paths.

"You know, you really should smile more often, Mr Darcy." Elizabeth trailed her free hand across glistening bushes, causing a cascade of tiny jewel-like droplets.

"And why is that?" He inched closer.

"You may not have a big, open grin like Mr Hadley or Mr Bingley, but you must be conscious, sir, that one's countenance appears to greatest advantage when smiling."

"Ha! You are perfectly right." He then smiled so handsomely that the outer corners of his eyes creased. "I shall endeavour to spend more time in your society, for that is when I smile the most. In fact, on this dreary morn, you already have dispelled gloom and brightened my day."

Disinclined to spoil their good cheer, Elizabeth was hesitant to repeat what she had overheard on Saturday in the great hall and what Miss Kensett had almost shared about Mr Fordham in her note. The lady was gone and could neither extort that gentleman nor be hurt by him. For her own part, Elizabeth had felt ill at ease about Mr Fordham from first acquaintance. There was something cunning about him, and she would remain cautious.

While the lady and gentleman wound their way round the flower beds, the morning's fine mist had gradually increased to a middling shower. As he opened the umbrella, Mr Darcy took a quick glance about the garden. "Where, pray tell, is our vigilant chaperon this morning?"

"*I* had not planned on this assignation, sir." Elizabeth grinned at him. "Ergo, I saw no need to advise Miss Rigby of it."

"Nevertheless"—he lowered his voice and twitched his head to the right—"we *are* being watched." He increased the distance between them.

From under the umbrella, Elizabeth peered across a bed of purple cone-flowers and espied the same gardener who had been trimming the shrubbery on Friday and the junipers on Saturday. That morning, he was raking gravel. Smiling sweetly, she waved and wished him a good day. Her greeting was gruffly returned.

Strolling arm in arm with Mr Darcy beneath their silk canopy, it did not seem life could possibly supply any greater felicity. The perfumed garden was at once both tranquil and alive, its floral displays ranging from delicate to showy.

Darting out from under the umbrella's protection, Elizabeth stopped to admire a bed of heliotrope in shades of purple, blue, white, and pink. A sign indicated the flowers were traditionally symbolic of eternal love and devotion. Behind the heliotrope, arranged in an arc, were pots of roses in a variety of hues from white to wine. "Beautiful!"

She thought she heard Mr Darcy softly whisper, "Yes, so beautiful."

When she turned to face him, his gaze was fixed on her face, not the flowers. *Have I been elevated from tolerable to beautiful?* Unaccustomed to compliments but warmed by the possibility of one from him, Elizabeth blushed and looked at the ground.

Instantly, the toes of his boots appeared a fraction of an inch from hers; and there he and she stood together beneath the umbrella, sheltered from rain and shielded from prying eyes.

"I am not one to speak in false or extravagant praise, Miss Bennet. You must know you are lovely. I thought so even at that ill-fated assembly in Meryton, and I should not have spoken so falsely that night." He passed her the umbrella, then reached past her to pluck one of the roses. After removing the thorns from its stem, he handed the flower to her.

Elizabeth accepted the exquisite bloom and held it to her nose, inhaling its sweet fragrance. Grateful for the suspension of Mr Darcy's compliments, she returned the umbrella to his care and said, "Speaking of Hertfordshire, I cannot say that I am in any hurry for the conclusion of our present visit. I shall miss Oakwood." *And you.*

"Perhaps your leaving this place will be but temporary."

"Do you think I shall win?"

"That is but one hypothetical ideal that could become reality." He looked not at her but at a thorn embedded in his glove. "Another possibility is that one of the gentlemen here

—Mr Hadley, for instance—might claim the prize and consequently be in want of a wife."

Mr Darcy waggled his eyebrows at her, and she smiled at him. "Seriously, madam, I have been meaning to ask what you will do with Oakwood Manor should you win the tournament. As per the terms of Miss Armstrong's will, this property cannot be put up for purchase. Ownership and inheritance must remain within the winner's family for a specified number of generations."

Elizabeth spoke then of how dearly she would love to win —needed to win—and why. He had entrusted her with the secret of his sister's near downfall, and she had no qualms about confiding in him about the Bennet family's situation. Certainly it was no secret.

Trust was significant. If the two of them were to further their acquaintance, what could be more important than mutual trust?

Mr Darcy stood looking into her eyes, attentively listening; and when she finished speaking, he remained silent, still gazing at her but seemingly deep in thought. So intent were they on one another that they jumped apart upon hearing a familiar voice.

"And why was I not invited to this cosy little tête-à-tête of yours?"

Elizabeth thought it odd that Mr Darcy chose that moment to glance at his watch and mutter in an unmistakably cynical tone, "Of course. Eleven o'clock. Right on the dot."

❧ 16 ❧

IT NEVER RAINS BUT IT POURS

With professions of pleasure, Elizabeth had greeted Miss Rigby more warmly than Darcy had; but he suspected she was as disappointed as he by the chaperon's ill-timed arrival.

Just prior to that, a pair of fine eyes had been fixed on his face with such a remarkable expression of pensive admiration that he could not help but have hope. And what he would not have given for some privacy, such as they had enjoyed—or at least he had enjoyed—in Kent. Nevertheless, even had they been alone, and as much as he longed to do so, Darcy would not have dared to make her an offer again so soon. And there were recent complications to consider.

He turned up his collar and walked alongside the ladies, envying the chaperon's advantageous position. Of course, he had done the proper thing and invited Miss Rigby to huddle beneath the umbrella with Elizabeth. As they advanced towards the manor, Darcy listened to their chatter but contributed nothing to it.

"And I assure you, Miss Rigby, that our being together

was not because of an assiduous endeavour to meet but rather the result of fortuitous timing. I have been having difficulty with my current puzzle and was feeling low because of it. Hence, I came to the garden seeking solace and inspiration."

The chaperon patted her charge's arm. "And who could not find comfort and inspiration in such a place as this? Rain has enhanced the colours and makes everything look so clean and smell so fresh."

Even above the patter of raindrops hitting their umbrella, Darcy heard Miss Rigby quietly add, "I assume you have found that which you seek, dear."

Catching Darcy's eye, Elizabeth smiled. "I believe I have, yes."

Does she mean me? He felt almost weak for an instant. Then such profound affection and happiness swelled within his heart that he feared it might burst from his chest.

"My spirits have been restored," continued Elizabeth, "and just as this sprinkle has washed away dust on plant life, the morning's freshness has cleared the cobwebs from my mind. I now believe I have the answer to my conundrum."

Darcy was confident he, too, had the answer to his most significant conundrum, namely Elizabeth Bennet herself. *But now I have eliminated one quandary only to find myself with a new one.*

But what was he to do about it? Disguise of every sort was his abhorrence.

※

IN HIS BEDCHAMBER, DARCY SAT AT THE WRITING TABLE IN HIS shirtsleeves and contemplated his newest puzzle, a charade:

My First is a Preposition.
My Second is a Composition.
My Whole is an Acquisition.

There was only one meaning for 'preposition'. Unfortunately, the English language had well over one hundred of them. As for 'composition', that could mean a number of things—the manner in which something is composed, a musical creation, a literary work, a writing exercise, the construction of a sentence, or the arrangement of objects in a painting. 'Acquisition' was either something obtained or the act of obtaining it.

Unable to hold his attention, the charade was set aside.

Although Miss Armstrong's legacy was of great material value, Darcy had been preoccupied with something else since the moment Elizabeth had explained she not only wanted to win the tournament, she needed to win it. It was a different sort of enigma, and it required a different sort of solution.

Were she and he still in a draw with Mr Hadley? For all Darcy knew, the younger man might be alone in first place at that very moment; and he realised that, other than in passing, it had been some time since he had spoken at length with the amiable gentleman. The barrister-in-the-making spent most of his time with Mr Monroe, having deep discussions concerning the legal profession.

Gaining his feet, Darcy stood at the window, one palm braced against its frame. The wet had not let up, and the view through the pane was distorted by runnels of rain. It hardly signified. His thoughts were turned inwards. A desperate resolution began to form; but its groundwork was interrupted by a sound from the door and the subsequent entry of the butler and a footman.

"Pardon the intrusion, Mr Darcy," said Mr Atwater. "Christopher and I are here under the instruction of Mr Monroe." The senior servant seemed embarrassed. "We are to conduct a search of your room, sir, so please have a seat at the writing table whilst we do so."

Darcy had forgotten about that day's planned search; and while he understood the necessity of it, he did resent the intrusion at that moment. Unworried, though, he knew a thorough examination of his apartments would neither take long nor prove fruitful.

As directed, he sat upon the Windsor chair and watched Christopher search beneath the massive oak bed and behind its pillows. Next, the footman inspected the cupboard wash-stand in the corner and then the cabinet concealing a commode. He even peeked behind the fireplace screen and in the grate.

Meanwhile, the butler had gone to examine the dressing room, where most of the space was taken up by a massive, centuries-old armoire that Darcy had been told once held a knight's suits of armour.

Minutes later, Mr Atwater emerged, stern-faced and flushed. "Christopher," said the butler, "fetch Mr Monroe."

"Why?" Darcy shot to his feet but received no response.

Half an hour later, after a hushed conference with Mr Atwater, the attorney ordered Christopher to fetch his brother.

When Alfred came in, Mr Monroe said to him, "As Christopher no doubt informed you, the Japanese vase has been found, wrapped up in Mr Darcy's greatcoat, inside the armoire. However, the gentleman tells me you can vouch for the fact it was not there earlier this morning. Is that correct?"

"Indeed it is, sir." The staid footman seemed indignant on Darcy's behalf. "After helping Mr Darcy dress, and knowing his intention was to walk through the gardens, I brought out the greatcoat and suggested he wear it in case of rain."

Standing with arms crossed, Darcy said, "As I already explained to you, Mr Monroe, I declined. Alfred then returned the greatcoat to the dressing room."

"Where I carefully folded it," continued the footman, "and replaced it on the armoire's top shelf. I am certain the Japanese vase was neither in that dressing room nor out here at any time prior to Mr Darcy departing for his walk."

Alfred sent Darcy an apologetic look, then said to Mr Monroe, "The gentleman is fastidious about his belongings, sir. 'A place for everything and everything in its place'. I have memorised his preferences. Top drawer—cravats, stick pins, and fobs. Bottom drawer—stockings of silk, cotton, and worsted. Boots and shoes on the bottom shelf, breeches and trousers on the next, shirts and waistcoats above, then tail-coats. Topmost are hats and the greatcoat. His satchel, writing desk, and trunk all have locks, and the keys are always kept on Mr Darcy's person except when he is abed."

Despite himself, Darcy smiled, although it may have looked more like a grimace to the others.

"Alfred," said the butler, "did you say you put the great-coat on the topmost shelf?" The footman replied in the affirmative, and Mr Atwater turned to the attorney. "When I found the vase, sir, with the garment maladroitly wrapped round it, it was on the next shelf down with the tailcoats."

Mr Monroe stood stroking his chin. "A shorter person could have dragged down the coat from the top shelf but would have had trouble neatly putting it back up there, especially if they were in a rush."

Darcy sat bolt upright. *Is he thinking the same thing I am? Peter Fordham probably stands no more than five feet five inches tall.*

But, if beneficiaries were being watched constantly, as Mr Monroe once had indicated, how was it that both Miss Kensett and Mr Fordham had been able to enter forbidden bedchambers?

FULLY EXPECTING TO BE ALONE WHILE HE VENTED HIS frustration, Darcy arrived in the games room only to be greeted with Mr Hadley's customary hail-fellow-well-met alacrity. "I say, Darcy! Jolly good of you to come and save me from beating myself." He held an ornate, ivory-capped mace in his left hand and a leather-tipped cue in the other.

Although he had entered in a surly humour, Darcy could not help but be amused. "Whatever, may I ask, did you do to deserve self-inflicted corporal punishment?"

"Eh? Oh. Ha! No, not that sort of beating. Billiards! I was going to play against myself, you see. Left-handed with a mace and right-handed with a cue. Instead, I hope you will join me, although I am rather poor at it."

Other than Bingley, Darcy had never known anyone who would so deliberately suppress his own merit. "I shall be delighted to prove you either right or wrong." He accepted the proffered cue from Mr Hadley. "You presently seem at leisure, spending time in a pursuit unrelated to the winning of Miss Armstrong's legacy." Was the younger man just biding his time, waiting to claim the grand prize? *My solution will be to no avail should either of the other gentlemen prevail.*

"Yet here you are, Darcy, doing exactly the same as I."

But Darcy's aim had been to vent his spleen by hitting something other than Mr Fordham. *And where is that weasel? What underhandedness is he hatching now?*

Opening a wooden marquetry box, Mr Hadley presented

it to Darcy. The padded interior held a red ball and two ivory ones. After choosing the white ball with a small black dot, Darcy bounced it upon his palm. "Do you happen to know Fordham's whereabouts?"

"No." After he thought for a moment, Mr Hadley added, "I dislike being unjust to the merit of another, but I fear he is not to be trusted." Taking the two remaining balls from the box, he placed them on the billiards table. "Christopher ironed the baize a while ago, so there should be no wrinkles to impede us. But, since daylight is rather dull in here and there are no lamps above the table, let us say thirteen points to win. By the bye, Darcy, speaking of light, have you seen the delightful Miss Bennet today?"

"She went for a walk in the gardens this morning." Darcy chalked the tip of his cue. "Why do you ask?"

"Simply curious. I missed seeing her this morning." Mr Hadley leant over the table, lining up his shot. "I had to stay in my apartment while it was being searched."

Jaw clenched, Darcy managed to grind out six one-syllable words. "They found the vase in mine."

The other gentleman's ivory ball shot past the padded rail and rolled across the floor, reminding Darcy of alabaster balls in the boudoir. Mace in hand, Mr Hadley advanced on him. "You? You!"

"Not me! Apparently, while I was walking in the gardens, someone entered my dressing room and rather ineptly hid the vase there. Mr Monroe summoned Alfred, and the footman confirmed it was not there earlier this morning."

"Good. I am glad." Relieved, it seemed, at Darcy's innocence, Mr Hadley grinned. "So, while you were walking in the gardens this morning, did you happen to see anything in bloom there? Anything cheerful or lovely?"

The very thought of Elizabeth brought a smile to Darcy's face.

Mr Hadley soon grew serious. "The vase, though... Who would have done such a thing? To steal it in the first place... But then to implicate you! And let us not forget that someone drugged your wine. Unconscionable! Do you suppose it was"—he lowered his voice—"Mr Fordham?"

"That is what I would like to determine. So now, future barrister, despite your hesitation at being unjust, tell me everything you know or suspect about Peter Fordham. But do so quietly. I once caught him listening at a door."

❧ 17 ❧
POCKETS

Elizabeth walked about her bedchamber in agitation. *What must he think of me?*

Whatever Mr Darcy thought of her, for better or worse, was thanks to Charlotte Lucas. Her dear friend once had stated that being guarded would be disadvantageous to a woman and that in concealing one's affection from the object of it, one risked losing the opportunity of fixing him.

Fixing him. La! I either have fixed him for good or sent him running for the hills.

Earlier, while the three of them had been leaving the gardens, Miss Rigby had enquired whether she had found that which she sought. Elizabeth had smiled sweetly at Mr Darcy and said yes, she believed she had.

Well, there is nothing to be done about it now, brazen girl.

That walk in the wet gardens, however, had removed the clouds from Elizabeth's mind...though perhaps not the part of her mind that controlled her tongue. Nevertheless, she hoped she finally might have an answer to 'Hearts shall weave'. She grabbed a shawl, rushed to the great hall, and approached the dais.

At the peep-hole, with the conversation she had over-heard echoing in her mind, Elizabeth felt a draught, real or imagined. It was wrong to observe or listen to others furtively, but she had heard Miss Kensett and Mr Fordham's conversation without their knowledge. *The walls in this room have ears as well as eyes.* 'The walls have ears'. On her fingers she counted again the letters in that sentence. *Sixteen. Perfect!*

Wetting her lips with cautious hope, Elizabeth lifted a corner of the tapestry that disguised the peep-hole. Then she closed her eyes, unable to look without saying a prayer. "Please, please, please, let it be there." Hopeful and fearful, she took a deep breath and held it. Slowly, she opened one eye, then the other.

There, pinned to the tapestry's backing, was the hoped-for piece of foolscap. Finally, she exhaled, then covered her mouth with trembling fingers. Not only was Elizabeth close to tears, but she was also one step closer to winning Oakwood Manor.

While she unpinned, unfolded, and read the paper, her stomach fluttered. The page indicated the puzzle written on it was the ultimate conundrum. Heart rejoicing, she set off in search of Mr Monroe.

Leaving the great hall with spirits elated to rapture, Eliza-beth startled when, across the way, the door to the games room creaked open just wide enough to accommodate Mr Hadley's head. He looked left, then right, then began to close the door. At the last second, he spotted her and opened it fully.

"Ah! Miss Bennet, good day to you!"

Mr Darcy appeared behind him and asked her to join them. Elizabeth hesitated. "Who else is with you?"

"No one else." Mr Hadley held an index finger against his lips and beckoned her inside.

Frowning, Elizabeth approached and shook her head. "I cannot risk either my reputation or disqualification from the tournament."

"Of course," said Mr Darcy. "But perhaps Miss Rigby could be convinced to sit with us. Shall I have her summoned?"

The folded paper in the concealed pocket of Elizabeth's gown screamed at her to decline, but the gentleman's eyes drew her in.

Upon receiving her reluctant consent, Mr Darcy passed a cue to Mr Hadley and swept past them both. A moment later, Elizabeth heard him, in the vestibule, speaking to Christopher. In a matter of minutes, Miss Rigby appeared, and the two ladies joined the two gentlemen in the games room.

"I shall just sit here at this card table with Miss Bennet," said the chaperon. "Pay me no mind. I have my embroidery to occupy me." She smiled when Mr Darcy pulled out a chair and held it for her as she sat. Then he did the same for Elizabeth.

"All I ask," said Miss Rigby, "is that the three of you not enter into any sort of conversation about the tournament."

While Mr Hadley talked and the others listened, the two gentlemen played billiards; but it seemed to Elizabeth that they did so more for appearances' sake than any real attempt at skill or friendly rivalry.

"...and whenever I visited here, Mr Fordham spent most of his time skulking about the place. I wish I could recall something approaching charity or benevolence in him, but, sadly, I cannot. More than anything, he and his wife seemed to enjoy the pleasures to be had while living off Miss Armstrong's generosity."

As Mr Darcy leant over the billiards table, Elizabeth admired his tall, lean, athletic build. His muscles were not as obvious as a labourer's, but they were well-defined and in proportion to the rest of his body. *Nature has given him no inconsiderable share of beauty.* He sank the red ball into a pocket and called out that he had scored three points for something called a hazard, but there was little enthusiasm in his voice.

"What was Mr Fordham's bequest from Miss Armstrong?" asked Elizabeth. "I do not believe I ever heard it mentioned."

"If you were to ask him, which I did," said Mr Hadley, "Mr Fordham would say he received a 'little bauble to present to his lovely wife'. Lovely, by the bye, is not a word I would use to describe her, but that is beside the point. I suspect the professed little bauble is a sixteenth-century Burmese ruby ring that was made much of by Mrs Fordham. It was too large for Miss Armstrong's slim fingers, so she sometimes wore it round her neck on a gold chain. Personally, I thought the ring hideous." He lined up a shot, and there was a double clack as his plain white ball, in succession, hit Mr Darcy's then the red one. "My word! Did you see that? A cannon! I scored a cannon!"

"Well done." Mr Darcy patted the younger man's shoulder. "So, in your opinion, the Fordhams do not have any better principle to guide them than selfishness, is that correct?"

"They are regardless of everything but their own gratification," grumbled Mr Hadley. Setting aside his mace, he pulled out a chair from one of the card tables and sat, knee bouncing. "What I am about to say is simply my own conjecture, but I fear the Fordhams imposed themselves on Miss Armstrong. They ingratiated themselves with an elderly lady and took advantage of her loneliness and infirmity. Eventually earning her trust and favour through flattery, Mr Fordham began taking her heirlooms to be valued. But I do not know that they ever found their way back to Oakwood Manor."

The billiards game abandoned, Mr Hadley rose and placed the three balls back in the decorative box. "Mrs Fordham told me they wanted to please Miss Armstrong, improve her mood, and restore a sense of physical well-being during her infirmity. But I never witnessed either of them seeing to her comfort. What I did notice was that every time one of them admired a valuable article, it soon thereafter was bestowed upon them. They were bilking her, I fear. I think they stepped in only because they knew she had no children to whom to leave her legacy. The Fordhams hoped they would inherit everything."

"I just remembered," said Elizabeth, "that Miss Kensett said Mr Fordham thought of himself before anybody else and that he was intent on snatching—yes, snatching!—everything he possibly could."

"Poor, dear Miss Armstrong." Mr Darcy sat perched sideways on the edge of the billiards table, one foot on the floor. "Manoeuvres of selfishness, cunning, and duplicity are revolting to me."

He seemed so angry and sad that Elizabeth longed to do something to comfort him but knew she could not. "I agree. Unscrupulous control and influence are despicable in every particular."

Miss Rigby patted her charge's hand. "There, there, my dear. Whatever a man sows, this he also will reap."

"Tell me," Mr Darcy said as he put away the cue and mace, "do any of you know whether opium was found in Fordham's possession?"

The younger gentleman glanced at the ladies. No one spoke up, so he did. "According to Mr Monroe, the only opium presently in this house is kept under lock and key in Mrs Vincent's medicine chest and only used for tinctures of laudanum. No other was found during any of the searches."

"I imagine a vial of powdered opium would be small enough to easily conceal," said Elizabeth.

To that, the chaperon muttered, "Probably on his person. Never before have I so wished to put my fingers inside a gentleman's fob pocket."

Elizabeth and the two gentlemen in unison cried, "Miss Rigby!"

❦

ALFRED HAD LUGGED PAILS OF STEAMING WATER FROM THE kitchen, and Rachel had poured them into a full-size copper tub.

Sweet-scented then and feeling singularly well, Elizabeth had her clean hair dressed and was helped into her best primrose gown.

Still smiling about the chaperon's fob-pocket remark, she was determined to maintain an acquaintance with Miss Rigby. *I must remember to ask for her direction so we may, at the very least, write to one another once the tournament ends.* She would be sorry to bid farewell to Mr Hadley also, but they would not be permitted to correspond. Then there was Mr Darcy...

"There is someone at the door, miss." Rachel, not quite finished with the back of Elizabeth's gown, went to investigate. When she returned, she held out a folded sheet of writing paper. "No one was there, but I found this on the floor."

While the maid went to work again on the gown's tiny buttons, Elizabeth unfolded the message. The writing was unfamiliar. Then again, the only person at Oakwood whose penmanship she would have recognised was Mr Darcy's. She could not remember what the attorney's hand had looked like, and she had never seen Mr Hadley's or Mr Fordham's. At any rate, the words were few.

Miss Bennet, meet me in the garret immediately. It is the only place we can be assured of privacy. I have urgent information to acquaint you with. Come quickly, please. And come alone.

It was unsigned.

Upon a second look, Elizabeth noted a particular elegance in the ornamental handwriting, the sort considered ideal for ladies. It had to be Miss Rigby's. There was no other possibility.

Had it to do with Mr Fordham? Was she in danger from him?

Was it because of the puzzle she had found behind the tapestry? But that had been verified by Mr Monroe, and all she had to do was find a solution and then the prize.

"Please hurry, Rachel. There is something I must do before dinner." Elizabeth glanced at the clock on the mantel. Already it was half past five, and they were expected in the parlour by a quarter to six. "How does one access the garret?"

"The garret? Do you mean the small tower at the very top?" Elizabeth nodded, and the maid's hands stilled on her back. "Surely you do not want to be going up there, especially in this gown."

"Yes, Rachel, I do."

"Then I shall go with you."

"No. I must do this alone." The instant her gown was buttoned, Elizabeth rushed to open the chamber door, then turned back. "Which way?"

The maid stood wringing her hands and looking wretched. Slowly she pointed left. "Go to the end of the hall and turn right. At the end of that hall, there are stairs that—"

"Thank you."

Within a few minutes, Elizabeth had found the narrow, spiralling staircase with steep risers. Hitching her hems in one hand, she held onto a rickety handrail with the other and climbed. Beneath her feet, wooden steps creaked.

At the top, in the shadows, was an alcove, large enough for a person. There was no window, and she wished she had thought to bring a candle. *Of all places, why would Miss Rigby want to meet here? I should turn back.* Peering into the dark, she groped blindly and tripped over a rumpled rug.

Opposite the stairs, Elizabeth located a latch, which she lifted, then pushed on the door. A shaft of sunlight slanted through a high window, and she momentarily closed her eyes against the dazzle.

The floor was uneven as she cautiously stepped inside. Nail heads protruded from the boards, and she felt every one of them beneath her soft slippers as she crossed the small room.

The garret was a dismal place. Its few pieces of blackened furniture were pockmarked and scratched. The ceilings were sloped, and she walked, face-first, into a series of ancient cobwebs. *So much for my clean hair and coiffure.* The air was dry, dusty, and cold. It smelt of old grains and onions.

Standing on a spindly chair, Elizabeth peered through the grimy window. All she saw were the manor's rooftops below. She stepped off the chair lest it collapse beneath her, and her gown caught on a large, sharp splinter protruding from a rung. *Bother!* It had pierced her thigh.

From behind, there came a noise. *Splendid. Mice.* The floor creaked. *Not mice.*

Turning her head, Elizabeth tried to determine who was on the landing, but it was too black out there to see anything. She did notice, though, an unexpected glow from the direction of the alcove.

Struggling to free her skirt, she called, "Miss Rigby?" *Why will she not answer?* The sensitive skin on her nape tingled, and she redoubled her effort to release her gown and thigh from the splinter.

The next thing Elizabeth knew, she was being roughly handled. She heard her skirt rip, then she was shoved through the doorway. After being in the sunlit room, her eyes had not adjusted to the dim light of the landing. "Please! *Please* do not throw me down those stairs!" Never had her fear been so strongly aroused.

Her assailant kicked aside the rug and opened a trapdoor in the floor. With a thrust, Elizabeth was forced inside. The last thing she saw before the hatch closed, leaving her in pitch blackness, was her attacker's face in the glow of a candle from the alcove. Then she heard the turn of a key in a lock.

18

THE GARRET

"...And, honestly, she did nothing to earn a place in this competition. In the year nine, when Miss Armstrong first moved here, Miss Kensett's grandmother, Mrs Amelia Delgrave, now deceased, called on the old lady several times and introduced her to some of the local women. Miss Armstrong made the granddaughter a beneficiary merely to honour Mrs Delgrave's memory."

With his back to the window, Darcy stood watching the parlour's doorway and paying scant heed to Mr Fordham's blather. He did notice, however, that, like him, Mr Monroe also consulted his watch a second time.

Elizabeth had yet to arrive in the parlour.

She was not even five minutes late; still, Darcy fretted. *Elizabeth is always prompt, never unpunctual. She would have sent a message with the maid if she was unwell or unavoidably delayed.*

He strode to the attorney's side. "Someone should enquire into her absence."

Mr Monroe seemed somewhat amused. "I assume you mean Miss Bennet."

Of course I mean Miss Bennet! "Yes, and it is unlike her to be tardy. The time is now ten minutes to six, and if you do not send someone, I shall storm her apartment myself."

"Very well, sir." Mr Monroe beckoned Alfred and spoke quietly to him.

The footman's eyes widened. Then he nodded to both the attorney and Darcy before turning on his heel.

"I suspect Alfred has become as fond of our Miss Bennet as the rest of us," said Mr Monroe. "But I am sure the young lady is simply having trouble deciding which earrings to wear or some such triviality."

"And I am sure that is not the case." Darcy went and stared through the window, waiting for word and fearing, knowing, something was wrong.

When Alfred returned with Rachel and moved towards Mr Monroe, Darcy reached them first. "What is it? What has happened?"

"I…I already…" Rachel wrung her hands, then took a gulping breath. "I already told Mrs Vincent… As soon as Miss Bennet left the room, I ran down and told the housekeeper that someone left a message by the bedchamber door. And Miss Bennet would not let me go with her! To the garret! Why would she go there?" The maid wiped away tears with her fingers. "If anything has happened to her, I shall never forgive myself!"

Miss Rigby rushed over. "What is this about Miss Bennet?" Mr Monroe took her aside and explained.

"Alfred, come with me." Without waiting for a response, Darcy was out of the parlour door and striding towards the staircase with the footman behind him. "How does one access the garret?"

"Sir, it will be faster if we take the servants' passages."

"Then lead the way."

"Wait for me!" Mr Hadley ran after them.

When he looked behind, Darcy noticed Mr Monroe had joined their sombre parade.

The footman opened a wood panel and a baize service door, and they all filed into a warren of whitewashed corridors and staircases that had been added over the centuries. The passages were lit by either tallow candles in sconces or rush dips—reeds soaked in hog fat—that had been clipped into holders. Both sources provided only a dim glow that flickered, sputtered, smoked, and emitted a foul, greasy odour.

Even Darcy, who had an excellent sense of direction, might have become hopelessly lost without the footman's guidance.

Finally, they reached a small spiral staircase. With each step taken, wood groaned under the men's weight. When the four of them reached the landing, Darcy heard a gentle female voice; but it was not Elizabeth's. Looking past the footman, he discerned a woman kneeling and holding a candle. She seemed to be talking to the floor.

"Mrs Vincent," said Mr Monroe, obviously relieved to see the housekeeper. "Is Miss Bennet in there? Is it locked? If so, do you have the key?"

The housekeeper stood. "Someone is down there. They must have heard my footsteps, for they have been knocking. And there has been a clicking noise coming from below. As for the key, it is missing, sir. I do not know how it happened, but someone took it."

"Wait!" Alfred flung out both his arms, impeding the men behind from moving forwards. The floor in front of him rattled. A trapdoor slowly opened.

Darcy could have wept when a head, full of cobwebs and unpinned brunette curls, emerged from what appeared to be a priest hole.

Elizabeth squinted in the candlelight. "What took you so long? I despaired of ever effecting my escape." With the footman and housekeeper's assistance, she climbed out of the centuries-old hiding place. "Have I missed dinner? I am hungry and filthy." She brushed off her dress and winced. "Kindly pardon my appearance. I broke ten hairpins and a fingernail trying to pick that stubborn lock. The eleventh pin worked like a charm."

Darcy ran his eyes over Elizabeth's form. A dark stain spread downwards on the side of her skirt from thigh to knee. It took every bit of decorum bred into him to stop himself from rushing forwards and crushing her to his chest, especially when fat tears slipped down her cheeks.

Mrs Vincent passed the candle to Alfred and enfolded Elizabeth in her arms. "There, there, dear. You have had an awful fright, but you are safe now. Come, let us get you washed and fed." With fire in her eyes, the housekeeper looked at the four men. "Find the wretch who did this to her!"

"I know who it was," said Elizabeth between sniffs.

Brushing past the others, Darcy handed her his pristine handkerchief, dearly wishing he could do more.

"Thank you." She gave him a watery smile and, leaving Mrs Vincent's embrace, wiped her eyes.

"Who did this to you, Miss Bennet? Who is he?"

Darcy had never heard Mr Hadley so full of anger and anguish; and when he glanced at the footman and attorney, they, too, appeared ready to tear the perpetrator limb from limb.

It was Fordham. It had to be. But he was already in the parlour when I arrived shortly after half past five.

Peering down into the pitch black of the priest hole, Darcy shuddered before kicking it closed. "How long were you in that hide, Miss Bennet?"

"I cannot be certain how much time might have elapsed, but I left my room at about half past five. While trapped, to dissipate a measure of panic, I sang 'Old Maid in the Garret' at least a dozen times." Rubbing her forehead, she moved unsteadily and looked terribly pale in the candlelight. "The person who…attacked me and…locked me…in…there… was…"

Moving fast, Darcy caught her before she could hit the floor, and he prayed she had not fainted from blood loss.

One arm round Elizabeth's lower back and the other behind her knees, mindful of her injury, Darcy lifted her limp form and held it close to him. Shoulders back and grip secure, he took a deep breath and a careful step forwards, maintaining his balance.

Thus, he began the treacherous descent of the staircase, fearful it might collapse under their combined weight, though she was as light as a feather and no burden to him. Almost immediately, she groaned and revived. He stopped on a stair and watched her fine eyes flutter open. "What…? Where am I? Mr Darcy?"

He felt her stiffen in his arms. "Mr Darcy! Put me down on my own two feet at once. I am perfectly well *now*. I merely was overwhelmed earlier. Please, put me down."

He would not hear of it, but he did have to listen to her constant fears of overtaxing his back. In gentle tones, he repeatedly assured her he was under no strain at all. If he took pride in exhibiting his physical prowess, no one else need know.

"Sir, allow me to carry Miss Bennet for you."

Darcy told Alfred that he could manage quite well himself, thank you. Under no circumstances was he going to surrender his precious cargo to anyone else's care.

"Watch Miss Bennet's head, Darcy! The stairs bend to the right just ahead." Mr Hadley, on Darcy's heels, kept up a running commentary on the twists and turns in the staircase.

All the while, Darcy relished the feel of the young woman in his arms, and he imagined carrying her across Pemberley's threshold.

"Why," she asked, "are you suddenly grinning like a Cheshire cat?"

Because you, my darling, never will be an old maid in the garret if I have any say in the matter. "This is not a grin, madam. This is a grimace—an ugly, twisted expression brought on by the pain of carrying a ton of bricks down a steep spiral staircase." His remark produced the desired effect.

She smiled, then spoke in no uncertain terms. "Put me down, sir. Now!"

He pretended he had not heard and concentrated on breathing in her fragrance, which customarily brought to mind a summer meadow or an autumn orchard. *Now I detect traces of a granary or vegetable cellar.*

"Mrs Vincent," called Mr Monroe from behind. "I will not hear of a genteel lady being carried through servants' passages. We shall take the longer but easier route."

"Easier for whom?" muttered Elizabeth. "I shall walk from here."

"No. I am perfectly capable of carrying you from here to Slough, if necessary."

Leading the way—though perilously walking backwards down the spiral staircase while guiding Darcy—Mrs Vincent softly asked whether Miss Bennet was ready to name the contemptible blackguard who had assailed her.

"Blackguard? It was not a man who attacked me and forced me into that horrid hide."

A collective breath was held as everyone waited. Darcy's mind raced. *Surely not Miss Rigby!*

"It was the maid Henrietta." Although she had whispered the name, Darcy was certain the others heard, for there came a collective gasp.

"This is our fault. Henrietta was hired by Pemberton & Monroe." In a tone of violent indignation, the attorney added, "She will be made to pay. Perhaps some time in the priest hole would serve as apt punishment."

"No!" Elizabeth tried to wriggle free of Darcy's arms, and he had a spot of bother trying to maintain his balance on the third last stair. "Please, please," she begged, "do not put Henrietta, or anyone, ever, in that awful place! So dark, so airless." She shuddered.

Darcy hugged her tighter and discreetly placed a light kiss upon her hair.

Mr Monroe spoke gently. "As you wish. In fact, I shall have the hiding place dismantled as soon as may be."

Arriving at Elizabeth's apartment, they found Miss Rigby and Rachel anxiously waiting at the door.

Lowering his body, Darcy allowed Elizabeth to safely place her feet upon the floor. He helped her stand but remained ready to assist if she stumbled. He need not have bothered. Together with Mrs Vincent, the women whisked the young lady into her bedchamber, and the four men were banished.

The instant the door closed in his face, Darcy was bereft. Still feeling Elizabeth's body against his, he turned and joined the other solemn men as they made their way downstairs.

At the bottom of the grand staircase, Mr Monroe rubbed his temples and ordered Alfred to have Henrietta brought to him in the library. "Secure her hands behind her back. Spare the wretched girl no mercy."

Grim-faced, Alfred nodded and set off to take the perpetrator captive.

Darcy approached the attorney and asked to be included while the maid was questioned. Mr Hadley was right behind him. "I wish to be there, too, sir. Miss Bennet is"—he glanced at Darcy—"our friend."

"Where the devil has Mr Fordham been during this entire incident?" Mr Monroe looked about the vestibule. "Why did he not accompany us to the garret? Was he not concerned about Miss Bennet's welfare?"

Darcy and Mr Hadley exchanged a look, then followed their host to the library.

I had not given Fordham a second thought, but I suppose he is in the dining room enjoying dinner. For his part, Darcy had no appetite, and he declined either a seat or a glass of brandy when they were offered. He paced, and his heart throbbed in rhythm with the clock's pendulum.

He, Hadley, and Mr Monroe turned at a sudden sound from the doorway. But it was Miss Rigby, who had come down to advise them of Elizabeth's condition.

"The poor dear is recovering. She has eaten a bite, and her wound has been tended. Now she is up there pacing and fretting over Mr Darcy's back, the tournament, and her ruined gown, in that order."

Finally, Alfred returned with Henrietta. The maid looked as though butter would not melt in her mouth, but the footman seemed ready to beat walls. "Here she is, Mr Monroe. She and Mr Fordham were in the coach house together, waiting for his carriage to be readied. It seems he was absconding and taking her with him. Mr Atwater and Christopher are detaining the gentleman, in case you wish to question him as well."

🏵 19 🏵

A TICKING TIMEPIECE

Sleep had come in fits and starts. Restless wakefulness had been followed by dreams of confined spaces and sensations of suffocation. Elizabeth awoke each time gasping for air but was comforted by either Rachel or Miss Rigby, who had taken turns sitting at her bedside.

Through a gap in the curtains, morning sunlight peeked into the room, and Elizabeth's eyes fluttered open. The splinter's gash on her thigh ached, but it had been cleaned and a poultice applied the previous night.

Bestirring herself, she squinted at the mantel's timepiece. Ten o'clock! Never had she arisen so late; and, it being Wednesday, only fourteen hours remained in the competition.

"Good morning, miss. Would you care for some chocolate?" Rachel patted a silver pot. "'Tis no longer steaming hot but still nice and warm."

"I would, but much time was wasted last night. My being close to victory must be the reason I was forced into that hide. I have a tournament to win, Rachel, and not a minute

161

to spare." Flinging aside bed covers, Elizabeth placed her feet on the floor. "A puzzle needs solving, and a prize awaits." She looked to the ewer on the washstand. "Is there warm water? And I shall wear my sprigged muslin this morning."

"Yes, miss."

"While you assist with my toilette, tell me what became of Henrietta."

"Etta was questioned by Mr Monroe," said Rachel, "but Alfred didn't stay in the room, so I can't tell you what transpired there. All I know is she has been dismissed."

It was not the news Elizabeth had anticipated, but she would not allow anger to damp down her fire to win the tournament. With cheerful predictions about securing Oakwood Manor for her family, she eagerly anticipated the day ahead.

The maid poured warm water into a basin and set out a cake of soap, a cloth, and a towel. "The magistrate and a constable came this morning. Now they, too, are gone." Rummaging round in the wardrobe, she called out in a muffled voice, "Sprigged muslin, was it?"

"Yes!" Elizabeth dried her hands and longed to sit quietly with her puzzle.

"I hear both of your gentlemen admirers are beside themselves with outrage due to the cruel treatment you endured."

Elizabeth firmly denied she had two admirers.

"Pish, I beg to differ." Rachel crossed the room with the muslin over an arm. "Even Mr Monroe and my Alfred are as cross as two sticks about your maltreatment at Etta's hands." She gasped, then covered her mouth with both palms.

"Oh! *Your* Alfred, is he?" Elizabeth smiled as a fine blush overspread the maid's face. "Come now, Rachel. He is a fine young man. There is no need for embarrassment."

As the muslin was slipped over her head and buttoned,

both women remained silent. Elizabeth was thinking ahead. No one knew what the future would bring; but if circumstances were favourable and she was granted the deed to Oakwood, she hoped Rachel, Alfred, Christopher, Mrs Vincent, and Mr Atwater would remain as part of the household, if they so wished it.

⚜

IN THE SUNLIT GARDENS THREE-QUARTERS OF AN HOUR LATER, Elizabeth sat alone with pencil and paper in her hand and aspirations of owning Oakwood in her head.

In that reverie, a sweet melody flowed from an open window in the music room, where Mary sat at the pianoforte. On the lawn, Kitty and Lydia giddily laughed while playing pall-mall without proper understanding or any degree of seriousness. Jane Bingley, of course, was at Netherfield with her loving husband, Charles; and Elizabeth's mother lived with the Bingleys because she would not hear of leaving her friends in Meryton.

But how was it all to work? If Mrs Bennet was at Netherfield and if Mary, Kitty, and Lydia were at Oakwood, that meant Elizabeth's dear papa was no longer alive, for that was the only reason her family would leave Longbourn.

Where do I fit into this picture? She did not. In her dream, Elizabeth resided with her own husband at a place called Pemberley.

"I thought I might find you here."

For an instant, reverie and reality became one, and Elizabeth stared stupidly at Mr Darcy. The smile on his face made him more handsome than ever as he advanced towards her. But she must have looked quite insensible to him, for the gentleman's smile disappeared as quickly as had the reverie, its permanence as fleeting as a bubble's. He asked whether she was well.

"Yes, thank you, I am."

"Did you sleep well?"

No. Hence my stupor. "Well enough. And you?" Elizabeth noticed a nick on his chin and supposed it had happened while shaving or being shaved. *Nick! Yes!* Smiling widely but wanting to laugh and dance a jig and, perhaps, kiss Mr Darcy, she schooled her features into something that hopefully resembled indifference.

"Hardly a wink. Yet I"—he gave her a pointed look, seemingly concerned about her odd state of mind—"feel no repercussions from lack of sleep."

"Forgive me. I was wool-gathering but should be working on this puzzle." Elizabeth indicated the pencil in her hand and the foolscap upon her lap. *I now know both words!* She could not help but grin again. Belatedly, she turned downwards both the paper and the satisfied smirk upon her face. In her head, she attempted to rearrange eight letters but needed to see them on paper.

"Ah. Then I should intrude no further upon your contemplation."

"No, please stay." After placing her pencil, the foolscap, and a bowl of cherries upon the ground, Elizabeth made room for him on the bench beside her. The gloves she had discarded earlier while working on her puzzle were quickly tugged onto their proper places.

Seated as indicated, Mr Darcy asked Elizabeth whether she might care to hear about the morning's proceedings. She nodded, and he half turned towards her, slinging an arm across the back of the bench. A whiff of juniper mingled with floral fragrances of the garden, and the air Elizabeth breathed was suddenly infused with a glorious, heady perfume.

"Due to your ordeal," he said, "Henrietta has been dismissed without reference."

Not for a moment did Elizabeth wish to rescind her entreaty to keep the maid out of the priest hole. Still, hearing Henrietta had got away with a mere dismissal was rather provoking.

"I know what you are thinking, Miss Bennet. However, she committed no punishable crime."

"No crime? She assaulted me and held me captive! And what of the missing vase and the tampering with your wine? Was Henrietta responsible for those offences? Then there is the housekeeper's missing key and the note I received. Although I abhor the very thought of capital punishment, I confess myself not at all satisfied with her penalty."

In a tone of gentleness and commiseration, Darcy said he understood and agreed. "I make no plea for mercy on Henrietta's behalf, and there can be no excuse for her cruelty towards you. However, her family's situation is deplorable. Her father, a widower, is deathly ill and unable to work, and like many other unemployed people, Henrietta's two brothers were forced into a life of crime to survive. When she was hired at Oakwood for the tournament, her menfolk were well pleased with the honest income she would bring home."

"I still do not understand. Why did Henrietta single me out? What did she gain by attacking and confining me?"

"She has been in Fordham's unscrupulous employ off and on for some time. His wife taught Henrietta to read and write and forged references so she could be hired here. They tasked her, as a maid, with finding a master list of the tournament's puzzles and answers, but Mr Monroe apparently keeps that on his person. When that plan failed, they attempted to obstruct Fordham's competitors instead. Henrietta stole the opium Fordham put in my wine, then she was ordered to detain you awhile. It was her idea to remove the key from under Mrs Vincent's ever-watchful eye using the sleight of hand her brothers taught her, write the note, and put you in the hide, but she maintains she did not assault you."

"Although I was roughly handled, I admit my only significant injury was from a splinter of wood."

"Does it cause much discomfort?"

"No." She grinned at him. "Unless you insist I dance a reel."

"Indeed, I would not dare." Darcy returned her smile but soon grew serious. "Before Henrietta left in disgrace, she levelled all the blame for recent nefarious activity on Fordham. She told Mr Monroe that the Fordhams' home is filled with antiques. As we speak, the magistrate and a constable are escorting Fordham to Slough, where they will search his house. At any rate, what they did to you and me was meant to impede our progress in the tournament. I realise that all you went through was deeply disturbing and distressing, however…"

"I am stronger than I appear, Mr Darcy. You may continue without fear of offending my sensibilities."

"Even had they attempted murder, they would have committed no crime. However, were you a kidnapped heiress, your family could claim property had been stolen from them. Theft of property is a hanging offence."

Elizabeth grasped at straws. "Theft, then! The missing items…"

"The vase is back in the parlour. Apparently, Fordham told Henrietta he was supposed to have had it valued last year—which I doubt—but forgot to do so. He paid her to move it from room to room during the searches, and I expect he hoped to abscond with it after the tournament. As for the key, rather mysteriously, it was on the housekeeper's desk by the time Mrs Vincent arrived in her office this morning. I had wondered why Miss Kensett and Fordham were able to enter forbidden bedchambers. Now I know that Henrietta assisted them."

Elizabeth offered the fruit bowl to Mr Darcy. "Henrietta and Mr Fordham are an artful pair. Poor Miss Armstrong! I am grateful everyone else here has been so kind...though Miss Kensett left much to be desired. What, other than the maid's dismissal, has been done?"

The gentleman absently twirled two cherries still attached by their stems. "A household inventory is being undertaken by Mrs Vincent, Mr Atwater, and their under-lings. The list they compile will be compared with one done when Miss Armstrong originally took possession of Oakwood in the year nine. I expect many heirlooms have disappeared and, or, been replaced by inferior items. But nothing has been proved. Yet."

Mr Darcy ate the cherries one by one, politely discarding the stones. "Now, Miss Bennet, enough dismal tidings. Since one more competitor has been eliminated from the tournament, the chance of winning has been narrowed. So, if you will excuse me, I shall leave you to work on your puzzle in peace." He bowed and wished Elizabeth success.

Making her wish a reality was the height of her ambition, so she reached for the paper and pencil, took off her gloves, and set about solving the poser.

A razor might do this, as might a thief with brio.

She scribbled the word 'nick'.

Extracted, I'm ebon; used, red; discarded, grey.

Beside 'nick' Elizabeth jotted down 'coal'.

Now rearrange your two words to then form a trio.

From those two small words—'nick' and 'coal'—she had to form three. Elizabeth saw the solution to the anagram straightaway but froze, overpowered by a sense of triumph and wonder. If neither Mr Darcy nor Mr Hadley preceded her, Oakwood Manor would be hers.

⚜

UPON ALBERT OPENING THE FRONT DOOR FOR HER, ELIZABETH entered the vestibule just as Mr Hadley hurried out from the library. He and she nearly collided.

"Miss Bennet! I do beg your pardon!" The young gentleman's coppery hair virtually stood on end, and it was evident he had been running his fingers through it. "I was just…ah… looking for…something. If you will excuse me." He sketched a bow and rushed towards the great room.

Something 'in a clock', perhaps? Elizabeth supposed she could eliminate the library since her opponent obviously had not found what he was looking for in there.

Arriving in the parlour, she was pleased to see the Japanese vase once again gracing the unlit fireplace, but she was only interested in the pink marble and gilt bronze clock on the mantel. It, however, was too disappointingly small to contain a deed and key.

She next peeked inside the great hall. Mr Hadley was still

wandering about in there, so she crossed to the games room. One glance at its transparent rectangular base proved the pyramid-shaped table clock held no prize.

Mr Hadley was encountered again between the two rooms, and he appeared twice as harried as before. With more at stake than friendship, they stood face-to-face, each anticipating the other's next move. The gentleman's eyes darted left, to the hall leading to the manor's breakfast and dining rooms. They were the only two places remaining.

For a moment, Elizabeth and he engaged in a dance of sorts. Mr Hadley moved left when she moved right, then he moved right and she left, causing an unseemly burst of laughter from both.

Startling when the Westminster chimes sounded from the vestibule's pendulum clock positioned against the parlour wall, Elizabeth thought it an ideal hiding spot.

It appeared Mr Hadley had the same thought, for his eyes widened, and they both set off in that direction, straining to neither run nor out and out race one another. Like the lady and gentleman they were, Elizabeth and he walked side by side with short, quick steps and in an affectedly refined manner.

❦ 20 ❦

SACRIFICE

The vestibule clock struck twelve as Darcy stood at the head of the stairs, gripping the railing and watching the goings-on below him.

Just days prior, he had been determined to claim Miss Armstrong's legacy of a country house and fifty thousand pounds. But in the gardens the previous day, although disguise was his abhorrence, he had decided to secretly cease trying to win the tournament. Miss Bennet's need to do so trumped all his own aspirations.

For appearance and curiosity's sake, he had continued to seek his series of puzzles and their solutions. Therefore, he knew the prize was 'in a clock'. If Elizabeth and Mr Hadley were hurrying towards the same location, it most likely meant they were in a head-to-head race for the ultimate reward.

No longer able to keep the competitors under observation from above, Darcy quietly descended to the bottom of the staircase. Holding a forefinger against his lips, he silently warned Alfred to not reveal his presence as he slipped behind the parlour door. Barely daring to breathe, he peeked out.

Elizabeth and Mr Hadley stopped at the same instant in front of the vestibule's walnut pendulum clock. The timepiece's trunk had beautifully rendered carvings of birds, and there were side viewing windows on the square hood that enclosed the clock's mechanisms and delicate face. Darcy assumed the deed to Oakwood Manor and the key to the money box—if, indeed, they were in that clock—would be hidden within a secret compartment in the base's footed plinth.

Use that clever mind of yours, Elizabeth. There should be a disguised spring mechanism somewhere—an unseen lever or button —that will release a concealed door, drawer, or panel.

Although restless, Darcy remained stock-still, not wanting to draw attention to himself. Conflicted, he wanted Elizabeth to win for her and her family's sake. Yet a selfish part of him wanted her to lose. Then he would provide for her and, if necessary, all the Bennets.

She, however, would gradually have to become intimately acquainted with all his strengths and weaknesses and learn to love him despite the flaws in his character. He was well aware that she would not marry for financial security alone, nor would he want her to do so.

The tournament was ending, and there were few opportunities for private, uninterrupted conversations. He was running out of time to win the lady's heart.

Darcy recalled his first offer, the horrid one made at Hunsford. He had asked whether she expected him to rejoice in the inferiority of her connexions or to congratulate himself on gaining relations whose condition in life was so decidedly beneath his own. At such audacity and arrogance, he nearly groaned aloud in mortification and shame.

Then there was his fear that if Elizabeth won the tournament and he made her another offer, she might suspect he was doing so only because of how utterly her situation had changed. Worse, if he admitted he had forfeited the competition for her sake, she might accept him out of a sense of gratitude.

He was the architect of every conundrum he faced.

Meanwhile at the clock, Mr Hadley had tried to open the hood. Then he joggled the lower door in which the weights and pendulum were housed. Both doors were locked, and a key was required to gain access.

All the while, a variety of polite remarks and civilities passed between the two contestants.

"Oh, I beg your pardon, sir."

"After you, Miss Bennet."

"That was clever of you, Mr Hadley. I am sorry it was to no avail."

"Good heavens, madam, I did not mean to touch you there!"

The young man, evidently thinking it best to distance himself from her, then stood on the left side of the clock and poked at the carved birds while the lady did the same on the right. They reminded Darcy of two lions facing one another with raised forepaws.

Crouching low, Elizabeth examined a wide, carved moulding on the base's footed plinth. *Clever creature.* Darcy had suspected there might be a secret drawer concealed within that decorative strip of mahogany. Such would demonstrate not only the cabinetmaker's ingenious skill, but it would be a perfect hiding place for papers and a key.

Mr Hadley also stooped and pressed a forefinger along the moulding on his side.

A loud, sharp, metallic sound made the four people in the

vestibule startle. But only two or three of them had witnessed the moment the secret button, a bird's eye, had been pressed by Elizabeth. The clang was followed by an elaborate six-note melodic chime pattern that resounded throughout the entryway and public rooms. Then, while Mr Hadley stood scratching his head, a secret drawer flew open and struck his shinbone.

Coming from behind the door, Darcy kept an eye on the young man lest he cease moaning and hopping about on one foot long enough to claim the drawer's contents. *No, Hadley is an honourable gentleman.*

With measured tread, Elizabeth rounded the clock, her eyes wide and singularly focused on the open drawer and the legal document within. Darcy doubted she had even noticed him.

The words 'This Indenture' were writ large upon the top of the page, and red wax seals authenticating the deed had been affixed along its bottom. A key with an attached ribbon rested upon the paper. Falling to her knees before the drawer, Elizabeth reverently reached for her prize with trembling fingers. Holding the deed and key to her breast then, she wept what Darcy assumed were happy tears. Behind her, he surreptitiously brushed his own eyes.

"Alfred," called Mr Hadley, "kindly fetch Mr Monroe."

"No need." The smiling attorney stood in the library's doorway. "I was summoned by the clock's unique chime."

"Miss Bennet has been the most skilful competitor, sir," cried Mr Hadley. "She has won the tournament!"

"Indeed, she has." Still smiling, Mr Monroe helped the winner to her feet and bussed her hand. "Congratulations, my dear."

Turning to the others gathered round—which by then included the entire household—the attorney declared Miss

Bennet the victor and called for a round of applause. As the clapping diminished, he beckoned the butler. "Mr Atwater, a bottle or two of wine, if you please, to celebrate our winner's sweet success. Now, young lady, if you will excuse me, I have an express to send to your father."

Elizabeth's eyes were bright, sparkling, and Darcy suspected she was overpowered by wonder of a most gratifying and delightful sort. Rooted to the spot, she beamed and cried and clutched to her heart the deed and the key. Surrounded then by well-wishers, she expressed herself with becoming gratitude for the kindnesses she had been shown by everyone from the butler and housekeeper on down to the stable-boy.

Having waited to come forwards, Darcy simply bowed to her when what he really wanted to do was hold her as closely as he had while carrying her from the garret. "Congratulations. Your worries have been obviated and your diligence well rewarded."

"Thank you. Yes, matters have taken a most favourable turn." Her happiness overflowed, and laughter escaped. "I suppose, at length, after this ebullition of shock and delight have subsided, something like composure may succeed it. For now, I am dazed and hardly know what to do or feel or say or even think. How I wish my family was here with me!"

How I wish to become part of your family!

At once, there seemed to exist an unexpected and unwelcome reserve between them; and, like Elizabeth, Darcy hardly knew what to say. In looking about, he noticed Mr Hadley awaiting his turn to congratulate the winner. The manner in which the young man was bouncing from foot to foot indicated his shin had not been badly injured.

Excusing himself and stepping aside, Darcy joined Miss Rigby and Mrs Vincent, who stood chatting just inside the parlour. While making the occasional comment, he could not help but listen to the conversation taking place beyond the doorway.

"Truly, I am not one who takes defeat with bad grace. I am utterly delighted for you." Mr Hadley sported a wide, genuine smile. "On our first day here, I told you I had no expectation of winning a contest of mental acuity. Indeed, I was completely perplexed by this clock's secret. At any rate, what would I do with a country house that I could not put up for purchase? No, that is not a case of sour grapes. Even had I won this place and the fifty thousand pounds, I most likely would still want to be hard at work in London at the Inns of Court, learning to be a barrister. Eventually, East-meadow Park, the estate in Eton Wick, will be mine some-day. My brother is considerably older, and he never married."

"Well, sir, you must come and visit me, although I have no notion of how or when I shall take up residence here at Oakwood. There is much to be decided...or decided for me, as I have not quite reached the age of majority, though my birthday is nigh."

"How happy I shall be to see you as mistress of these venerable walls! But I should very much like to visit you, wherever you may be. Perhaps I shall have to call on you and Darcy at Pemberley one day."

"Good heavens! Why would I be at Pemberley?"

"Come now, Miss Bennet. You must know Darcy is violently in love with you. It is plain to see."

Plain to see? Darcy *was* violently, ardently, passionately in love with her. Still, he winced at having made his feelings so easily perceived by another. For such a private gentleman, those sorts of displays, clear demonstrations of intense emotion, were unprecedented. Even Elizabeth herself had not been aware, in Hertfordshire or in Kent, of his admiration and love. Only Miss Bingley, at Netherfield, had suspected his interest in the young woman.

But if I thought for a moment that such a public display was what Elizabeth desired, I would run to the top of that staircase and shout of my love for everyone to hear. Yes. That is as likely to happen as to see a hog fly!

Having accepted a glass from Christopher's tray, Darcy took a sip and tried not to pull a face at the wine's sweetness. He suspected barrels of the *vin de pays* had been imported—that is to say smuggled—from France's northeastern region. Then sugar had been added and the champagne allowed to further ferment before being poured into superior English glass bottles. Nevertheless, he heartily joined the others and raised his glass in a toast to Miss Elizabeth Bennet and drank to the health of the new mistress of Oakwood Manor.

Half tempted to propose to her on the spot, admit what he had done, and let her accept him in appreciation for it, Darcy knew neither of them would be happy in a marriage where one's love was unreciprocated. *Besides all that, Elizabeth has enough to occupy her time and energy for the nonce.*

Just then, Mr Hadley came up to him. "Well, Darcy, as soon as Mr Bolton and Jimmy have my Cleveland bays and curricle ready to go, I shall take my leave of Miss Bennet, give my thanks to Mr Monroe and Miss Rigby, and be on my way to Eastmeadow Park, four miles distant as the crow flies. After spending the night there, I shall continue on to London in the morning. I must say this has been the most diverting se'nnight I can remember. Although I came here with no expectation of winning a contest of mental acuity, I am rather proud of myself for having made it as far as I did. Remember when I…"

Soon the two gentlemen were sharing a bit of a laugh about the epergne puzzle.

"It has been a genuine pleasure," said Mr Hadley, "to make your acquaintance, sir. Perhaps somewhere, sometime, our paths may cross again, eh? I am sure that you and a certain young lady will find your way to one another." For an instant, it seemed the amiable fellow was going to give Darcy a nudge or a wink, but he simply grinned at him.

"It has, indeed, been a pleasure, Hadley." Darcy passed one of his calling cards to the younger man. "I hope you will call sometime while I am in residence at my town house. If for no other reason, you should come and see your old friend Biscuit. And if you ever find yourself in Derbyshire, Pemberley's doors will be open to you, always."

The two shook hands, and Darcy was sorry to see Mr Hadley go.

I, too, should leave, but... Blast! A brilliant idea formed. *Why did I not consider such beforehand?*

After ascertaining from Alfred that Mr Monroe was in the library, Darcy went there and conveniently encountered not only the attorney but also Elizabeth and the chaperon.

Immediately upon bowing, he blurted, "Has the express already been dispatched to Mr Bennet?" At their surprised expressions, Darcy added, "To save her father the trip, I could take Miss Bennet to Longbourn. 'Tis almost on my way."

"On your way? Are you for Derbyshire, then?" asked Mr Monroe, eyebrows shooting upwards.

"No." Too late, Darcy realised his folly. "I shall first go to my town house."

The attorney exchanged a knowing look with the ladies. "Then what a strange route you would take from Oakwood to London, sir. Rather than simply travelling due east from here, you first would go north into Hertfordshire, would you?"

"I said almost, not directly." It had been a daft idea, and Darcy was paying the price for it.

Miss Rigby, too, appeared entertained. "And would you have Miss Bennet travel alone with you, an unrelated gentleman?"

"Of course not. I would ask someone to accompany us. Perhaps a mature woman with experience in being responsible for the decorous behaviour of a young, wealthy, unmarried lady."

"Well," said Miss Rigby. "You are fortunate that I happen to know where you might find both a meritorious chaperon and such a young lady."

"I thank you for the offer of transportation, Mr Darcy," said Elizabeth. "However, my father has been staying in London with my relations on Gracechurch Street, near Cheapside. And Mr Monroe and Miss Rigby will be escorting me there on the morrow. Papa and I shall remain with the Gardiners awhile. There are legal matters to settle, you see."

She looked apologetic and, Darcy liked to think, disappointed. "I see," he said. "Well then, Mr Monroe and Miss Rigby, may I impose upon your hospitality for another night? I should like to leave at the same time as your party. We could travel in tandem. Safety in numbers and all that."

"Perhaps, Mr Darcy," said the chaperon, "you should ask Miss Bennet whether you may remain here. This is, after all, her house."

21

BOMBOONS

The celebratory air in Oakwood Manor's library was immediately damped when Alfred announced the arrival of Mr Sumner and Mr Wright, respectively the magistrate and parish constable.

After polite greetings and necessary introductions, Mr Monroe said, "Mr Darcy, you are welcome to stay. In fact, you should."

"Now then," said Mr Sumner, "if the ladies will excuse us, we shall report on the findings at Mr Fordham's home."

"I shall stay as well," said Elizabeth.

Before she obligingly left the room, Miss Rigby gave both her charge and Mr Monroe encouraging smiles and the magistrate, constable, and Mr Darcy a negligible curtsey.

With everyone seated, Mr Sumner glanced at Elizabeth, huffed, and looked to the attorney as though to say 'do something about her'.

"If you expect Mr Monroe to send me away, sir, you will be disappointed. I am staying and shall brook no opposition." *That sounded like something Lady Catherine de Bourgh might say.*

With new respect for Mr Darcy's formidable aunt, Elizabeth sat a little taller, raised her chin, and met each of the men's eyes. *They will not forcibly remove me. Will they?*

Mr Monroe winked at her. "Proceed with your report, Sumner. As I told you, Miss Bennet is the new mistress of Oakwood Manor. Ergo, any of the missing heirlooms found at the Fordhams' residence rightfully belong to her now."

Heaving a dissatisfied sigh, the magistrate gestured to Mr Wright, whereupon the constable opened a notebook and reported that a pearl necklace with matching earrings, brooch, and bracelet had been found in Mrs Fordham's bedchamber.

"Mr Monroe, I believe you mentioned something about genuine pearls being exchanged for imitation ones," said Mr Sumner.

Elizabeth cleared her throat to gain the magistrate's attention. "The genuine parure belongs to Miss Sophia Kensett in Maidenhead. Please ensure it is returned to her."

Mr Wright jotted down her instruction. "Mr Monroe, you also said opium was slipped into a guest's wine. We found this"—he showed them a vial—"during our search." The constable then read from his notes. "Also, Mrs Fordham wore a ruby ring that her husband asserted was a bequest from Miss Phoebe Armstrong. Is that correct?" He seemed unsure whether he should look to the attorney or Elizabeth.

"That is a barefaced lie," said Mr Monroe. "Mr Fordham was bequeathed a book. I did not understand Miss Armstrong's intention at the time, but now I do. Her dictation to me was: 'To Mr and Mrs Peter Fordham, I leave a dictionary. Hopefully, they will consult it to find the proper words they need to apologise for what they have done.'"

"I do not understand." Elizabeth's mind raced, searching for an explanation. "If Miss Armstrong knew, or suspected, they were stealing from her, why would she have included Mr Fordham in the tournament?"

"Good question." Tapping his fingers on the table, Mr Monroe slowly nodded. "The old dear may have been too embarrassed to tell me what Fordham was doing. I suspect she rather slyly wanted him to be caught and trusted he somehow would trip up during the tournament." The attorney then placed upon the table the inventory newly completed by Mr Atwater and Mrs Vincent. "Mr Wright, may I compare this against your notes?"

From the music room, where Miss Rigby must have taken refuge, came the strains of 'Greensleeves', and while the others compared inventories, Elizabeth took that opportunity to have a good look about the library—the decoration, the books, the globes, the art. *My own book-room!*

Her eyes then rested upon Mr Darcy, and she longed to also call him her own. In character, in intelligence, deportment, looks, and attire, in every way, he was superior to any man she had known. His close friend Mr Bingley looked to him for advice; and, as far as she knew, neither of them engaged in debauchery of any sort. He was a dutiful nephew; and from his letter, Elizabeth knew he was a good brother. The balance of approbation was tipping heavily in his favour.

Mr Monroe, after some minutes of study—accompanied by tut-tuts, humphs, and other expressions of disdain—held up a handful of receipts from the constable's notebook. "These are acknowledgments from London merchants who purchased antiques from the Fordhams. Many of the items match heirlooms on Miss Armstrong's original inventory but are missing from our current one."

Mr Sumner turned to Elizabeth. "Unless you have an objection, I shall consider those receipts and inventories as evidence presented by you, the victim, and sufficient to support a trial by jury. You, of course, are expected to pay expenses incurred by Mr Wright. When this goes to trial, you also must pay the prosecution." The look he gave her seemed to say, 'And that is what you get, young lady, for sticking your nose in men's business'.

If that, indeed, was what he was thinking, he was not half wrong. *I am at sea. All this is out of my depth, over my head.* Despising herself for it, Elizabeth looked to Mr Monroe, then to Mr Darcy, for guidance.

The latter gentleman at once responded. "I also was a victim of Mr Fordham's wrongdoing. Although I suffered no lasting effect, the opium dosage could have killed me. He cannot be charged for that, of course. However, I shall bear the cost to take the Fordhams to trial for their thievery."

"I do not want them hanged." Elizabeth was emphatic. "I do not even want them pilloried."

"What do you want, Miss Bennet?" asked Mr Monroe.

"I want them far away from our shores. I want the Fordhams transported for what they did to that dear old lady."

❦

"MISS BENNET," SAID MR DARCY AS THEY LEFT THE LIBRARY together, "I cannot begin to imagine the differing throes of emotion you have contended with during the events of last evening and today. You told me you are stronger than you appear. But are you truly well? Is there anything I may do for you?"

Hardly knowing whether to laugh or cry, Elizabeth said, "Could you possibly snap your fingers and make my entire family suddenly appear? How I long for my parents and sisters!" Tears gathered for an onslaught, but she fought back. Collecting herself as well as she could, she smiled and thanked him for offering to pay the expense of legal proceedings against the Fordhams. "I was at a loss in there. But I expect, someday very soon, I shall be able to repay you."

"That will not be necessary."

With thoughts that could rest on nothing, she chose to be bold. "There is one thing I would ask of you."

"Anything." He raised her bare hand to his lips. "Ask anything of me."

She closed her eyes. *Will you do that again, please?* "Will you accompany me while I take the air? Otherwise, I honestly shall not know what to do with myself. Until I am reunited with my father, and we meet with Mr Pemberton in London, there is little I can do in the way of planning for my future. So, for now, I shall do something requiring physical rather than mental effort."

"It will be my pleasure to accompany you, madam. Shall we say in…ten minutes? And will you invite Miss Rigby?"

As she set her foot upon the second stair, Elizabeth rather flippantly replied, "I would rather not."

Fifteen minutes later, sporting a pale-green spencer over her sprigged muslin and wearing bonnet, gloves, and her half-boots, she strolled arm in arm with Mr Darcy. "How unusual," she said. "Neither my chaperon nor a gardener within sight."

"Nevertheless"—he lowered his voice and twitched his head across the lawn towards the stable—"once again, we are being watched."

Jimmy was espied lurking about and observing them while playing with a stick. "Surely, sir, a stable-boy has not been tasked with watching us."

Mr Darcy beckoned, and Jimmy came running. "What

mischief have you been getting into today, young man?" He ruffled the boy's hair.

Jimmy shrugged. "Nothing, sir. There's not much work to do since the only two carriages left are yours and Mr Monroe's. I've been playing quoits with this rope ring and broken broom handle, but it's not much fun by myself." The boy sounded terribly downcast, but his eyes lit up as he turned to Elizabeth. "Do you have any of those comforts with you, miss?"

"Comforts? Well, as you see, I do have Mr Darcy here with me. And, indeed, his presence is a great comfort." She squeezed the gentleman's arm and smiled at the boy.

"Aw, miss, not *him*! I meant those sugary-sweet comforts you had."

Elizabeth caught Mr Darcy mouthing, "Com*fits*."

"Alas, all I have today are"—from the concealed pocket of her gown, she presented four wrapped sweets—"orange bomboons."

"Hurrah!" The boy danced in place. "But will bomboons give me the toothache?"

She bit her lip, subduing a smile. "Most likely."

Jimmy shrugged. "May I have one in any case? Please."

"You may take two. The others are for Mr Darcy and me."

"Good heavens!" cried the gentleman with an exaggerated shudder. "I recently read a report saying baboons were very big and hairy and horrible to look at. And now I discover they may cause the toothache. I shall pass, thank you. Jimmy may have mine."

Delighted, Elizabeth smiled while the boy grinned. Mr Darcy was being frivolous, and she expected it was as much for her benefit as Jimmy's. *Be still, my heart! He has a sense of humour and is good with children.*

Speaking then round a mouthful of chewy bomboon,

Jimmy asked whether they wanted to play quoits with him. "I know I'm not supposed to bother you folks, but you looked like you weren't having much fun either, just walking about doing nothing." He put a finger in his mouth and unstuck a piece of bomboon from a tooth. "Miss Bennet, is it true you own Oakwood?"

Elizabeth said it was not yet official, but, yes, she had won the tournament.

"So, Mr Darcy," said Jimmy, frowning at him, "are you wooing Miss Bennet now?"

Her face grew hot. "Quoits! What a wonderful idea. I saw metal rings and a hob amongst other equipment in the games room cupboard. Shall I fetch them?" She began to move away, only to be stopped by the gentleman's hand upon her arm.

"I *am* trying to woo you, Miss Bennet," he whispered, "but not because you are an heiress. My affections and wishes have been unchanged since April."

Her eyes grew wider. Was he going to make an offer of marriage in front of Jimmy?

Heedless of grass stains, Mr Darcy then went down on one knee in front of the stable-boy, looked into his eager, young eyes, and...spoke too softly for her to hear what he was saying to him. *Botheration!*

Regardless of whatever was being said between the two—and Elizabeth suspected it had to do with either wooing or quoits—she replaced her image of giddy Kitty and laughing Lydia playing a game on the lawn. In her mind's eye, she pictured her own children, the next generation of Darcys, playing quoits with their father.

That gentleman stood, and Jimmy nodded solemnly at him. Then the sad-faced boy waved to Elizabeth and walked towards the stable, head bowed, feet dragging.

"Goodness! Whatever did you say to him?"

"That," said Mr Darcy, shaking his head, "was one of the most distressing communications I ever have had to impart to someone."

Not knowing what to expect, Elizabeth clasped her hands in front of her. All concern and anticipation, she prepared for the worst. "Will you tell me of it?"

He offered his arm, and they walked towards a small, walled garden. "If you insist. But prepare yourself for something very dreadful." The nudge Mr Darcy gave her prompted a remembrance of her own words at Rosings.

Then he was all seriousness again. "I had to inform your ardent admirer he could not marry you. The age difference, you see. Now, though, I have distressing news to impart to you."

"Humph," Elizabeth said. "I no longer know whether to believe your solemnity. Remember, sir, I already remarked on your commendable theatrical talents. But go on, then. Tell me this distressing news of yours."

"I am sad to report that the loss of Jimmy's matrimonial aspirations, due to the age difference, was borne with stoic resignation. He was, however, utterly heartbroken to realise his source of comforts would depart on the morrow."

Mr Darcy stopped at the garden wall and gazed into Elizabeth's eyes. "On the other hand..." He kissed her gloved fingers, and his voice was a husky whisper. "A mere seven or eight years is not a great age difference between husband and wife. Is it, Miss Bennet?"

Is this the moment? Is he going to make me a—

A giggle erupted from somewhere very close, followed by, "Oh, Mr Monroe!"

22

LONG & SHORT ANSWERS

'*One wedding, the proverb says, begets another.*' That quote —from John Gay's 'Wife of Bath'—was Darcy's first thought upon waking on Thursday morning from a pleasant dream in which Elizabeth Bennet was his bride.

The previous afternoon, he and she had come upon Miss Rigby and Mr Monroe on a gravel path just beyond the garden wall. Standing face-to-face, holding one another's hands, the chaperon and the attorney had been engaged in an earnest and, perhaps, amorous conversation. Had their closeness not been sufficient cause for suspicion, the faces of both would have told it all. Upon being discovered, they had moved away from one another as though burnt.

The older couple's situation had been awkward enough, but Darcy suspected his and Elizabeth's was worse still. For a long moment, not a syllable had been uttered by any of them, and he had been about to turn away and go when Mr Monroe cleared his throat.

"Miss Rigby and I have an understanding."

"Indeed, we do," said the smiling chaperon. "We are

engaged to be married. Neither of us thought such a future was, as they say, on the cards. But here we are. And at our age!"

Upon their happy announcement, heartfelt congratulations had been expressed and graciously accepted. That had been the moment Darcy had first thought of Gay's quote.

Thus, after the sun made its first appearance of the day, he leapt from bed with a smile upon his face. Such uncustomary alacrity was ascribed to Elizabeth's agreement to meet him early that morning. Hoping to have a private conversation with her before joining the others for breakfast, Darcy did not bother to ring for either Alfred or Christopher. Using tepid water from a pitcher, he soaped a cloth and performed his morning ablutions with uncustomary haste.

Only a few servants were about at that hour to witness either the quick tap of his walking stick upon the marble floor or his hastily tied cravat as he crossed the vestibule and opened the front door.

BIRDS CHIRPED AS HE STRODE ACROSS THE DEW-COVERED lawn, and morning's soft light had already grown stronger and warmer. As promised, Elizabeth awaited him at the archway leading to the walled garden. To Darcy she was like daybreak, instilling in him the hope of a new beginning and better things to come.

People, men and women alike, always wanted so much from him—his time, his advice, his wealth, his very soul. He had become wary, jaded, and reticent. But with her by his side as Mrs Darcy, he could be himself and once again enjoy life to the fullest as he had done before the deaths of his beloved parents.

When he first had proposed in Kent, Darcy had thought his affection for Elizabeth was sublime, but each moment spent in her company had him falling more violently in love. He would broach such thoughts aloud if he thought she would welcome them, for his mind overflowed with inspiration.

As they softly greeted one another, her dainty hand wound round his proffered arm, and he noticed her fingers were bare. "Where are your gloves?"

"In my rush, I left without them. Perhaps I should return and—"

"Do not do so on my account."

They set off then, with no particular destination in mind. "Even now," she said, "I scarcely can believe this entire place will be mine. I am enraptured by Oakwood's beautiful gardens." Her free hand trailed along lavender tops as she walked and talked.

It seemed to Darcy that Elizabeth enjoyed physical contact with the world around her, and he longed for her touch. "My father often said that if a person had a garden and a library, they had everything they needed."

"That is Cicero, is it not? Papa often repeats that quote... except he purposely omits the garden part. I understand from Miss Bingley that you are always buying books and that Pemberley has a delightful library."

"Most of the credit belongs to my ancestors." Hopefulness lent fervency to his voice, and he came to a standstill. "But if you could see it, I believe it would be your favourite part of the house. Pray tell, who is your favourite author?"

"It is impossible to choose just one. I do greatly admire Mary Astell, though. Like my own father, hers gave her a good education. But it was a cleric uncle, noticing her quick, natural parts and thirst for knowledge, who became her teacher. Her delight in learning made her wish education was readily available to all women. One of her published treatises was on"—she looked at him with a sparkle in her eyes and a smile upon her lips—"the improvement of their minds. There was opposition, of course, but the authoress defended her position with wit and intelligence."

Darcy stood grinning down at her. "I am not surprised she is a favourite of yours, nor am I opposed to ladies being educated."

"There is much to admire in her writings." She recited then in a higher voice than her own, "'If God had not intended women should use their reason, he would not have given them any.' You cannot argue with that, sir. Nor can you dispute the fact that if a woman can neither love nor honour, she does ill in promising to obey."

Egad. Tick, tick, tick… Darcy counted as eleven seconds elapsed. "Obey *is* part of the marriage solemnisation. And I would expect a…degree, at least, of obedience from the woman who would be my wife. However, I do not wish for one who always agrees with everything I say."

"A degree." Fists on hips, she regarded him with both challenge and that characteristic twinkle in her eye. "Alas, an education and a *degree* are exactly what a woman cannot obtain. Instead, we must become obedient wives."

She is toying with me. Darcy grinned at her.

"Speaking of wives," she continued, "'He who does not make friendship the chief inducement to his choice of a wife —and prefer it before any other consideration—does not deserve a good wife and, therefore, should not complain if he goes without one.'"

"That, my dear friend, I enthusiastically agree with, support, and applaud."

She gently ran the tips of her fingers across the tops of

delicate flowers in the nearby bed, and Darcy read a sign naming them as melancholy gentleman or Hattie's pincushion.

"What think you of tulips, sir?"

If there had been tulips in the garden, they were long gone by June. *What a mysterious mind she has.* "I...suppose I... like them." There were *two lips* Darcy very much wanted to plant his upon, and he watched them with fascination and desire as she spoke.

"Mary Astell asked of womankind: 'How can you be content to be in the world like tulips in a garden, to make a fine show, and be good for nothing?'" Elizabeth looked him in the eye. "Think on it, sir. To be free to sway in the breeze and be admired in one's natural environment, only to be cut down and brought inside, placed in a pretty vase to wither, die, and be discarded."

Darcy's heart landed in his boots. "You paint a dismal portrait of being a wife."

"Based on my parents' marriage, I cannot paint a very pleasant picture of it."

Overcome with disquiet, Darcy tried to swallow, but his mouth was a desert and his future a bleak landscape without Elizabeth Bennet in it. He barely managed to choke out, "Do you... Do you intend to never marry?"

Sliding her hand from his arm, she looked to the horizon. "Because of my family's situation, I formerly had little choice. The only privilege I had was to accept or reject an offer. Now I could be an independent woman. Truth is, though, I long to marry and raise a family with a man I trust, respect, and love and who reciprocates those feelings. I desire a marriage with a balance between romance and reason, somewhere between Jane's idealised view of it and Charlotte's more sensible perspective. Having witnessed Mr and Mrs Collins's harmoniousness, I wish I had not been so harsh when my friend told me of her engagement."

Glancing about at the thriving flowers, she spoke almost to herself. "It is a garden's nature to be forgiving. I pray those I have wronged may be as understanding and merciful."

"You know you have *my* forgiveness, although there was nothing to absolve."

She thanked him for being so understanding.

He poked his walking stick at the loamy soil of the flower bed. "I imagine understanding and forgiveness must be as essential to a married couple as rainwater to a parched garden. As a landowner and gentleman farmer, planting is not entirely new to me—though I rarely get my hands dirty."

A barn owl, with its distinctive heart-shaped white face, flew low and silently over a nearby hedgerow. They both watched it disappear amongst distant trees.

From behind, Christopher came running into the walled garden. "Miss Bennet! Oh, and Mr Darcy. Mr Monroe and Miss Rigby are at breakfast and asked me to find you both. If you wish for a repast before departing, you had best come in now."

Blast! Another lost opportunity. Darcy had been prepared to make Elizabeth another offer of marriage, but he would not see her go hungry during the carriage ride to London. So, to the breakfast room they were to go.

⚜

AN HOUR LATER, RACHEL RUSHED OUT TO BID FAREWELL TO Elizabeth. In fact, it seemed the entire household had done so.

Darcy knew the new mistress of Oakwood Manor

deserved everyone's respect and esteem as well as all the good wishes bestowed upon her at parting.

Arm in arm with her former chaperon and the maid, Elizabeth approached Darcy's carriage, which was drawn up before the front door. He had insisted they travel in his well-sprung one rather than the attorney's inferior conveyance, though Darcy had not referred to it as such.

Miss Rigby was heard saying, "Rachel here spent hours washing the stain from your pale-yellow gown, mending the rent in it, and embroidering a spray of primrose flowers over the flaw, concealing it completely."

"It is carefully tucked up inside your trunk now, miss." Rachel seemed close to tears over their leave-taking.

Elizabeth thanked the maid for that kindness as well as for her exemplary service over the past se'nnight. Then, rather impulsively—and imprudently in Darcy's opinion—she gave Rachel a quick hug. Restraint had been used when she had taken leave of the butler, housekeeper, and the footman brothers; however it had appeared to Darcy as though she wanted to embrace them one and all. Such behaviour spoke of her warm-hearted nature.

After the attorney had given final instructions to the housekeeper and butler, he and Darcy joined the two ladies in the carriage. Then, with Mr Monroe's own equipage following behind, they began the journey to London with a quick stop at the coach house so Elizabeth could bid farewell to Mr Bolton and Jimmy and leave with them a packet of comfits.

Underway, and with all the nonchalance of perfect amity, the four engaged in unreserved conversation. But it was not as chaperon, attorney, and beneficiaries. Rather, it was as four friends. Soon the gentlemen had dispensed with 'mister' before one another's names, and the ladies were on first-name terms.

Good-humoured pleasantry continued and progressed to frivolity when Elizabeth, in the highest of spirits, suggested a few rounds of Short Answers.

"In this game," said she, "you must reply to each question with a single syllable word. If your answer is too long, a penalty will be exacted for each additional syllable." Mirthful eyes turned his way as she added, "I fear Mr Darcy will be at a disadvantage in this exercise. I have it on good authority he studies too much for words of four syllables."

Had Miss Rigby not been looking his way, Darcy might have winked.

"To make things more difficult, neither enquiries nor replies may be repeated. Any player who does so incurs a forfeit. And because the aim is to become better acquainted with one another, your responses should be truthful. Grace, please begin by asking something of Mr Monroe."

"At this moment, sir, what do you most like about your life?"

Darcy glanced at the attorney beside him on the rear-facing seat. *Tread carefully, Monroe. There is only one possible answer to that question.*

Mr Monroe replied, "You." In turn, he asked the smiling woman across from him which colour she would recommend for a carriage's leather interior.

"Blue."

"Then blue the interior of our new carriage will be."

Elizabeth's turn was next. "In your opinion, Mr Darcy, what is the silliest word in the English language?"

Is that what you truly wish to know about me, Elizabeth? Very well. He was about to reply 'bomboon' but remembered the one syllable rule. *Flibbertigibbet...taradiddle...widdershins.*

Three times he had opened and shut his mouth. *By Jove, I do favour polysyllabic words.* "Erf," he blurted.

"Erf?" Elizabeth smiled at him. "Surely erf is not a word. Is it?"

"From the Dutch word for 'inheritance', erf means a plot of land."

"But I clearly said in the *English* language, sir."

"Yes, I know. But Cape Town was retaken by our troops in the year six," said Darcy. "I predict one day the cape will become part of our empire. Ergo, erf will become part of our language."

He incurred a forfeit.

Before he could ask her any sort of question, the game was abandoned in favour of further discussion of Elizabeth's inheritance and property.

Darcy wondered and worried what she would think, feel, or do if ever she found out he had let her win the tournament. *Elizabeth must never discover the truth.*

But deceit was despicable. What a conundrum he had created for himself.

23

UNTIL MR DARCY

Their journey from Oakwood to London had not ended as auspiciously as it had begun.

After the 'erf' dispute, Mr Darcy had become an altered creature, reverting to the reticent gentleman with whom Elizabeth first had been acquainted in Hertfordshire. Rather than aloofness, though, he seemed to have been deep in thought or mired in melancholy, and she had no notion what had caused such a change in him.

When Mr Darcy's carriage stopped in front of the Gardiners' house on Gracechurch Street, the attorney hopped out to assist the ladies to alight. Mr Darcy was the last to step down; but when he did, he smiled and offered his arm to Elizabeth, who said, "I am pleased to see the return of your smile, sir."

"I would by no means suspend any pleasure of yours, madam," he responded with a wider grin.

Her joy could have no moderation when three of her favourite people, who must have been watching for their arrival, appeared at the door. "Aunt Gardiner! Uncle

Gardiner! Papa!" She flew into the latter's embrace, and it took several minutes to give any degree of tranquillity to her heart.

"Congratulations, my dear Lizzy," said her father. "I knew you could not be so intelligent for nothing." He looked over her shoulder. "But I see you have brought guests with you. Including Mr Darcy, of all people."

Once Elizabeth had made the necessary introductions and received congratulations from her relations, everyone was invited into the pretty parlour that Mrs Gardiner had made so warm and welcoming.

Mr Darcy spoke of how pleased he was to meet her relations, and he even complimented her aunt on the lovely room. Unprepared for such civility, Elizabeth barely suppressed a smirk at his acceptance of the very people against whom his pride had revolted during his offer to her at Hunsford.

As he entered into conversation with Mr Gardiner, she could not but be exulted to claim some relations for whom there was no need to blush. She listened most attentively to all that passed between them and gloried in her dear uncle's every expression and sentence. Each utterance marked his intelligence, his sense, taste, and manners, all superior to his sister's. For a man who lived by trade and within view of his own warehouses, he was more of a gentleman than many who could claim that title by birth.

Meanwhile, Mr Bennet and Mr Monroe were immersed in a tête-à-tête that she assumed involved her inheritance. Although Elizabeth longed to be included in their conversation, she trusted she would hear the gist of it from her father once the guests were gone.

Settled upon the sofa with her aunt and Miss Rigby, she again glowed with pride. Mrs Gardiner was an amiable, intelligent, and elegant woman as well as a consummate hostess. Already, after ensuring everyone was comfortably situated, she had ordered tea, sweetmeats, and fruit.

When Miss Rigby momentarily turned away to answer a question posed by Mr Monroe, Mrs Gardiner took that opportunity to lean in and say, "So, Lizzy, the infamous Mr Darcy also was a beneficiary, was he? Goodness, I trust his presence at Oakwood was not too unpleasant for you." She gazed at the gentleman with evident admiration. "I must say he seems perfectly amiable to me. And terribly handsome."

"Indeed, he is," whispered Elizabeth, also leaning in. "I was utterly mistaken about him, Aunt, and for that reason I have been duly ashamed of myself for some time now. Truth be told, Mr Darcy had more reason to be disgusted by my behaviour in Hertfordshire and Kent than I by his. Fortunately, we have forgiven one another, and I fully expect—" Mrs Gardiner elbowed her, and Elizabeth's eyes grew wide upon noticing the subject of their discourse standing before them.

"I beg your pardon, Miss Bennet," said he. "Mrs Gardiner, I have just learnt from your husband that you once resided in Lambton. I also understand you have seen Pemberley and that you knew my father by character."

The difference between Mr Darcy's animated air at that moment and what it had been for the last hour in the carriage was striking, and Elizabeth was heartened by the further improvement in his spirits.

He and her aunt spoke at length about Derbyshire and about mutual acquaintances until a blur of blond hair, blue clothing, chubby little arms and legs, and bare feet flew into the room.

"Mama, Mama!" Stopping short upon seeing what must

have seemed a roomful of strangers, the child buried his head in Mrs Gardiner's skirts and whimpered.

Setting aside her teacup and crouching down beside her cousin, Elizabeth stroked his fine flaxen hair. "Jonathan, where is your nurse? Never mind, angel. I shall take you to the nursery while your mama speaks with her guests. Or... you could stay and sit quietly with me. I do love cuddling you, you know." She nuzzled his neck and tickled his ribs. "Would you like me to read a story? Would that make you feel better? We could snuggle together over there in that cosy armchair and share a cake and some strawberries." Standing, she held out her hand for him to take.

As she and the burbling Jonathan walked away, Elizabeth heard her aunt remark to Miss Rigby and Mr Darcy, "Lizzy will be a wonderful mother some day."

Unable to help herself, she glanced over her shoulder and caught the gentleman staring after her with a fond smile upon his face. All of a sudden, the child's hand in hers was not that of a blond cousin but of a dark-haired, dark-eyed son or daughter. The warmth then emanating from within Elizabeth's heart set her face aflame. She despised blushing. And embarrassment because of it only served to increase its intensity.

Minutes later, with Jonathan curled contently upon her lap, she watched Mr Darcy approach her father. The two spoke quietly, had a quick word with Mr Gardiner, then excused themselves. As they left the room, Elizabeth craned her neck and saw them entering her uncle's study. Immediately offended that her father's consent was being sought before her own, she hugged her cousin and attempted to remain calm while her pulse pounded. *The audacity of the man!* But she grinned and had every expectation of being engaged to marry Mr Darcy by day's end.

Rather than abating, Elizabeth's anxiety increased a quarter of an hour later when the Gardiners' guests—*all three of them!*—politely took their leave and her father called her into the book-room.

Seated behind her uncle's desk, Mr Bennet succinctly explained exactly why Mr Darcy had requested a moment of his time. "I was taken aback when the arrogant gentleman admitted responsibility for not making Mr Wickham's proclivities known to us last autumn. And, while I appreciated the recommendation that my youngest daughter be removed—hopefully, in the nick of time—from a scoundrel's influence, I cannot comprehend why a mere acquaintance came to be involved at all in our family's private concerns. Perhaps you can explain it to me."

So, Mr Darcy's conference with her father had not been about her at all but about her silliest sister. While pleased that belated action was being taken, Elizabeth was disappointed her own concerns were being swept aside and that she would not be made an offer of marriage that day.

"Lydia's being in Brighton with the Forsters arose in a conversation Mr Darcy and I had at Oakwood. You should be grateful that he has shown us such benevolence."

"Yes, yes. And so, my dear, I shall be bound for the south coast in the morning. I realise you are eager to have matters settled regarding your fortune. However, we must consider the unthinkable consequences should Lydia not be rescued from both Mr Wickham's clutches and her own stupidity. I shall stay the night either with the Forsters or at an inn, then Lydia and I shall leave early Saturday morning and travel all day, stopping only as necessary to change horses or have a bite to eat. Our meeting with Pemberton & Monroe must be postponed until my return."

Mr Bennet's expression quickly shifted from unalloyed amusement to annoyance.

"By the bye, Lizzy, Mr Darcy subtly hinted at a romantic interest...in *you*. Ha! Let me congratulate you on a very impressive conquest. But rest assured that I wished him much good luck should marriage be his intention. He will need it, eh? Can you imagine it? Mr Darcy! The haughty gentleman who never looks at any woman but to discover whether there is an exalted title or princely fortune behind a pretty face and form. What makes it all so delightfully absurd is your pointed dislike of the man."

"I do not dislike Mr Darcy. He and I became friends at Oakwood, where he gained my respect and esteem. Admiration gradually swelled to deep affection. If he makes me an offer of marriage, I shall accept."

"You will *what*? Lizzy, you greatly disappoint me. *Think*, my dear! He was not clever enough to win Miss Armstrong's legacy himself, so he intends to have it by another means. Unless I can be convinced otherwise, I shall refuse my permission for that man to have you as his wife and your wealth as his own."

Remembering Mr Darcy's whispered words at Oakwood —*I am trying to woo you, Elizabeth, but not because you are an heiress*—she was resolved to soften her father's resentment. "I promise you, Papa, he is not at all like that. He is a gentleman of complete integrity."

"Do you not remember he said you were not handsome enough to tempt him? Have you forgotten about his disdain of your family, your relations, friends, and neighbours? Do you think his opinion would change so rapidly? How can you not share my suspicion? No, Lizzy. I am sorry to say so, but that proud Mr Darcy is more interested in your inheritance than in your person."

How earnestly then did Elizabeth wish her former opinions had been more reasonable, her expressions more moderate. "He has no improper pride, Papa. In fact, although he is reserved and fastidious, Mr Darcy can be perfectly amiable. Even Aunt Gardiner thinks so. And, yes, his opinion of me did change over time, as did mine of him."

"Mere infatuation on your part, my dear, and avarice on his. So let us not be hasty." Mr Bennet rose and kissed the top of her head. "Now I must send a note to Mr Monroe. We had arranged to meet on the morrow, so I shall inform him of the change in plans and fix a time on Monday morning. I wish to leave here as near to midday as possible."

Yes, let us not be hasty. If Mr Darcy proposes, Papa will change his mind and give his consent. He must! Coldness gripped Elizabeth's heart. Fingernails biting into her palms, she gave her father a long, pained look and came to a shocking realisation: she would give up Oakwood Manor and the fifty thousand pounds in a moment if it meant she could have Mr Darcy.

But the moment passed. She had her mother and four sisters to consider before her own hopes and needs.

A tiny voice inside her head asked why she felt responsible for remedying her father's dereliction of duty. And did she not have to make provision for her own future children? As those considerations occurred to her in quick succession, Elizabeth climbed the stairs to her guest room in a state of uncertainty and anxiety.

Nevertheless, she thought she could—even then, under the first sharp twinges of disappointment and trepidation—command herself well enough to join the others at dinner only two hours after she had learnt of her father's dissent. No one would have supposed from her appearance that Elizabeth was fretting over obstacles that might divide her from the object of her love.

At least until I turn twenty-one. But, once she reached her majority in less than a month, she might be compelled to sow dissension with the one man she had loved with her whole heart for her entire life. Never had she even dared to rebel against her father's authority. Estrangement had been unthinkable.

Until Mr Darcy.

ON FRIDAY, AT FIRST LIGHT, MR BENNET HAD SET OFF TO fetch Lydia.

No doubt she will leave Brighton kicking and screaming. Elizabeth did not envy her father for having to listen to a querulous sixteen-year-old for endless hours on the road. But she, too, could be petulant. *It will serve Papa right for being so hard-hearted where Mr Darcy is concerned.*

That thought seemed to have summoned the gentleman, for at that very moment, at the stroke of eleven o'clock, Mr Darcy presented himself at the Gardiners' front door, and Elizabeth was summoned. Fleeing to a mirror, she was relieved her eyes were neither red nor puffy, although there would have been nothing to be done about it had they shown evidence of her having cried herself to sleep the previous night.

He had come, he told Mrs Gardiner and her, in the hope they might join Georgiana and him for a ride round the park. "It is a fine day, and I have a barouche with its hood folded down."

Mrs Gardiner's eyes grew wide as she looked from Elizabeth to their caller. "We shall be delighted, sir." She summoned her maid to fetch their bonnets, gloves, and reticules.

It was with astonishment that Elizabeth beheld a luxurious black barouche at the kerb. The carriage was drawn by two sleek black horses, driven by a liveried coachman, and it sported a noble crest upon its door. Pointing at it, she cast Mr Darcy a puzzled look. "Have you gained a title overnight, sir?"

He smiled and shook his head, then spoke to the young lady perched upon the rear-facing cream leather seat. "Georgiana, may I present to you Mrs Gardiner and her niece, Miss Elizabeth Bennet. Ladies, I am pleased and proud to introduce my beloved sister, Miss Georgiana Darcy. I fetched her this morning from her residence on North Audley Street. And, from our relations' town house on Park Lane, I fetched this equipage"—he paused to catch Elizabeth's eye—"which belongs to my uncle, the Earl of Matlock, Colonel Fitzwilliam's father."

As she and her aunt were being assisted into the carriage, Elizabeth remembered hearing from Mr Wickham that Miss Darcy was exceedingly proud. She knew, however, from Mr Darcy's letter and by the sweet girl's shy demeanour that the lieutenant's information had been false.

There was sense, good humour, and a becoming blush upon Miss Darcy's face as Elizabeth smiled at her and began a conversation. "I have heard much good of you from the Bingleys, Lady Catherine, Colonel Fitzwilliam, and, of course"—she glanced at Mr Darcy—"a proud brother who absolutely dotes on you."

"You are too kind, Miss Bennet." The young lady's manners were perfectly unassuming and gentle, and she spoke softly and in monosyllables. *She would do exceedingly well in the game of Short Answers.*

Less than an hour later, in a nobleman's fancy barouche, with Elizabeth and her aunt seated opposite Mr Darcy and his sister, the four of them smoothly glided round the gravelled carriageway known as 'the Ring'. While the Darcys received many greetings and warm salutations, their two guests attracted unwanted attention—mostly consisting of jealous looks from the fine ladies of the *ton*, young and old alike. Elizabeth realised that being with her and Mrs Gardiner in Hyde Park demonstrated Mr Darcy was not ashamed to be seen with two females not of the *beau monde*.

At one point he said, "How fortunate I am this morning to be in the company of the three most handsome ladies in the entire park."

It had been hyperbole as far as Elizabeth was concerned, but his outrageous comment had brought a bit of a smile to her face. *I am the fortunate one. Mr Darcy is a much sought-after marriage prospect. Of course, he would be fortunate to gain me as his wife...should he ever propose again.*

For several hours, she almost had been able to forget the troubling conundrum looming overhead. And, in Miss Georgiana Darcy, she had gained a new friend. *And, I hope, a future fifth sister.*

❧ 24 ❧

THE MULBERRY BUSH

Earlier that same morning, Darcy had urged his sister to join him in asking the Gardiners and their relations to dine at his town house before the three Bennets had to leave for Longbourn.

In the park, Georgiana had readily complied, although it was done with a diffidence that proved she was not at all in the habit of extending invitations. Mrs Gardiner had accepted with alacrity, but she looked to her niece for an indication of mutual agreement.

"I thank you, yes," said Elizabeth. "However, I can speak for neither my father nor my sister. Which day did you have in mind?"

Darcy wondered at her perfunctory response. "The next two evenings, I fear, will be inconvenient. I imagine Mr Bennet and Miss Lydia would rather rest upon their return tomorrow. On Sundays my servants work reduced hours so they may rest. I assume you and your father will meet with Pemberton & Monroe at some point on Monday. Would that evening be favourable?"

"I regret we must decline, sir. Papa said we are to leave at midday."

Elizabeth then spent the remainder of the drive mainly speaking to his sister about her cousins, the Gardiner children—two girls of six and eight years old and two younger boys. Darcy fretted over her otherwise languid indifference.

Upon their arrival at the house on Gracechurch Street, he approached Mrs Gardiner. "Would it be possible for Georgiana and me to be shown round the delightful garden I espied here earlier? Our se'nnight at Oakwood gave me a new appreciation for horticulture, and I caught but a mere glimpse of the profusion of beauty you have created out there." He gave his sister a pointed look.

"Brother, as much as I should be pleased to join you, I had hoped to meet the four children Mrs Gardiner and Miss Bennet spoke so lovingly of during our jaunt round the park."

Darcy wished his sister's little speech had not sounded quite so rehearsed and that she had not looked so desperate when she appealed to the proud mother of said children, but he was pleased she had made the effort.

Then out to the garden, arm in arm, Darcy and Elizabeth went. When he had set out that morning, he had had every intention of asking for the young lady's hand in marriage. But at that moment his priority was getting to the bottom of whatever was preying upon her mind, for something surely was. Had she learnt of his relinquishment of the tournament? Impossible. No one knew of it. Had it to do with the Fordham affair?

He longed to tell her he would, with his life and until the end of his days, safeguard her from all perils and unpleasantness. "I was wondering whether Mr Monroe apprised you of Mr and Mrs Fordham's situation."

When she indicated the attorney had not, Darcy said, "Until the next assize court, the accused—under Mr Sumner's supervision—are to be held separately in the parish gaol. There, the Fordhams will be forced to perform useful manual labour and exist on fare far inferior to that which they had become accustomed at Miss Armstrong's expense. I expect they eventually will be transported."

Without as much as a glance in his direction, she told him she was grateful for the information, but she spoke between shuddering breaths.

"What is it? Tell me, and I shall do my utmost to alleviate your suffering."

Shaking her head, she peered at the ground beneath her feet.

"Elizabeth, look at me."

She would not, so Darcy stepped round and searched her countenance for signs of distress. As he expected, tears glistened in her dark eyes. *Decorum be damned!* He enfolded her in his arms. "Whatever it is, you may depend on me. I love you, Elizabeth, now and for evermore. Allow me to share in your troubles. Together we shall banish them."

She sniffled but remained silent.

"Come now, madam. I shall not go away until you confide in me. I shall cling to you as tenaciously as sugary-sweet comforts stick to Jimmy's teeth."

She giggled into his chest, then looked up at him. "Very well. You deserve to know the truth, but prepare yourself for something dreadful. I mean it this time."

"My constitution is in fine fettle, and I have strong shoulders. Let me bear this dreadful burden of yours." He touched his forehead to hers.

"My father said you hinted at having formed an interest… in me."

"Interest is putting it mildly. As recently avowed, I love you." Darcy held his breath, waiting, hoping, to hear those three little words repeated back to him.

"It may be rather presumptuous, Mr Darcy, but I have been expecting...or, rather, hoping to receive another—"

"Marry me."

Her eyes grew bigger. "That is what I have been hoping, and dreading, to hear you say."

"Dreading?" Darcy thought he might be sick, and he took a step backwards. *Please, not another rejection!*

Catching both his hands, she gave his arms a shake and would not let go. "I would *love* to marry you, but—"

"But?" It was the worst, the best, the most confusing few moments of his life. *But? What condition will be attached to her acceptance?* Why was the confounding woman hoping for his proposal but also dreading it? Never had he felt so distressed, then happy, then vulnerable.

"My father may not grant his consent for us to marry."

He nearly laughed in relief. "What do you mean? Of *course* he will. I am the sort of gentleman no father would dare refuse, unless he be a duke or a monarch...or mad. In fact, your father wished me good luck, if matrimony was my intent." He frowned. "Oh. He did not mean it in *that* way, did he?" He gave her fingers a little squeeze. "No matter. Eventually we shall win him over. Trust me."

"I do trust you, sir. And only with trust can there be respect. And only with respect can there be love. I trust, respect, and love you, Mr Darcy."

He was certain his smile grew wider than either Mr Bingley's or Mr Hadley's. "Then trust me to make your father change his mind."

"'Tis doubtful he will."

"Why is he so opposed to me?"

"Oh, let me count the reasons. And I apologise in advance if what I am about to say causes you pain."

"Fine fettle, strong shoulders. Remember?"

"You looked ready to swoon a minute ago."

Darcy drew himself up. "Gentlemen do *not* swoon."

"To be on the safe side, perhaps we should sit." She let go of one of his hands, turned him round, and led him to a bench beneath a massive but lopsided mulberry.

Once seated, she enumerated her father's objections while counting them upon her fingers. "One, he believes I still dislike you. I tried to convince him otherwise. Two, he thinks that because you could not win the tournament yourself, you intend to seize Miss Armstrong's legacy by marrying me. He will not give his consent because once I marry, my husband will have control of my property. Three, he remembers that I was not handsome enough to tempt you."

Darcy tried to interrupt, but she held up a hand, forestalling him.

"Four, he resents your disdain for our family, relations, and neighbours. Five, which perhaps is the same as two, he thinks you are only interested in my inheritance, not my person." Her eyebrows danced up, then down. "I think that was all."

"All? Egad. Did you not tell him of my first proposal?"

She whispered a faint, "No."

"Then I shall." *And I shall confess that I withdrew from the tournament for your sake. And I shall negotiate a settlement he cannot refuse.* "All will be well, my love." Darcy took her hand in his. "You are the best part of my life, and I truly believe we were meant to be together, you and I. Call it fate or call it destiny."

She nudged his shoulder. "Or give it a more fascinating

name. Call it love." She tilted her head back and gazed up at the tree. "We could elope, of course, but that will not be necessary. There are but twenty-two days until my twenty-first birthday. Then we shall not require my father's consent to wed. I fear that choice, though, might lead to my being estranged from him."

She released his hand and plucked a flower, a developing berry, from the tree. "Do you know Ovid's story of the black mulberry's curse?"

"I know it inspired Shakespeare's *Romeo and Juliet*, but remind me of it."

"Two star-crossed lovers, Pyramus and Thisbe, decide to elope because their parents will not allow them to wed due to a rivalry between their families. The lovers plan to meet late at night under a mulberry tree. Thisbe arrives first but flees from a lioness, its mouth dripping red from a recent kill. When Pyramus arrives at the scene, he finds the blood-stained cloak Thisbe dropped in her haste. Heartbroken, believing his lover is dead, he takes his own life. The tragedy continues when Thisbe returns and finds Pyramus expired beneath the mulberry tree. Grief-stricken, she takes his sword and plunges it into her breast."

Darcy picked one of the flowers and twirled it between his fingers. "Now I remember. Before her death, Thisbe put a curse on the mulberry. And these trees bear the reminders—fruit of a dark, mournful hue—of the blood Pyramus and Thisbe shed." He tucked the flower into her bonnet's ribbon. "Enough morbidness, my dear. Mulberry jam is delicious. We are engaged to marry, and marry we shall."

"I am here only until Monday at midday." She heaved a sad sigh. "Then you and I shall part."

Darcy was silent awhile, studying her profile. "Bingley is

soon coming back to town and is planning a return to Netherfield. I shall ask to accompany him."

"I hope he goes to Hertfordshire without delay. I want to be near you."

"You know, if you keep pouting like that, I shall have to kiss you."

Brazenly, she pushed out her lower lip like a sulky child. Darcy carried through with his threat, but it was a mere peck on those pouty lips. Then she latched onto his cravat and pulled him in for a lingering kiss that he wished would never end. Eventually, the gentlemanly part of him broke the sweet contact. "Name the date, madam, but please make it soon."

Her eyes brightened. "The eleventh of July! My birthday."

Darcy drew back. "You were born on the *eleventh*? You wish us to wed on the *eleventh*?"

"Yes. It would be the loveliest gift imaginable." Then her shoulders slumped. "But even if you are able to convince my father to grant his permission, there is insufficient time to arrange for the banns to be read on three consecutive Sundays in both parishes."

"Once we have his consent, I shall purchase a common licence." *If all goes well, we might marry before the eleventh.*

⚜

WHAT HAD HE BEEN THINKING? HE SHOULD HAVE STAYED AT home. He knew being at Gracechurch Street so late on Saturday afternoon—exactly when Mr Bennet and his youngest, most rebellious daughter were expected—was ill-advised; but he had been eager to see Elizabeth again and to have his future settled. Then Mr and Mrs Gardiner had invited him to remain for dinner.

A commotion in the vestibule heralded the travellers'

return and sent the two Gardiners and their niece from the parlour. When they returned, it was with an evidently grumpy Miss Lydia leading the way and an annoyed, weary-looking Mr Bennet in tow.

Darcy stood and squared his shoulders.

"Lord, Aunt, I am so tired! Going to Brighton with Harriet and Colonel Forster was such a merry lark, but today's journey was long and tedious and—" Miss Lydia stopped short. "Lawks! Why is *he* here? Lizzy," she said over her shoulder, "why is Mr Darcy, the man responsible for all Mr Wickham's hardships, standing here in my uncle's parlour? Papa, make him go away."

"Hush, Lydia," hissed her aunt. "Remember your manners."

"Mr Darcy is our and Lizzy's guest," said Mr Gardiner, "and, Niece, I should like you to remember you, also, are a guest in this house."

"Perhaps," said Darcy, stepping up to Mrs Gardiner, "it would be best, after all, to take my leave." He was loath to do so.

His hostess kindly insisted he remain.

During the meal, Elizabeth's father had been neither hostile to Darcy nor willing to initiate conversation with him. When directly spoken to, Mr Bennet answered with cold civility, preferring, it seemed, to simply listen to every word and—with an unwelcoming look in his eyes—watch every move made by his favourite daughter's suitor.

Although Darcy had been made aware of Mr Bennet's many objections, he admitted that such a rebuff from a far less affluent country gentleman than himself was an affront. But the man was Elizabeth's father and, therefore, worthy of clemency.

Perhaps Mr Bennet is torn between gratitude towards me for warning him about Wickham and mistrust of me where his daughter is concerned. I shall set his mind at ease; Elizabeth's happiness depends upon my doing so.

So it was that after a dinner that included two courses of huffs and lamentations from the youngest member of the Bennet family as well as stiffness of manner and resentful silence from the eldest, Darcy requested a conference with the gentleman who—despite opposition—very soon would be his father-in-law.

The two of them sat facing one another across Mr Gardiner's rosewood desk. Libation had been offered, but Darcy had declined, preferring to keep a clear head. He was a private person and not accustomed to divulging intimate information; but for Elizabeth, he would bare his very soul.

Frankly and eloquently, he avowed his abiding admiration and love for the man's second daughter; and he spoke of the offer he had made at Hunsford and of being rejected and why.

"Also, for Miss Elizabeth's sake, I secretly withdrew from the tournament so that she might have an added advantage. Please keep that to yourself. She knows nought of it."

Mr Bennet merely raised his eyebrows. "If you are trying to convince me you are worthy of my Lizzy, you are going about it all wrong. My clever girl would have won the legacy without your forfeit." He paused for a sip of port. "You come in here, boasting of your sacrifice and your chivalry. But, no matter what you say of such generosity, you merely want control of my daughter's wealth."

Fairly vibrating with indignation, Darcy put his final card upon the table. "As my wife, her fifty thousand pounds and Oakwood Manor itself will be safeguarded within the marriage settlement, in Elizabeth Darcy's name. And, if you truly have her best interests at heart and want to maintain the special bond the two of you have shared, you will let Miss Elizabeth marry as she wishes. Withholding your consent will not achieve your goal, Mr Bennet. Once she reaches her majority, she and I shall wed, with or without your blessing. If you refuse to sanction our union, you risk estrangement from your favourite daughter."

You do not deserve her precious love. Darcy sketched an obeisance and strode from the room, leaving the man to ponder a course of action.

Mr Bennet was right about one thing: chances are that clever Elizabeth would have won without my interference.

25

HER FATHER'S HOUSE

After attending Sunday services at St Peter upon Cornhill, the seven of them—Mr and Mrs Gardiner and their two daughters and Mr Bennet with a pair of his— walked along Gracechurch Street. While Mattie and Evie behaved like genteel young ladies, Lydia did nothing but loudly complain; and her father did nothing to correct her recalcitrant, childish conduct. The little boys, who had been left at home with their nurse, probably would have been better behaved than their sixteen-year-old cousin.

Duly ashamed of her father and sister, Elizabeth was thankful Mr Darcy was not there to further witness her family's delinquencies. Her thoughts could not long stray from images and thoughts of him. *Someday he and I shall be announced as Mr and Mrs Fitzwilliam Darcy.* She smiled to herself.

Her love had not been a sudden thing, although physical attraction had begun the instant Elizabeth had set eyes on him at the Meryton assembly. Her dislike of his general behaviour had sharpened into particular resentment that same night because of a disrespectful remark. The cutting barb had wounded her pride and festered into prejudice; but the passage of time had healed the injury.

In Kent, seeds of love had been planted by a heartfelt declaration and by words upon pages written to her. A change of sentiment had taken root with each subsequent reading of that letter. At Oakwood, in sunshine and in rain, gratitude and esteem had sprouted. Affection had grown stronger, and her love bloomed and flourished with each passing day.

Was it not strange how quickly a person's profound feelings could change? Feelings she once thought immutable. Dislike to romantic love. Paternal love to disappointment. The special bond she had shared with her father withered on the vine. Perhaps that was natural.

The sermon given during that morning's service had included a psalm encouraging women to forget their people and their fathers' houses to live harmoniously in their husbands' homes. To Elizabeth's disgust, there also had been a quote from the Bible advising fathers to utterly refuse to give their daughters in marriage to men they did not approve of.

The eleventh of July could not come quickly enough.

Lost in thought, Elizabeth had outpaced the others and was startled when Lydia caught up with her.

"Lizzy, what business do you have with an attorney? I just overheard Papa mention to my aunt and uncle something about a meeting you and he have in the morning."

"I promise that Mama and all my sisters will learn of it when we are reunited on the morrow."

"You might as well tell me now, for I shall have far better things to do tomorrow. Kitty will be wild to hear all about Brighton...as will Maria Lucas and Harriet and Pen

Harrington and Aunt Philips. La! I shall be ever so busy and in demand!" She sighed dramatically. "But how shall I survive without the officers? Particularly my very own lieutenant! But I suppose you do not care to hear about my Wicky lest you become wretchedly unhappy and expire from jealousy."

"My infatuation was but a momentary lapse—a slight, thin sort of inclination." Elizabeth smiled secretly, remembering a conversation at Netherfield with Mr Darcy on the effects of poetry. "I pray, Lydia, that your little fever of admiration will be as fleeting."

Lydia stopped and stamped her foot. "No. It is not like that for Wicky and me. My misery upon parting from him is of the highest extreme, and I imagine his is far worse. Why do you smile so?"

"It was just something you said, my dear giddy sister. Honestly, I can sympathise with you."

"And well you should. I do not know what is to become of me without my Wicky. What am I to do?"

"What are you to do? You could begin by ceasing all reference to him in that manner. That sobriquet sounds positively vulgar. *True* ladies are supposed to feign a swoon upon hearing anything remotely crude."

"Oh, what do *you* know, Lizzy? Besides, *I* am too lively to ever faint. I had such fun in Brighton! What were you doing while I was gone? Oh Lord, I forgot. Your letter mentioned a house party somewhere. Did you meet any handsome men? Did you flirt? If you asked me those questions, I would answer yes to both. How I long to return to the seaside! We all should go there for the summer. What a delicious scheme, do you not think so? I dare say it would cost hardly anything at all. And we must have new gowns for all the balls we shall attend." Glancing behind at the

CONUNDRUMS & COINCIDENCES

others, she whispered, "But Papa is being terribly disagreeable."

He is, indeed, sister dear.

In such affliction as rendered her careless to surrounding objects, Lydia nearly tripped over a broken cobble. "Lord, Lizzy, why did you not warn me? I could have fallen and broken my head. Alas, it is my heart that breaks." She placed a hand upon her bosom. "Where *is* my heart? I cannot feel it. I cannot feel my heart!" Turning, she ran back, calling, "Aunt Gardiner! Aunt Gardiner, I cannot feel my heart!"

Elizabeth wanted to be diverted by her youngest sister's folly, but her own best source of happiness was somewhere in the west end, on some fashionable street or square, in a town house she had yet to set eyes upon. Already, she missed him. What was she to do? If she acted in a manner that would constitute her own happiness, she would be compelled to forget her family and her father's house.

Lydia's was not the only heart breaking.

⁂

SEVERAL HOURS LATER, WHILE EACH OCCUPANT OF THE HOUSE on Gracechurch Street was quietly engaged in some activity or other—reading, sewing, playing on the floor with the children, or pulling apart a hideous bonnet bought in Brighton on a whim—the maid announced Mr Darcy. If groans were heard from the youngest Bennet daughter, the others, including the caller himself, pretended not to have noticed.

After greeting everyone in the room, Mr Darcy crouched down beside Elizabeth and the children. Surreptitiously, her little finger touched his, and he smiled.

"Who are these handsome young ladies and gentlemen?" He winked at the four gaping children. "I have heard much about you from your cousin here, so let me see whether I can guess your names." He proceeded to assign each of them an endearment Elizabeth had used during the ride round the park.

While the children laughed and cried out in protest, Elizabeth was well pleased he had been paying attention when she had effusively praised her beloved relations. He had remembered each affectionate term but had incorrectly assigned them, perhaps purposely. "Your coming here today is a pleasant surprise, sir."

He whispered that he had not been able to stay away, then he glanced over his shoulder. "Your father watches us like a hawk and wishes I *had* stayed away. Is there a chance we might arrange a modicum of privacy?" As he helped Elizabeth gain her feet, he added, "I wish to consult with you on an important matter."

"And I have something to discuss with you." After a moment's thought, Elizabeth said, "Aunt, would you like Mr Darcy and me to take the children out to the garden for air and exercise?" Mrs Gardiner readily agreed.

Immediately Mr Bennet stood and stretched. "I could use some of London's infamous air myself. Children, would you like your uncle Bennet to chase you round the garden? Mr Darcy may chase your cousin, but he will not catch my Lizzy."

Whatever his design might have been, Elizabeth's father soon was hoist by his own petard. Once in the garden, the children chased after him, pestered him to run after them, clung to his arms and legs, and generally gave him neither peace nor any opportunity to eavesdrop on his daughter and her gentleman caller.

Meanwhile, Mr Darcy stood beneath the mulberry with Elizabeth, kept an eye on her father, and spoke in a whisper.

"As your future husband, I would like to accompany you to tomorrow's meeting at Pemberton & Monroe. Although I have my own attorney, it is my intention to hire Monroe to draw up the marriage settlement since he is familiar with your inheritance. I shall not touch even a halfpenny of your wealth, Elizabeth. It is yours and yours alone, I promise. However, do you have any objection, should we be so blessed, to leaving Oakwood Manor to a second son or a daughter? I realise your mother and sisters will need a place to live should, God forbid, your father die before all your sisters are happily wed. But it will be quite a while before *our* children leave home to set up their own nurseries."

"Agreed. And thank you. However, there will be no meeting tomorrow. I have decided to wait until I have reached my majority to claim my inheritance. In that manner, it may pass to me without the encumbrance of a guardian. Uncle Gardiner has written a letter stating my intention, and he will have it delivered to Mr Monroe first thing in the morning."

Elizabeth held her head high but fidgeted with her bracelet. "Also, because ownership of Oakwood Manor must remain within my family for a specified number of generations, once we marry and have children, I wish for any sons to somehow bear the name Bennet."

It took a moment for Mr Darcy to reply; and when he did, it was with a frown. "I trust you mean any sons would be given two Christian names rather than a double family name."

"If you prefer it, our children still would be Darcys, not Bennet Darcys. However, I should like to have a peace offering to present to my father when I inform him of the cancelled appointment and my intentions." *And so, as it should, begins the compromising between Mr Darcy and me.*

Elizabeth watched as her four cousins dragged their uncle to the ground and piled atop him. "I fear this is the last time we shall be together until you come to Hertfordshire with Mr Bingley. I expect Papa, Lydia, and I shall be returning to Longbourn earlier than expected tomorrow."

"Then I shall take my leave now, unless you wish me to stay. I would be happy to hold your hand while you speak to your father."

"I would like that, thank you. But your presence at this juncture will only antagonise him further and— Edwin! Stop jumping on your uncle this instant!" With amused frustration, she shook her head. "I should rescue my father. So, my dear Fitzwilliam, I bid you farewell." At her endearment, Mr Darcy looked upon her with such tender solicitude that she longed for a more intimate leave-taking.

Bending over her hand, he raised it towards his lips. The lightest but exquisite touch upon her skin was interrupted by the exaggerated clearing of her father's throat.

ON MONDAY MORNING, THE WILDLY JOLTING AND SWAYING Bennet carriage rumbled over road surfaces damaged by subsidence, its wheels hitting hard at each hole and rut.

Within, its occupants suffered their own sinking depression. Both daughters were in Mr Bennet's black book. One was out of favour because he could approve of neither her suitor nor her intention to postpone claiming her inheritance; the other was in disgrace for having been found in Brighton seated upon Mr Wickham's lap.

Sullen, Lydia had discovered that Mr Darcy was responsible not only for her favourite's loss of the living in the village of Kympton but that he also had been to blame for her own expeditious removal from a lovely seaside sojourn. Angry and resentful about being abducted by her father, she was not best pleased with Elizabeth either for having brought Mr Darcy back into their lives.

From without came the creaking of leather, thudding of hoofs, jingling of metal rings on harnesses, shouts of the coachman, and the swish of his whip as he urged on the team.

Inside, no one spoke, not even Lydia, which was a blessing even though she probably thought she was punishing her father and sister by withholding her scintillating remarks.

Watching the passing scenery and eager for the awkward carriage ride to end, Elizabeth silently egged on the horses as enthusiastically as the driver; but the ride was rough and the going slow. Due to its clay soil and the heavy loads transported along it, the final section of road between London and Meryton was notoriously bad. The lane from the market town to Longbourn was worse. Blame for that could be laid to her father's charge. The task of keeping that portion in good repair was beyond him, so he had put very little effort or expense into it.

I imagine the road to Pemberley is in excellent condition due to Mr Darcy's diligence as a responsible landowner.

Elizabeth's happy spirits, which seldom had been depressed before, were so much affected that morning as to make it almost impossible for her to appear even tolerably cheerful as they finally pulled up in front of her home. *My father's house.*

From rows of lavender in full flower lining the gravel sweep, a herbal scent greeted her. Above, near the eaves, barn swallows swooped, feeding on insects. Chatting, her mother, Jane, Mary, and Kitty filed out of the front door, then greeted the travellers and welcomed them home.

Yes, home. But for how long shall I be welcome here? Elizabeth feared that when she left Longbourn as Mrs Darcy, she might be forbidden from returning. *Soon, for me, 'home' will mean wherever Mr Darcy is.*

"Lydia!" cried Mrs Bennet. "Why on earth are *you* here? Mr Bennet, what is the meaning of this? Why is she not in Brighton still? Oh, my nerves! My dear girl, are you unwell? Did the Forsters treat you poorly?"

"Mama, my heart is broken. Papa tore me away from all my friends and admirers, and I shall tell you about it once I have had something to eat, for I have not slept nor eaten anything worth mentioning since Friday night. When I awoke this morning, I was allowed only a roll and a cup of tea before we left town. Then at the coaching inn, we had only a crust of bread, a scrap of meat, and hard cheese. I am famished."

"Well, I have news of a happier sort, Lydia," said Mrs Bennet, patting her favourite daughter's arm. "Netherfield is being opened anew, which means Mr Bingley is coming back for our dear Jane."

Entwining her arm with her elder sister's, Elizabeth said she, too, had heard of Mr Bingley's plan. "I believe he will bring people with him again, Mr Darcy included. I am uncertain of Mr Bingley's purpose for coming back"—she nudged Jane's side as if to say otherwise—"but I am sure he will pay us a call as soon as may be."

❧ 26 ❦
FLUMMERY

"**B**rother?" Georgiana stood in the doorway of his study in the Brook Street town house.

He shot to his feet. "How are you, m' duck?" Darcy used the Midlands term of endearment only when the two of them were alone. The visit was unexpected, but he was always delighted to see her.

Georgiana resided with a companion, Mrs Annesley, who presided over the establishment Darcy had formed for his beloved sister on nearby North Audley Street. Music and dance masters went thither to further the young lady's education and assist her along the path to becoming a truly accomplished woman.

Rounding his desk, Darcy pulled her in for a hug. "Are you well? Is Mrs Annesley with you? Have you come to rescue me from this pile of paper, lest it bury me alive?" Having just waded through correspondence accumulated over a se'nnight, he shook cramped fingers, then indicated his sister should sit upon the sofa adjacent to his desk.

A year past, she might have flung herself upon it, toed off

dainty slippers, and tucked her feet up under her. Since the incident at Ramsgate, Georgiana sat demurely, shoulders back, hands folded upon her lap. "Yes, I am in perfect health, thank you. Yes, Mrs Annesley walked here with me, but she has gone to speak to Mrs Walker. No, I am sorry to say I had no intention of digging you out from beneath paper when I set out this morning."

"What is it then, Poppet? You seem slightly perturbed."

"Good heavens, Fitzwilliam. One minute I am a water-bird with a waddling gait, next I am a wee poppet again."

Whenever she smiles so sweetly like that, she reminds me of our late mother. And I wish Georgiana still was a waddling tot. "Is there a problem, dearest? Does your doll need rescuing from atop your bed curtains yet *again?*"

"As you well know, I threw Mag atop my canopy only the once, the summer when I was but six years of age and you were home at Pemberley from Cambridge. No, the problem is that Miss Bingley sent round a note, filled with her typical style of flummery, informing me of their party's arrival at Grosvenor Street. You and I have been invited to dine with them this evening at half past six."

"Tonight? Terribly short notice. Did she mention when they returned to town?"

"Yes. A whole hour ago. I wonder what took her so long."

That sounds like something Elizabeth might say. I wonder what she is doing at this moment. Does she miss me as much as I miss her? Has she been able to allay her father's concerns? Is she—

"Did you hear me, Brother?"

"Yes, of course." *What did I miss?*

"Very well, then." With the slightest hint of a grimace, Georgiana sighed. "I shall send round our acceptance at once."

Blast!

Darcy glanced at the mantel clock. Its hands both pointed at eleven. *Of course.*

⊗⅊⊗

AT PRECISELY QUARTER PAST SIX THAT MONDAY EVENING, Darcy and his sister arrived at the Hursts' modest town house. Although the sun would not set for at least another two hours, the place was aglow with sweet-scented beeswax candles. *Such waste, simply to make a show of one's wealth.*

A footman had barely received their hats and such when Miss Bingley, elegant and smiling, swept from the drawing room into the vestibule, a large, green silk shawl billowing behind her.

"Mr Darcy! Georgiana! How punctual you are. And how happy I am to see you both. It is so very courteous of you to be the first to welcome us home."

You invited us to do so, madam. And Georgiana is Miss Darcy to you. Darcy gave the woman a dignified bow, and the two ladies performed their curtseys with practised precision.

Linking arms with both Darcys, Miss Bingley said, "That lilac colour is nothing short of perfection on you, Georgiana. And Mr Darcy, Charles informed us that you recently attended a little house party in Buckinghamshire. You must tell us all about it. I insisted the smaller table be used so that your scintillating conversation may be heard by all."

Scintillating?

"In the meantime, do come through, dear friends. We await a couple more guests. A cousin dropped in earlier, so I had no choice but to invite him to dine as well. Then, of course, the number was off with one too many men. So I asked Miss Grantley to come. Both of them should be here directly, but separately."

Why does Mrs Hurst, who should be tonight's hostess, allow herself to be overshadowed by a younger sister? The manner of interaction between the two women brought to Darcy's mind Miss Catherine and Miss Lydia Bennet.

Upon entering the drawing room, as though her sister and brothers—the latter already on their feet—could not see well enough, Miss Bingley said, "Louisa, Hurst, Charles, our most important guests have arrived."

Darcy bowed respectfully to Mrs Hurst, the *de facto* mistress of the house, and greeted the men. Having ensured his sister, after shyly extending her own courteous regards, was comfortably situated, he then stood beside Bingley and enquired after his Scarborough sojourn.

Miss Bingley soon sidled up to them. "Mr Darcy, can you not talk some sense into my brother about this foolish scheme of his to return to that country house he leased in the wilds of Hertfordshire? Charles, having just arrived in town, we should stay here at least a se'nnight to be with our true friends."

Turning to Georgiana, she said, "If we *must* go to that wretched place, I hope, dear Georgiana, you will accompany us this time. If you are not so compassionate as to agree, my family and I shall be in danger of hating each other for the rest of our lives. There is so little to do in that dull neighbourhood, and being confined in such close quarters with one's sister and brothers for more than a se'nnight must end in horrid discord. Of course, you would know nothing of disharmony, for you are of such a sweet disposition, and you have the very *best* of brothers."

The woman's flummery was turning Darcy's stomach, which was unfortunate since dinner soon would be served. Speaking for his blushing sister who seemed at a loss for words, he said, "I thank you on *Miss Darcy's* behalf. She and I shall discuss the possibility, and you will have our answer tomorrow." Turning to his friend, he asked when Bingley intended to go to Netherfield.

"I had planned to leave by week's end, but now I have changed my mind."

"Oh, thank goodness!" cried Miss Bingley, pressing a palm to her heart.

Voice firm and lower pitched than was customary, Bingley said, "We shall leave on the morrow. I am keen to spend as much time as possible with our Hertfordshire friends."

Unseemly cries of outrage issued from his sisters.

Mrs Hurst turned to her husband. "The least you could do, Freddie, is support Caroline and me in our objection."

"It makes little difference to me where I spend my time," said he. "'Tis much of a muchness, really. Like your brother, when I am in the country, I never wish to leave it. When I am here in town, it is pretty much the same. Each place has its benefits, and I can be equally happy in either as long as there is food, drink, and a pack of cards to be had."

In Darcy's opinion, and to his disgust, Hurst's time was trifled away without benefit from books or anything else worth his while.

A footman announced another guest's arrival, and Miss Bingley went to fetch her.

With everyone in the room already acquainted with Miss Grantley, no introductions, only polite salutations, were necessary when the young lady entered. Darcy knew that due to their newly acquired wealth, the Grantley family was considered *nouveau riche* by members of the nobility and often referred to as upstarts.

Between Mrs Hurst and Miss Grantley, Georgiana sat primly and softly responded in monosyllables when directly spoken to by anyone. Taking a seat adjacent to her and watching from the corner of his eye, Darcy sympathised, knowing full well that small talk was as distasteful to his sister as it was to him.

Contrasting her demure demeanour with the brazenness of another young lady of sixteen years, he recalled Lydia Bennet's insolent words upon seeing him at the Gardiners'. *I cannot imagine Georgiana uttering anything even remotely close to 'Lawks! Why is he here? Make him go away'.* Rousing himself from those thoughts, Darcy consulted the mantel clock and tapped fingers upon his thigh. *Whoever this inconsiderate final guest might be, he is tardy by eleven inexcusable minutes.*

When a commotion in the vestibule heralded the man's arrival, Mrs Hurst gave a nod to her sister, upon which signal Miss Bingley again excused herself. She moved in such an ostentatious and provocative manner that Darcy suspected it was a ploy to capture his attention, as was Mrs Hurst's relinquishment of duties for the evening.

Upon her return to the drawing room, Miss Bingley was arm in arm with a gentleman who stopped short and cried out in surprised delight, "I say! Darcy!"

"Good heavens." Darcy shot to his feet and smiled so widely that everyone gaped at him. "What an unexpected but pleasant surprise, Hadley."

All the gapes turned to puzzlement.

Bingley approached and shook Hadley's hand. "How do you do, David? How on earth are you acquainted with Darcy?"

"He and I met at a house party in Buckinghamshire."

"When I first saw Hadley," said Darcy, "I thought he could be your twin. I even told him he reminded me of a very good friend of mine not only in appearance but in character, which, I said, was a compliment to him."

"By Jove, Darcy," said Hadley, "I remember that conversation, but I had no notion you were referring to good old Charlie here. Our mothers, you see, were sisters."

"Gentlemen," said Miss Bingley, tugging Hadley's arm, "perhaps we could continue this conversation in the dining room. Dinner was ready to be served a quarter of an hour ago."

"Am I late? Oh, I do beg your pardon, everyone. There was a bit of a to-do while passing through Soho. A herd of cattle was being driven towards Greek Street, perhaps destined for one of the butchers. Speaking of which, I am famished. Lead on, Caro."

Miss Bingley gave him a glaringly false smile. "First, *Davy*, you must come and meet Miss Grantley and my dearest friend Miss Georgiana Darcy."

After those introductions, everyone went through to the dining room.

Seated on Mrs Hurst's right and left respectively, Darcy and Hadley exchanged grins when the latter twitched his head towards the centre of the table, which was taken up by an elaborate ormolu epergne overflowing with seasonal blooms and fruits.

During the first course, sitting between Darcy and Miss Grantley, Miss Bingley leant to the left. "May I enquire, sir, about that house party you and David attended?"

Darcy spoke of Oakwood Manor's history and architecture, its gardens, a bit about the late Miss Armstrong, and he mentioned by name Miss Kensett and Mr Fordham. "Also among us was someone who can claim an acquaintance with you."

Miss Bingley preened. "And who might that be, sir?"

"It really was quite a coincidence to see her there because I was also in her delightful company two months ago while visiting Lady Catherine de Bourgh in Kent. Can you not guess, madam? The young lady with fine eyes has a cousin who happens to hold my aunt's living at Hunsford."

The clang of a Sheffield knife hitting Spode porcelain preceded Miss Bingley's outcry. "No! You cannot mean Miss Bennet!"

From between Hadley and Miss Darcy, Bingley startled and said, "What is this about Miss Bennet?" He looked round the table for an answer. "What have I missed? Of which one do you speak? The eldest? Is Miss Jane Bennet well? Is she not at Longbourn?"

"Oh, Charles," hissed Mrs Hurst, "do be quiet and let Mr Darcy answer."

The table went silent but only because the second course was about to be served.

Peering round the epergne, Hadley said, "Are you also acquainted with the charming and delightful Miss Bennet, Caroline?"

"Of *which* Miss Bennet do you speak?" Bingley stood, all the better to have his voice heard and to glare at his sister across the epergne. "There are five Miss Bennets."

"Miss *Elizabeth* Bennet," said Hadley. "The heiress."

Face drained of all colour, Miss Bingley flinched. "What do you mean 'heiress', David? We cannot be speaking of the same Elizabeth Bennet if the one you know is an heiress. The young woman with whom we are acquainted is an impertinent Hertfordshire country chit with a laughable dowry of one thousand pounds, a vulgar family, and relations in trade."

Georgiana spoke up. "I, too, have met Miss Elizabeth Bennet, and she is perfectly charming." She gave her brother a pointed look. "I pray she and I may become, at the very least, the best of friends before long."

It was the most Darcy had heard his sister utter in public since Ramsgate, and he was proud of her. He also was well pleased she and Elizabeth were fond of one another.

Not bothering to lower her voice, Miss Grantley turned to her left. "Caroline, what was the name of the poor young lady deeply in love with your brother? Was she not a Bennet?" Evidently not the brightest candle in the chandelier, she added, "Remember? You separated them by tricking her into believing your brother has an understand with Miss Da—"

"This ham is not to my liking." Miss Bingley's face had turned from ashen to red. Beckoning a footman, she demanded that the third course be served.

Ears hot, Darcy lowered his fork and looked round the table. No one but Hurst, not even Miss Bingley herself, had sampled a second course dish, nor, to his relief, had anyone accused him of conspiracy. *But...another course? She certainly is trying to impress someone. In all likelihood that someone is me.*

While Hurst made a grab for a meat pie, the epergne and untouched dishes were being removed, and new dishes—of pigeon pie, prawn, and crab, garden crops galore, and sauces for everything—began to appear on the table. Where the centrepiece had been, a mound of quivering, sugary-white jelly moulded into the shape of a temple was set down.

At opposite ends and corners of the table, Darcy and his sister mouthed a word at one another and exchanged grins.

The punctilious Miss Bingley, on the other hand, seemed to have lost not only her appetite for dinner but all interest in impressing the Darcys with her flummery.

27

KING MINUS

I n a near swoon—real or imagined—upon having learnt of her youngest daughter's rescue from Mr Wickham's clutches, Mrs Bennet was restored to her usual querulous self after inhaling spirit of hartshorn.

Elizabeth's despondency, however, received no palliative. Surrounded by her chattering sisters, she waited in painful suspense for whatever her father would say as he closed the sitting room door.

Standing then in front of the unlit fireplace, he cleared his throat, demanding everyone's attention. "So, daughters, according to your mother, Netherfield's housekeeper has received orders to prepare for the arrival of Mr Bingley by week's end."

Mrs Bennet smiled knowingly at Jane, who gave no indication of having noticed.

"Have any of you wondered," continued Mr Bennet, "why that man is returning to his country house at *this* particular time and, I hear, bringing Mr Darcy with him?"

Apparently thinking it all a game, Kitty said, "Perhaps they are coming to fish."

Taking up her book of extracts, Mary flipped through it. "It is possible that, like the prodigal son, he went away to lead an intemperate life but wishes to make a repentant return."

"Both Kitty and Mary are wrong," said Lydia, "although I do not know what Mary was talking about. And I care not a groat why gentlemen in blue coats are returning. I would much rather see the militia come back."

With a hint of pique colouring her tone, Jane said, "Can Mr Bingley not come to a house he has legally rented without raising such speculation? At this time of year, many families leave town for their country homes."

"How odd to have not heard an opinion from you, Elizabeth," said Mr Bennet.

"Papa," said Kitty, looking from her father to the sister she most resembled in appearance, "why do you address Lizzy so formally?"

"Well, Kitty," said he, "does 'Lizzy' sound like the proper way to address the mistress of a grand old manor or a lady in possession of a good fortune? And while we are at it, answer me this... Why would a wealthy woman be in want of a husband? Would she not be required to hand over Oakwood Manor and her fifty thousand pounds to her lord and master?"

"What nonsense you speak, Mr Bennet," said his wife. "Who is this wealthy woman?"

Wide-eyed, Jane clutched Elizabeth's hand. "Lizzy, is Oakwood Manor not the name of the place where you spent a se'nnight? Oh! Oh, my dear sister, did you—"

"Yes, Jane, my clever girl," said Mr Bennet. "You have hit

the nail on the head. As only you knew beforehand, Elizabeth went to Buckinghamshire for the sole purpose of participating in a tournament. And you now may congratulate her on winning the prize. Your sister soon will be mistress of the aforementioned country house and possess a staggering amount of wealth."

Struck dumb, his wife and four of his five daughters sat staring at him. Then, as one, they turned and gaped at Elizabeth.

Finally comprehending what she had heard, Mrs Bennet rose and danced round the room. "A country house and fifty thousand pounds! But is it really true? Oh, my sweetest Lizzy, how rich and how great you will be! What finery you will be able to buy for not only yourself but for all your sisters and me! Dear, dear Lizzy. A house in Buckinghamshire and a staggering amount of wealth!"

Silently rejoicing that such an effusion could not be heard by the entire neighbourhood, Elizabeth said, "There is more, Mama."

"More?" Mrs Bennet stopped dancing and stared stupidly at her.

With a defiant look at her father, Elizabeth said, "I am engaged to Mr Darcy."

"Oh, my dearest child!" her mother cried, taking Elizabeth's face between her hands. "Fifty thousand pounds and ten thousand a year! An estate in Derbyshire, a country house in Buckinghamshire, and a house in town! And a tall, handsome gentleman to boot! I hope he will overlook the fact that you do not like him."

That was enough to prove her mother's approbation need not be doubted. *As for Papa...*

From across the room, Mr Bennet said, "Must I remind you, Elizabeth, that you require my consent?"

"Of course they will have your consent," said his wife, waving her handkerchief at him. "Lizzy will marry Mr Darcy, and she will be richer than King Minus!"

Her husband scoffed. "Ah yes, good old King Minus... Everything he touched was taken away."

Elizabeth winced. *Why must he mock my mother so?* "Mama, the king's name was Midas, not minus. The myth of his golden touch warns about the tragedy of avarice and"— she turned to her father—"of what happens when *true happiness* is not recognised."

"We shall continue this conversation in my library. Now, Elizabeth." Mr Bennet opened the door and waited for her to follow him.

Once she was seated in his private domain, he paced. "So, child, tell me your theory. Why *are* the gentlemen returning to Netherfield at this particular time?" Shaking his head, he muttered, "From whence have all these worthless young scoundrels come? Bingley—the man who made love to Jane, then deserted her. Wickham—the seducer of almost thirty who preys upon girls half his age, working on their innocence and stupidity. Darcy—who looked down on all of us until you became a wealthy woman. Pah! From what woodwork have they all crawled?"

It had been a rhetorical question asked only to make a statement, but she refused to respond to her father's provocation.

Hands behind his back as he paced, Mr Bennet seemed deep in thought. "Perhaps I should set Lydia upon your lover. I am confident she could frighten him back to the Midlands from whence he came." He stopped in front of her. "Do not look so downcast, child. If Mr Darcy is too squeamish to bear connexions with a little absurdity, he is not worth a groat of regret."

"I truly do have much to regret, Papa. I regret my hasty judgment of those two men from the Midlands. I regret not being more moderate and private in my opinions of them. I regret my ill-treatment of Mr Darcy while we were in Kent."

"Oh yes, I heard all about that. Although he has a disposition tending towards self-congratulation, your admirer actually lowered himself enough to speak of his mortification at your hands. Well done, child. Well done. I wish I had been there that evening to have given him one of my own set-downs."

"I do not understand this bitterness and vitriol towards the gentleman I love."

"Love! Pshaw. What do you know of it?"

"I know I love him enough to surrender Oakwood Manor and fifty thousand pounds if it means I can marry him. Except my conscience will not allow me to do that because of the entail on Longbourn. But Mr Darcy will not fritter away my inheritance. He is a good man, and you will understand that when he presents the marriage settlement to you. He will not touch my wealth. His sole condition is that Oakwood Manor be preserved for a second son or daughter, and that is only after Mama and any of my sisters might have need of it. Papa, do you not realise that if—no, *when*—I marry him, my fortune will benefit my future children, *your* grandchildren?"

That seemed to give him pause.

From above the open window somewhere, probably under the eaves, the musical twittering of barn swallows seemed incongruous with the rancour inside the library. All the discord Elizabeth experienced with her father made each minute of harmony she had spent with Mr Darcy all the more precious.

What she needed to impart next would cause additional pain and acrimony, but it had to be said. "I realise you wish to retain control of my wealth for as long as you can. However, as I told you in town, only when I reach my majority shall I claim my inheritance. Mr Darcy and I shall marry on the eleventh of July. Soon afterwards, he and I shall meet with the attorneys at Pemberton & Monroe. I trust Mr Darcy to do whatever is best with my property. He is conscientious that way." Her vehemence made reserve impossible. "Unfortunately, I must question whether or not *you* would have been capable of managing my inheritance, considering how poorly you have provided for your wife and daughters."

As though she physically had wounded him, Mr Bennet winced and pressed a palm against his breastbone. Shaking his head, he muttered, "How could I have let this happen? What a state my imprudence has reduced me to."

Overcome, Elizabeth required several moments to keep her emotions under any sort of regulation. *How unpleasant must be his reflections!* "Papa," she said, barely able to hear herself speak above the wild pounding of her heart. "I hope to honour you and our ancestors by bestowing a second Christian name, 'Bennet', upon any sons I may bring into the world. Mr Darcy has agreed. So, please, give him and me not only your consent but your blessing."

Her father remained silent. *Listening, no doubt, to the reproaches of his conscience.*

Gaining her feet, she felt a bout of light-headedness while moving towards the door. She had taken only a roll and a cup of tea in town and had eaten nothing since. "Consider this, Papa. Unless you gain a son-in-law willing to take on your surname, this line of Bennets ends with you." Hand upon the latch, she spoke without turning to face him. "And do try to remember that King Midas failed to find pleasure in all he had wrought."

"Do you know what I think, Lizzy?" Jane pulled the boar-bristle brush through her sister's hair as they sat upon her bed. "I think Papa is jealous of your Mr Darcy."

"Perhaps." Elizabeth winced as Jane tugged at a tangle. "Such a kind and honourable gentleman is likely to arouse jealousy in lesser men, and my Mr Darcy is immensely enviable."

"You did not always think of him in such terms."

"True." Elizabeth gazed into the teardrop-shaped flame of the bedside candle and could not resist a tease. "In his friend's presence, do you suppose Mr Bingley ever feels inferior?"

The tug grew positively vicious. "Such errant nonsense! Mr Bingley may be fickle, but I cannot imagine him capable of discontentment or resentfulness. His amiable and cheerful disposition is *entirely* different from Mr Darcy's."

Elizabeth turned so quickly that the brush flew from her sister's hand and skidded across the floor. Laughing and apologising, she leapt from the bed and fetched it. "Seriously now, do you suppose jealousy is the only reason Papa continues to be so contrary?"

"My father has his faults, but I believe that initially he was trying to be protective of the person he loves most in the world. You. Now he is being obstinate. You get your stubbornness from him." Jane turned down the coverlet and climbed in. "You have my support and that of Mama and all my sisters. Well, *most* of them."

"I presume you mean Lydia. She had a matrimonial

project in mind when she went to Brighton—to be the first of us married—and Mr Darcy ruined her scheme. Besides, she thinks he is too staid for me. Her next project is to persuade Papa to take us all to Brighton, where she intends to, and I quote, 'find husbands for all my sisters'." Elizabeth crawled beneath the covers and extinguished the candle.

"Jane," she whispered after a minute or two, "are you asleep?"

"If I answer yes, would you believe me?"

"No." Elizabeth yawned. "Has Mary said anything to you about my situation?"

Bed linens rustled. "She struggles between 'honour thy father and thy mother' and 'forget thine own people and thy father's house'. But, Lizzy, surely the psalmist did not mean a prospective bride should erase all memory of her family." Jane sounded close to tears. "I could not bear it if you severed ties with us."

"Never! Besides, you and Mr Bingley will purchase an estate in Derbyshire, and the four of us will live happily away from our father's house."

◈

MUCH LATER THAN WAS CUSTOMARY, FOR SHE HAD SLEPT poorly on Monday night, Elizabeth went downstairs. Upon reaching the bottom, she was met by her father.

"Good morning, Lizzy. I was just going to look for you. Come into my library, please."

His entire demeanour seemed altered, and she was intrigued but wary.

Once they were comfortably settled—he at his desk and she in an armchair across from him—Mr Bennet said that over the past hour and a half he had been worked upon by his wife and eldest daughter. "Then Sir William paid a call. Apparently, the whole neighbourhood knows our business because Lydia spoke of it to Maria. At any rate, I have had some sense talked into me, have been made to see the error of my ways, and have been persuaded. So, if you will allow it, I very much would like to remain a part of your life." He steepled his fingers, and behind his spectacles, his eyes twinkled. "I wish to know these future grandchildren of whom you spoke."

Feeling a measure of relief, Elizabeth remained cautious. "Then...do you consent to my marrying Mr Darcy?" She sat forwards, all hopefulness.

"Yes, and you have my blessing." Mr Bennet removed his spectacles and scrubbed a palm across his eyes. "Having been a young man once, and a bit of a scoundrel, I simply wanted better for you. I believed your young man was not good enough, but I should have trusted your judgment."

"Based upon on my first impression of Mr Wickham and of Mr Darcy himself, I know my judgment is not infallible." She beamed at her father, grateful to have proof that his affection was not lost to her. She, however, had lost a degree of respect for him. "Thank you for wanting the best for me, Papa."

"Yes, well, who could be better for my dearest daughter than a gentleman who is madly in love with her? He has, you see, some sense and good taste after all. And he is a man with his own fortune and no need of yours." Mr Bennet shook his head. "I acted despicably, accusing Mr Darcy of avarice when all along the greedy one was me. The thought of all that wealth went to my head, I suppose. The inheritance is yours, of course, not mine."

He stood and kissed the top of her head. "My dear Lizzy, just as you defeated your opponents during the tournament, you, your young man, and others have prevailed over me. I concede. Mr Darcy is the better man. Who else would have given up a chance to claim fifty thousand pounds and a country house just so that you might have a better chance of doing so?"

Elizabeth gasped. "I beg your pardon? He did *what?*"

❧ 28 ❧

HIS GOOD INTENTIONS

Eleven more miles. The wheels could not turn swiftly enough for Darcy's liking on that Tuesday. At least he was in pleasant company, although it had been a narrow escape.

More flummery, not the sweet dish kind but rather the meaningless flattery sort, had been offered to him; but, try as she might, Miss Bingley had managed to neither curry his favour nor inveigle herself into Darcy's carriage. By design, the rear-facing spot beside him was already occupied by Hadley, who had been fetched from the Inns of Court. The forward-facing seats were taken by Georgiana and Mrs Annesley. Barely discernible through the raised dust of the road, the equipage following behind held the Bingleys and Hursts. Both conveyances were Netherfield bound.

Keeping Miss Bingley out of his carriage had been a trivial thing compared to Darcy's design of grander proportions. The previous day, during his sister's visit to his town house, he had explained the scheme to her and secured her cooperation. Later, Bingley's assistance would be enlisted. As for Hadley, he had been made aware of the plan; and even though he had not been there on the night in question, he was most eager to see Darcy succeed. Bingley's sisters would baulk at such a course of action, and Hurst would be of no use in any case; but things would shift along well enough with or without their cooperation.

His main objective was to please no one but Elizabeth. Of course, the fact had crossed Darcy's mind that such a scheme, as seen through the eyes of her family, friends, and neighbours, might shed a better light on him. Already he had spent countless hours setting his plan in motion, and Darcy was eager for its execution on Thursday.

Elizabeth will be so pleased with what I have done.

HAVING JUST ARRIVED AT LONGBOURN IN COMPANY WITH HIS sister, Bingley, and Hadley, Darcy made the necessary introductions while looking about for Elizabeth.

With a wink of her eye, Mrs Bennet said, "If you are wondering about Lizzy's whereabouts, she is out there on the lawn." She pointed through the window. "She intends to teach Lydia and Kitty to properly play pall-mall."

Thither Darcy went, content to leave his two friends and his sister in the sitting room with Miss Jane Bennet, Miss Mary, and their mother.

Rounding the corner of the house, a pretty picture greeted him—an unclouded sky, verdure, barn swallows darting about, creeping buttercups, common daisies, and three young women in summery gowns.

The instant Elizabeth espied him, she, mallet in hand and fire in her eyes, rushed in his direction.

Almost fearing for his life, Darcy—no coward, he—stood

his ground but kept an eye on the long-handled wooden stick she wielded. A flush stained her cheeks, and he suspected she might have wept recently.

Coming to a halt, she gave his chest a powerful push. "Why would you *do* such a thing?"

Not the welcome I was expecting. "I might ask you the same question, madam," said he, rubbing his sternum. "But, whatever I have done, I regret incurring your displeasure." It sounded like a husbandly thing to say.

"Oh, you regret *incurring* my displeasure, do you? Displeasure is putting it mildly. I cannot recall having suffered any vexation equal to that which I experienced at eleven o'clock today when Papa told me what you did."

Gently relieving the lady of her weapon, Darcy racked his brain. What had Mr Bennet said to cause such pique? *Oh. Blast.*

Darcy's need for Elizabeth had become as vital as the need for air and sustenance, and the mere thought of losing her created a physical pain not unlike the first time she had spurned him or the time he had broken his arm.

Thinking it best to ascertain the cause before panicking, he said, "I assume you mean..." He had hoped she would complete the sentence; otherwise, he might put his foot in it by confessing to another transgression, if there had been one. She, however, was not obliging. *Tread carefully, man.* He cleared his throat, trying to delay that which could not be avoided. "You must mean...that thing I did." He tossed the mallet aside with force. "At Oakwood."

Watching the mallet's trajectory, Elizabeth nodded. "You did not believe I could win the tournament on my own merit, *did* you?"

Cradling her chin with both hands, he turned her head and looked into her eyes. "Of course I did. You are a clever lady, my love. I had, *have*, every confidence in your abilities. I simply wanted to eliminate some of your competition, meaning me."

"But Papa had the right of it. You withdrew from the tournament *after* winning my heart, knowing the prize would be yours either way."

"The prize is *you*, Elizabeth. And it never was about winning or losing. It was about wishing to see you happy." His heart broke at having caused sorrow instead. "When Monroe told me about the tournament, I dithered about even participating. In the end, I went to Oakwood thinking, if nothing else, the competition might, at least for a se'n-night, keep my mind off the woman I loved and had lost. And there you were."

She backed away from his touch. "But...I thought I had won fair and square."

He followed. "You did! Elizabeth, you solved the puzzles on your own, using your quick understanding and keen intelligence. You claimed the prize by unmitigated determination to do so. I witnessed the moment you pressed the button releasing that secret drawer. You triumphed. On your own."

"If you were there, witnessing the moment of my so-called triumph, you must have solved the puzzle already. You knew the deed and key were in that particular clock." She looked at the sky, at the ground, anywhere but at him. "And you just stood there and let me win."

"It was my wish to give happiness to you and, through you, your family." His voice lost some of its power. "Honestly, Elizabeth, I did it with the best of intentions."

That she was not formed for ill-humour was a well-known fact, and Darcy hoped he was forgiven when her beautiful eyes turned his way and softened.

"Knowing what you did, how could Papa not have fallen to his knees in gratitude? How could he have treated you so cruelly? You saved Mama and my sisters from being forced into reduced circumstances. How can we ever thank you?"

Moving ever closer, he took her hand in his. "*You* saved them, my love. But, if you will thank me, let it be for yourself alone. Your family owe me nothing. I thought only of *you*."

He then expressed himself as passionately as a man violently in love can be supposed to do while under the watchful eyes of the two youngest Bennets. Gently, he peeled back the cuff of Elizabeth's glove and placed a kiss upon her wrist.

Raucous laughter was not the response he had hoped to elicit. Scowling in Miss Lydia's direction, he noticed Miss Catherine placing a hand over her own heart and closing her eyes. He even imagined he heard a sigh.

"Shall we walk, sir?"

"You are, indeed, a clever lady." Darcy offered his arm.

Strolling round Longbourn's park, he continued praising Elizabeth's abilities. "...and I suspect your father encouraged knowledge through book learning." He dared not utter it aloud, but he doubted Mrs Bennet had much of a hand in that regard. "I also suspect you learnt through observation and experience. But who was the person you looked to as an example to be imitated?"

Running her free hand across a juniper's spiny needles, she said, "My Grandmama Bennet. Then, when that dear lady died, I took Aunt Gardiner—yes, a tradesman's wife—as a model. Much as my grandmother had done, my aunt loves and supports her husband, is a good mother, an exemplary housekeeper and hostess, is charitable with her time, and remains patient and elegant while doing it all. I want to be that sort of woman...for you."

"You will be a magnificent mistress of Pemberley." He wanted to say more, about what a loving wife and mother she would be, but such thoughts of her in those roles incited ungentlemanly passions. Instead, Darcy merely patted Elizabeth's hand and said he did not deserve her.

"I once tried to emulate my friend Charlotte, who is more than five years my senior and a very sensible woman. She shares many of Aunt Gardiner's good qualities."

Many, not all. Mrs Collins, Darcy suspected, supported her husband; but theirs was not a grand love. *Not like ours.*

"Charlotte thinks I am too much of an incurable romantic to practise prudence."

They had strolled as far as the barn, and a tabby cat came trotting out to greet them. "Good day, Abby." Crouching, Elizabeth cooed at it, stroked its head, and scratched beneath its chin. The cat purred loudly, then was gone in a flash, chasing two brimstone butterflies.

Hand upon Darcy's arm again, Elizabeth suggested they walk towards the meadow. "To continue what I was saying, Miss Bingley and her ilk might not approve of my Gardiner relations, but I never thought of my aunt and uncle as anything other than ladylike and gentlemanlike, although neither is of gentle birth. And think what you will of my mother, sir, but she taught me about housekeeping, setting a fine table...and catching an eligible gentleman." Elizabeth grinned at him. "Mama is inordinately proud of me, for I have caught the very best. And I love him so."

"I return your love tenfold." Longing to kiss her but noticing her bootlace was untied, Darcy bent down on one knee to secure the lace in a double knot. "Since you are such an incurable romantic, I suppose I, like a medieval knight, should have proposed to you on bended knee as a sign of allegiance to a superior. But I am no sentimental noddy,

Elizabeth. In fact, if I remember correctly, my second proposal was a rather curt 'marry me'. But I do promise you my respect, fidelity, and everlasting devotion."

Standing tall then, he shook his head. "I fail to understand how a man is supposed to gain experience in offering marriage. Practice makes perfect, they say, but if he has chosen well, he should have to make a proposal only the once. Or twice."

"What could be more clearly expressed than 'marry me' or 'I love you'? Succinctness, at times, has its own charm."

"Do you have suggestions for how one might go about speaking to your youngest sister? I wish to apologise to Miss Lydia for her removal from Brighton, although I firmly believe it was done for the best."

"I wish you success in trying to talk any sense into that girl." Stopping at the edge of the meadow, where farm horses grazed and clumps of tall Timothy grass grew, she plucked a stem from the ground, pulled seeds from the long, cylindrical flower heads, and released them to the breeze. "Might your sister also be willing to speak to Lydia?"

"About Wickham? Certainly not!"

"Who better to make Lydia understand the danger she faced than a young lady of similar age who suffered at the hands of that ne'er-do-well? They are to be sisters, after all."

That gave him pause. "You are correct, and your wish is my command. I shall ask Georgiana whether she might be willing. Shall we return to the house now? Bingley and Hadley are there."

"Mr Bingley and Mr *Hadley*? Yes! It will be wonderful to see both of them."

You were not so enthusiastic about my arrival.

"I never mentioned it before, but I think those two share certain similarities. Do you not agree?"

"Yes, clever lady. Their mothers were sisters."

They returned to the house, where Darcy was pleased to see his sister sitting and chatting with Miss Jane Bennet, Miss Mary, and Bingley. Their mother was nowhere to be seen. Nor was Hadley.

At an opportune moment, he took Georgiana aside to quietly make the necessary enquiry, and, to his utter astonishment, she readily agreed.

"Where is Hadley?"

"He saw you and Miss Elizabeth through the window and went out to the lawn."

So, to the lawn went Darcy and the two most important ladies in his life. There, they joined Miss Catherine and Miss Lydia, and introductions were made.

"I thought Hadley was out here," said Darcy.

"Oh, he was." Miss Catherine had either caught too much sun or was blushing. "Mr Hadley spotted you and Lizzy walking towards the house and thought you were ready to leave. You just missed him. He must have gone round the other way."

Between Georgiana and Miss Lydia there ensued so much of friendliness, of flattery, of everything warm, and of so many polysyllabic words from his sister that Darcy had to give Georgiana a discreet nudge.

"Miss Lydia," she said, reminded of her mission, "I noticed a pretty little tangled garden on one side of your lawn, and my brother and I should like to take a turn about it, if you will accompany us."

As the three walked towards the little wilderness, the youngest Bennet linked arms with her new friend but frequently looked back towards the lawn. "Where did Lizzy and Kitty go? No matter. There really is nothing special to see in this neglected garden but... Oh, look!"

On one side of the garden was an overgrown jumble of bramble thickets, vines, and bracken. Against a crumbling wall, fragrant, sprawling rose bushes ran wild over everything in their path. The gurgle of a spring could be heard; and amidst the wildness, in a little clearing, stood a massive willow with branches trailing to the ground. From a nest somewhere above, within the gnarled crooks of its branches, hatchling robins chirped, begging to be fed.

"Mother Nature has prevailed here, but someone has been busy. See? Flowers have been planted in the tree stumps over there. Perhaps it was Kitty. She told me she had taken up gardening again." Dropping onto a weathered, splintering wooden bench, Miss Lydia beckoned Georgiana to join her.

"I shall stand, thank you."

"Kitty is so odd. La! I cannot abide rooting in soil like a pig after truffles. Nor can I abide muddy hems. Hereabouts there is little point in wearing such a fine gown as yours, Miss Darcy, to trudge along muddy cart tracks. How I long for the clean, raised walks of Brighton and the company of officers in their scarlet coats."

"I regret," said Darcy, with not a whit of remorse, "that it was necessary to curtail your Brighton sojourn. But I assure you it was done with the very best of intentions."

Best of intentions, indeed. Such had been the case when he had warned Bingley away from Miss Bennet and when he had withdrawn from the tournament at Oakwood.

But this is different. "Mr Wickham is not to be trusted. And you, young lady, were in peril there...and, perhaps, here, should he return."

"You are wrong about him." The girl's tone was both defiant and smug. "And I hope the lieutenant *does* return for me. Then we shall wed, as he promised."

One glance at Georgiana's concerned face convinced

Darcy that she, too, feared for her future sister. "Should Mr Wickham discover my affiliation with your family," he said, "the reprobate may try to destroy our happiness by coercing or tempting you into a situation that ultimately would result in your ruin and risk the good reputation of all your sisters. I am sorry to say that the lieutenant will not *willingly* marry you. He is a scoundrel of the highest degree."

"It is well known, sir, how badly you treated that dear man." Miss Lydia's tone had become as cold and sharp as icicles.

You take an eager interest in that gentleman's concerns. "My sister wishes to have a private word with you, but whatever Georgiana tells you must remain a secret. She will be entrusting you with what could be incendiary information. Miss Elizabeth knows of it. Otherwise, we have been able to keep the matter strictly confidential. May I have your solemn promise that you will not tell a soul, not even Miss Catherine? May we depend on you?" *Am I mad, thinking Lydia Bennet might be trustworthy?*

"Why should I keep this secret of yours? What shall I gain by doing so? Besides, I shall not believe a word said against my dear Wickham."

Georgiana's eyes flew wide at such impertinence. "What will you gain? My brother just explained that very thing to you. It is not what you will *gain*. It is what you will not *lose*. Our aim is to keep you safe from harm." She sat beside Miss Lydia and made a shooing gesture at Darcy.

While the two young ladies spoke within the garden, he paced outside its gate. Finally, he heard them bidding one another 'good day'. Miss Lydia ran off towards the house without so much as a glance at him.

Looking enervated, Georgiana approached. "I told her all, Brother. Then, I am ashamed to confess, I bribed her."

"You did *what?*"

"If Miss Lydia does not breathe a word of all that I have revealed, I promised to purchase a lovely new gown for her."

As they walked towards the house, Georgiana added, "Every quarter day."

❦ 29 ❦

MUSICAL MAGIC

At Longbourn on Wednesday, between the fragrant cutting garden and the shrubbery, Kitty chatted with Elizabeth while they took turns on the swing suspended from a massive oak. The tree had been there for over three hundred years, the swing since Mary had been a young child.

Seated but not setting it in motion, Kitty said, "I did not admit as much to you yesterday when we were chatting, but I was angry and jealous when Lydia went to Brighton. Then, after three or four days of vexation and moping round the house, I felt free to do as I pleased rather than follow wherever Lydia's fancy might take us. I did a bit of gardening and, you may be properly shocked, read an entire novel while she was gone. Lydia never has patience for either reading or needlework, but I rather enjoyed sitting by the open window, embroidering handkerchiefs and listening to Mary play the pianoforte. I even begged her to teach me a few simple tunes. Just imagine what I might have accomplished had Lydia stayed away the anticipated three months instead of one."

"My dear sister, I am exceedingly proud of you." *Imagine. An entire book in one month!*

Kitty scuffed her feet on the patch of dirt beneath the swing and glanced about uneasily. "Lizzy, what can you tell me about that nice Mr Hadley? I understand you met him at the country house in Buckinghamshire. *Your* country house." She heaved a sigh, then coughed. "How very fortunate you are to own a grand old manor and possess a huge fortune."

Elizabeth kept to herself the fact that she had decided to use most of that wealth to provide dowries for her four sisters. "I first became acquainted with Mr David Hadley in Cheapside during the autumn of the year ten, a twelvemonth before we met Mr Bingley. Similar to his cousin in looks and in amiability, Mr Hadley is a delightful young gentleman... emphasis on *young*. His ambition is to become a barrister until he inherits Eastmeadow Park, a modest estate in Eton Wick, where his elder brother lives. Why do you ask about him?"

Standing behind her sister and pulling on the ropes, Elizabeth eased the swing towards herself. Then resting her chin upon Kitty's shoulder, she whispered, "As though I cannot begin to guess at your interest." Releasing the ropes, she watched as her sister's legs pumped to and fro, propelling the swing higher and higher into an azure sky.

Shading her eyes, she watched as the top of Kitty's head touched the bottom rim of the sun, which was not quite at its zenith. "In several hours you will have a chance to become much better acquainted with Mr Hadley. He and the Netherfield party have been invited to dine here this evening."

Her sister uttered a surprised squeak. "Why was I not told of this?" Her feet flailed as they sought to gain purchase with the earth. "I must make haste! The seam on my peach muslin needs mending. And I shall ask Patty to dress my hair differently. And Lydia will be wrestled to the floor if she does not return my pale-green ribbons, and…"

CLAD IN HER ALTERED AND EMBELLISHED PRIMROSE GOWN— the one last worn the evening she had been trapped in Oakwood's garret—and with all her sisters in pretty muslins, Elizabeth thought the five of them appeared to great advantage. Lydia was in white with green dots, Kitty in peach, Jane in pale blue, and Mary in cream with brown stripes.

Then Miss Darcy entered the drawing room wearing an elegant ivory satin with dainty lilac and green sprigs.

I shall purchase bolts of silk in each of my sisters' favourite colours and have them made into lovely gowns by London's finest dressmakers. And for Mama too. A thrill ran through Elizabeth at the thought of having deep enough pockets to do such things for her family.

Rushing over and latching on to her new friend's arm, Lydia cried, "La, Georgiana, I just realised something. Today is Midsummer quarter day. What a laugh! You now owe me an elegant new gown, like yours, for I have not yet breathed a word about…you know what."

Grateful that Messrs Bingley, Hurst, and Hadley were too occupied with greetings and welcomes and being seated to have heard Lydia's remarks, Elizabeth warmly acknowledged Mr Darcy. Then, speaking barely above a whisper, she said, "Do you have any notion what Lydia just alluded to?"

"I shall tell you whenever we have a private moment. In the meantime…" From behind his back, Mr Darcy brought forth and presented to her a posy of crimson and yellow. "I picked this bouquet of wildflowers for you myself. I noticed them in a meadow on my way to Meryton earlier today. I was there delivering...messages. I see that, providentially, the yellow ones match the gown you wear."

From those flowers, Elizabeth surreptitiously brushed off two ants and trod upon them with her slipper. "Thank you. Common cow-wheat looks lovely with the great burnet. But how odd you should go about our neighbourhood delivering messages. Could you not have relegated such tasks to Netherfield's errand boy?"

For a second or two, his eyes widened with what seemed to be alarm. "Ah. Yes. But as I already had calls to make"—his look of disquiet was back—"I decided to kill two birds with one stone."

While frowning at him in puzzlement, Elizabeth noticed Mr Darcy swallowing so hard that she suspected he might have the aforementioned stone lodged in his throat. "Calls to make? You? In Meryton? How very..." *Unlike you.* "Mysterious."

Mrs Bennet bustled over. "Lizzy, why are you lingering about holding weeds? I assure you, Mr Darcy, that all my daughters know better than to keep guests standing in the doorway. How unfortunate that Mr Bingley's sisters both should be indisposed at the same time! But believe me, with five daughters unmarried, *I* know how horrid headaches can be. Of course, soon you will take our Lizzy away. And I fully expect another offer of marriage soon will occur." A pointed look was directed towards Jane and Mr Bingley, who sat with their heads together speaking quietly to one another. "What congratulations will then flow in! And have I told you, sir, about my—"

"Mama, let us not keep our guest standing here. Apparently, he has been traipsing about Meryton all day."

"Oh! Do come in, Mr Darcy, and rest your weary feet. Dinner soon will be served."

Indeed, dinner was announced almost immediately. And during the first course, Lydia said, "Afterwards we all should play Musical Magic. What a laugh we had while doing so in Brighton! My Wick— Um… One of the officer's tasks was to remove my locket and fasten it round Colonel Forster's neck. But it would not fit, for Harriet's husband has such a fat—" Having placed a hand at her own neck, Lydia gasped. "Oh Lord! Wick— The officer quite forgot to return my locket. Papa," she said, as she leant across in front of Miss Darcy, "we all must go to Brighton and retrieve my necklace. Then we must stay there for the remainder of the summer."

"Aunt Philips is sure the salt water and air would do me a great deal of good." Kitty added a little cough for good measure.

"Have you both forgotten," said their father, "that we have a wedding to attend on the eleventh of July?"

To everyone's surprise, Mr Bingley stood and cleared his throat. With all eyes upon him and everyone silent, he said, "Weddings. Plural. I have asked for Miss Bennet's hand in marriage, and I am elated to announce that she has agreed to be my wife."

With lively emotion, Jane nodded and declared herself the happiest creature in the world; and the endearing smiles of the betrothed couple soon had everyone else grinning.

Mrs Bennet's prediction had come true. Congratulations flowed forth and were received with sincere warmth and delight. Copious amounts of wine also flowed forth, and toasts were made to both happy couples.

Even Mr Hurst raised a glass to them. Then he raised a glass to his hostess and said her venison was roasted to a turn. "Never have I seen such a fat haunch as yours, madam."

Perhaps Mr Hurst has ingested a bit too much wine.

When the happy babble subsided to a dull roar and

everyone focused on their plates, Elizabeth looked round the table and saw Kitty was in particularly good spirits. *Is it the wine or...*

Earlier in the day, Kitty had expressed an interest in Mr Hadley, and the attraction seemed mutual.

Obviously smitten, he listened with rapt attention to every word she uttered; and rarely had the young man, directly across from the object of his admiration, taken his eyes from her during the two courses. In fact, Elizabeth had to stifle a grin and pretend she had not witnessed the moment Mr Hadley missed his mouth. *Is not stabbing one's chin with a fork the very essence of infatuation? Perhaps I, too, have had too much wine.*

Prior to winning an inheritance, Elizabeth had imagined Mary, Kitty, and Lydia would marry men in a profession—the clergy, military, or law. But soon all her sisters would have ten-thousand-pound dowries.

Might they do better than one such as Mr Hadley? Good heavens! Has wealth robbed me of my senses? Am I becoming like Papa? If it was proved that Kitty and Mr Hadley loved one another and that he easily could support a wife and children, then she would be happy for them.

While Elizabeth had been wool-gathering, the topic of after-dinner entertainment evidently had been reconsidered. It had been agreed that once the gentlemen had enjoyed their port, they would join the ladies in the drawing room where anyone who wished to do so could exhibit on the square Broadwood pianoforte.

I suppose the instrument is not as grand as Miss Darcy is accustomed to, but it does have a damper and more keys than the one the Gouldings have at Haye-Park.

As the least proficient of those exhibiting, Kitty went first and softly sang 'The Soldier's Adieu' while Mary accompanied her on the pianoforte.

That performance was followed by Elizabeth's rousing rendition of 'Old Maid in the Garret'. Sitting then beside Mr Darcy while Mary performed a concerto, she was rewarded by the touch of his bare fingers upon her wrist. She closed her eyes, savouring the sensation. *Can he feel my pulse race? Is it wrong to crave more?*

After a bit of coaxing, Miss Darcy agreed to take a turn at the instrument. Her audience sat in silent awe until she gracefully lifted her fingers from the keys. Then, with everyone applauding her exemplary performance of a Haydn sonata, she quickly moved away from the pianoforte and sat blushing on her brother's other side.

Elizabeth noted how he gave his sister's hand a gentle squeeze and whispered words of pride and appreciation for her courage, talent, and grace. *He is such a loving brother. And beau! And what an excellent father he will be.*

Just as she was about to slide her palm beneath his, he was approached by Mr Bingley, who requested a private word. As they quietly spoke across the room, she became increasingly suspicious, particularly when they kept stealing glances at her.

"Miss Darcy, is there some problem of which I should be made aware?"

"Oh no! I mean… There is nothing of which you should be aware." Blushing again, Miss Darcy seemed inordinately eager to change the subject. "Since we soon are to become sisters, please call me Georgiana. Lydia already does."

Lydia came then and, taking one of Elizabeth's hands and one of Georgiana's, pulled the ladies to their feet. "We are to play Musical Magic now. Papa invited the gentlemen to join him in his library for more port, but only Mr Hurst went with him. Jane and Kitty have agreed to play, as have Mr Bingley and Mr Hadley. Lizzy, Mr Darcy says he will participate only if you are willing. Dull Mary has agreed to provide the music for us, and Simon has been summoned to arrange chairs in a circle."

After declining and refusing to be persuaded, Georgiana said she would sit by Mrs Bennet and watch.

Perhaps realising she would be a fifth wheel amongst three ladies and three gentlemen, and although the scheme had been her idea, Lydia said, "I shall keep you company, Georgiana. It can be just as much fun to watch as to play."

Once Mary was at the pianoforte and the chairs in place, Elizabeth—having agreed to go first—left the room, closed the door behind her, and anxiously paced while the others decided upon her task.

Mere seconds had elapsed before Simon opened the door. Failing to hide a grin, the footman said, "They are ready for you, miss."

A faint melody from the Broadwood increased in volume as she approached the circle. By the time she reached its middle, the music had become moderately loud. Gathering courage round her like a cloak, Elizabeth stepped up to Mr Darcy. The volume increased, so she placed a quick kiss upon his cheek. The result was not only loud music but an outburst of laughter from the others. *Botheration! Why did I drink more than two glasses of wine?*

Colour high, she stepped over to Kitty. The melody softened, so she turned back to Mr Darcy. *A crescendo.*

She moved towards Jane. *Softer.*

Mr Darcy it is, then. Standing in front of him, she bent and kissed his hand. More laughter and loud music. *What do they expect me to do? Am I to sit upon his lap? Mama is watching! I shall strangle Lydia for suggesting this game.*

Elizabeth reminded herself that her courage always rose at every attempt to intimidate her.

So she tweaked the gentleman's nose.

The Broadwood could not be heard above the uproar. *Definitely too much wine with dinner.* Hands raised above her head, Elizabeth surrendered.

"Lizzy," said Jane, once her mirth was somewhat under control, "all you had to do was ruffle Mr Darcy's hair."

I loathe this game. "Very well, what forfeit must I pay?"

Holding his sides, Mr Bingley cried, "By Jove! I say tweak Darcy's nose again!"

"That is not what we agreed upon," said Kitty. "Lizzy, you now must ruffle *each* gentleman's hair."

No! Not without several more glasses of wine. Raising her eyes from the floor, she stole a glance at Mr Bingley and Mr Hadley and gulped.

Sitting in front of her, arms crossed, Mr Darcy waited with a smug, expectant expression on his face. In truth, Elizabeth very much longed to run her fingers through his hair, but not in public. *Oh, hang it!* She ruffled the soft, dark waves as she might have done to her little cousins Edwin and Jonathan.

Then she stepped up to the next gentleman, Jane's future husband. Elizabeth wanted to shut her eyes during the ruffle but feared she might poke out one of Mr Bingley's. Steeling herself, she lightly brushed her hand across the grinning gentleman's artfully tousled, reddish-gold hair.

Finally, she moved to Mr Hadley. The young man's leg bounced nervously, and Elizabeth did not know whom to feel sorrier for, him or herself. Taking a deep breath, she plunged her fingers towards his hair.

The instant her turquoise ring became entangled in Mr Hadley's shock of coppery, springy curls, her father and Mr Hurst walked into the room.

Elizabeth hung her head and sighed. *Please, let this be the culmination of my mortification. I cannot bear any more.*

Glowering at her, Kitty nevertheless came over and helped to untangle the ring. If a few strands of coppery hair were detached from the gentleman's scalp in the process and were secreted away in her younger sister's pocket, Elizabeth pretended not to notice.

To cap off the evening's entertainment, the parlour game —rather like a piece of music with a loud, powerful finale— reached its own conclusion under Mr Bennet's strident direction.

❧ 30 ❧

REASSEMBLY

On Thursday, after receiving and answering urgent correspondence and paying a call at Longbourn—an all too brief one for his liking—Darcy returned to Netherfield relieved that Elizabeth had suffered no repercussions, particularly of her father's doing, following the previous night's Musical Magic.

Darcy had enjoyed that quick kiss upon his cheek, the one upon the back of his bare hand, and the hair ruffling. He could have done without the nose tweak, though. Her mortification had become his own, and he silently repented of being jealous when Elizabeth had caressed other men's hair. *It was but a mere touch, you noddy, not a caress.*

Most of all he regretted that he had gone to Longbourn bearing ill tidings. Elizabeth's disappointment had nearly been his undoing. He prayed that, later that evening, all his time, effort, and expense might mitigate some of her sadness over the forthcoming separation—one of a fortnight's duration, longer than expected, and a distance of one hundred and thirty-eight miles.

There were estate matters to be addressed in Derbyshire, ones that could not be handled through the post. The most urgent was that Pemberley's venerable and long-serving steward was not long for this world. Darcy wished to be home for his friend's funeral, and Mr Ward's nephew would require guidance while settling into the position for which his uncle had been training him.

Then there was the matter of preparing the house for Mrs Darcy's arrival. Mrs Reynolds was a godsend, as always; but, needing everything to be as perfect as possible, Darcy wanted to oversee the refurbishment of the mistress's apartments and nursery himself. A thrill shot through him at the very thought of Elizabeth in those rooms.

Rubbing his forehead, he banished those images and reviewed details of his current project and was confident nothing had been overlooked. Even the sky had cooperated. The night was clear, and guests would be guided to and from the venue by the light of a full moon. But after days of preparation, he had gained a greater appreciation for the time and effort stage-managers put into theatrical productions.

"So remember, Bingley," Darcy had said to his friend hours ago, "the first with Miss Jane Bennet, the two third with Miss Maria Lucas, the two fourth with one of Mrs Long's nieces, the two fifth with Miss Jane Bennet, the two sixth with *my* Miss Bennet, and Le Boulanger with—"

"Yes, yes, Darcy! I remember!"

Once Jonesby had made the final touches to his cravat, Darcy inspected his valet's handiwork in the mirror and nodded his thanks. When he arrived downstairs at half past the hour, six of the Netherfield party stood waiting in the vestibule, but there was no sign of Miss Bingley.

"Georgiana, Hadley, Mrs Annesley, and I shall go ahead in

my carriage and await you outside the inn. Bingley, kindly ensure your sister does not cause a delay. We must make an entrance together, as we did on the fifteenth of October."

Reassembled outside Meryton's best—and one and only —inn, they paired up as arranged: Mrs Annesley on Bingley's arm, Georgiana on Darcy's, and Mrs Hurst on her husband's, leaving Miss Bingley to be escorted by Hadley. Together they climbed the stairs and entered the hired assembly room, for which Darcy had paid handsomely.

In general circulation within five minutes of their arrival was a report of his being in desperate need of a wife. *Want, not need. Well, yes, need.*

The Master of Ceremonies beckoned them over. Clapping while the musicians tuned their instruments, Sir William Lucas said, "Capital, capital! What a charming amusement assemblies are for young people, eh, Mr Darcy?"

"Certainly, Sir William. There is, after all, nothing like dancing. It is one of the first refinements of polished societies."

Miss Bingley sneered. "Then one should have *stayed* in London, where there *is* polished society." She and the Hursts were much as they had been in the autumn, and Georgiana and Hadley seemed duly shocked at their supercilious remarks.

Disregarding Miss Bingley and her fault-finding, Darcy nodded to Sir William. "I hope to prove tonight that I am adept in the science of dance." And off he went to do so.

In passing a gaggle of females frantically fanning their faces, he heard them complimenting his countenance and stature. "And he has such an alluring, inviting smile."

Egad! Darcy cringed, and the tips of his ears reddened. Glancing down at Georgiana, whom he was shepherding about the room, he noticed the pretty blush upon her cheeks and the grin she tried to subdue.

Needing to be on his very best behaviour, he walked about the hall reacquainting himself with all the principal people and introducing his sister, her companion, and Hadley and making a valiant attempt to be amiable, mannerly, very easily pleased, and not above his company. It was quite exhausting.

And if all that was not enervating enough, there was the dancing. Georgiana and Mrs Annesley would not be partaking, but, between the three of them, Darcy, Bingley, and Hadley danced almost every dance.

While his friends stood up with local young ladies, Darcy danced with Elizabeth, her sisters, Miss Bingley, and Mrs Hurst. His good character was decided, and everyone hoped he would return to Meryton again and again, with or without a wife.

During his first set with Elizabeth, she said to him, "Should I be worried or happy, Mr Darcy, that you, my future husband, can be so secretive and scheming? I thought Jane had gone quite mad this evening when she rooted round the wardrobe, pulled out this old gown, and insisted I wear it to an assembly about which I had no knowledge. Although, come to think of it, of late you have been acting suspiciously."

"Acting? Whatever do you mean?"

"Yes, acting. You belong on stage, sir, as I believe I told you at Oakwood."

"Oakwood? What is Oakwood? I have no notion of what you speak, madam." Darcy smiled and put his whole heart into it. *I am enjoying this a bit too much, I think.*

Halfway through the night, he was informed that—due to the trampling of her toes by an inept buffoon—Elizabeth had been obliged to sit down awhile, which, although terribly unfortunate for her, was fortuitous for him.

He fetched Bingley, and ensuring they stood close enough for Elizabeth to overhear a conversation between them, Darcy prodded his friend.

In a decidedly stiff, monotonous tone, Bingley recited, "Come, Darcy, I must have you dance. I hate to see you standing about by yourself in this stupid manner. You had much better dance."

Good grief. Has he never acted before? Put some emotion into it, man!

"I certainly shall not." Darcy feigned a groan. "My feet are killing me. Have you not noticed how many times I have danced thus far? Of course, at such an assembly as this, with ladies outnumbering gentlemen, it would be insupportable not to do so. Besides, it would be unwise of me to stand up with someone a second time, lest my intention be marriage. Gallantry is expected of a gentleman but is often construed as flirtation."

"Upon my honour, Darcy. I never danced with so many pleasant girls in my life as I have this evening." Bingley's intonation had improved. "And there are at least half a dozen of them who are uncommonly pretty."

"Indeed there are *many* uncommonly charming and attractive young ladies here, and you just danced with one of the handsomest."

"Oh, *yes*! Miss Jane Bennet is the most beautiful creature I have *ever* beheld!" Bingley's vocal inflections were masterful. "If I am *very* fortunate, I shall marry her some day! Oh, but look. There is one of her sisters sitting down just behind you. She is very pretty and, I dare say, very agreeable. Why not ask her to stand up with you again?"

"A second time! Why, I might as well announce to the

entire world that I ardently admire and love the lady and have chosen her as my bride. As you well know, Fitzwilliam Darcy does *not* dance twice with any woman at any ball. By the bye, which sister did you mean?" Turning round, Darcy looked fixedly at Elizabeth, never withdrawing his gaze. "By Jove, Bingley, thank you for bringing that exquisite creature to my attention. What fine eyes she has!" He lowered his voice a mite. "You know how discriminating I can be. She, however, is handsome enough to tempt me." His eyes caressed her.

Squaring his shoulders, he made a show of adjusting his cravat. "I presently find myself in excellent humour just being in the lady's presence. Why, my feet do not even hurt any longer. Return to your partner, Bingley, and enjoy those pretty smiles she bestows so generously. You are keeping me from the woman I intend to wed and carry off to Pemberley." With confidence, Darcy strode towards Elizabeth.

Her dark eyes were bright and, perhaps, laughing at him. Tempting lips smiled so invitingly that he almost forgot himself and kissed her then and there.

"Pray tell, madam, does your injury cause much pain?"

"No…unless you insist I dance a reel."

"Ha! I would not dare. But whenever you are ready to scandalise your neighbours, I hope you will stand up with me a second time. I want everyone to know my affection is not a slight, thin sort of inclination."

She stood and held out her hand. "Then let us leave them in no doubt, sir."

Elizabeth remained extremely cordial towards him during that quarter of an hour. She teased him, she held his fingers a little too long for decorum, and she moved a little too close for propriety. So much so that Darcy thought it wise to put a bit of space between them and find a less desirable partner for the second dance of that set.

Therefore, with Elizabeth's permission, he cajoled Mrs Bennet into dancing a reel with him. While doing so, he kept an eye on his intended as she walked about the room, smiling and laughing and speaking with her friends and telling them, with great spirit, the story of how he was putting to rights last autumn's event during which he had so cruelly slighted her. Of course, most everyone in the room had been in on the scheme, so they merely smiled and nodded at her and declared it a most excellent evening.

So lovely, so delighted with what he had done, so lively and playful was she that Darcy longed to whisk her off into the night and... *Best keep your thoughts under good regulation whilst dancing with the woman's mother. Soon, though...*

The instant the reel ended and he had escorted Mrs Bennet to her chair beside Mrs Philips, Darcy went in search of his love.

"Darcy! Darcy, did you not hear me hailing you?" Running a hand through his hair, Bingley approached from the side.

That sight evoked in Darcy a memory of Elizabeth's fingers threading through his wavy hair, fingernails scraping his scalp, eliciting a moan, and—

"Darcy, are you well, man? You just groaned. Are your feet truly killing you?"

"No. Yes." *That was just my own wishful thinking and not at all how it happened last night.* "What is it, Bingley?"

"I despair of doing this again to Jane...leaving so soon after a ball, but she and Miss Elizabeth wish for us fortunate men to marry them in a double wedding on the eleventh. So I must go to town and procure a common licence, and see about purchasing Netherfield, and arrange for—"

"Stop there, Bingley. Do not be so hasty in making such an important purchase. Give living within three miles of your mother-in-law a few months before deciding whether to renew the lease, buy, or run for the hills of Derbyshire. Trust me."

"I do trust *you*. I just wish I could trust Caroline and the Hursts not to pack up and follow me to town."

"Yes, well, speaking of going, I really must beg your pardon, my friend. There is an important matter I have yet to accomplish this night." With a nod, Darcy turned on his heel. Although others called out to him, he was finished with being amiable, mannerly, and easily pleased. There was only one person with whom he wished to be warm and engaging.

A glance at his watch informed him it was eleven o'clock, and the assembly would last only until half past the hour. There was no time to lose.

In passing the supper room, where light refreshments were being served at his expense, he noticed Hurst eating and drinking as though he was famished from dancing all night. The man had stood up once. With his own wife.

At the very end of the passage, Darcy espied the very person he sought, standing at an open window, looking out into the night. At his footfall, she turned, and he rushed to her.

Moonlight caressed her profile, and he perceived a silvery track of tears. "Elizabeth, my love, are you well?"

"I am...now that you are here with me." Her smile was forced, he could tell. "It is your leaving tomorrow that saddens me."

Darcy tenderly wiped away the vestiges of tears with his handkerchief. "I am sorry. 'Tis unavoidable, though. Mr Ward was, *is*, my very good friend, and I pray I shall not be too late to say my last farewell."

She reached for his gloved hand. "I understand, sir. Truly I do. Still, I shall miss you terribly."

"Terribly as in very much, or terribly as in very badly done?" He smiled as Elizabeth batted his arm.

"Horrid man. Why did I imagine I might be wretched without you?" She looked at him with a sombre expression. "Last night you told me you would be gone eleven days, which was bad enough. But *fifteen!* You are to return only just in time for our wedding. And I distinctly remember you saying, on at least two separate occasions, that you would by no means suspend any pleasure of mine." Moonlight captured a hint of mischief in her eyes.

Darcy tugged her into an embrace. "Of all horrid things, this act of saying goodbye is the worst. However, when we meet at the altar after this separation and all the longing and anticipation of a fortnight, our love will be stronger."

Tilting her head back, she looked up at him, eyes luminous as she swept a few curls from his forehead.

Just as he had done while carrying her from Oakwood's garret, Darcy firmly hugged her warm body to his. A whiff of summer meadows and autumn orchards. *Home.* The caress of sweet breath upon his cheek. He closed his eyes, indulging in sensation. Fingers stroking his nape. *Blasted gloves!* Lips brushing lips, sliding, parting. *Heaven.*

Unsure how the kiss had been initiated or by whom, he drew back to look into her eyes. They were closed. Her kissable lips were still slightly parted. *To indulge one's appetites without restraint is not the action of a gentleman. To indulge one's appetites without restraint is not the action of a gentleman. To indulge one's appetites without restraint is not the action of a gentleman.*

Nobility of restraint asserted itself. Gently, he moved her

hands from his neck and held them. "Elizabeth, we should go."

"No. Not yet."

"We must. But before we do, I have something to give you." He backed away and reached into his breast pocket. "This was the first gift, and sadly the last, that I chose for my mother. And it will be the first of many for you." He placed a tiny velvet pouch upon her palm. "'Tis nought but an amusing, decorative trifle, but I hope you might like it."

She pulled the strings and tipped the pouch onto her glove. "Oh, how lovely!" The silver brooch featured a pair of long-tailed barn swallows perched upon a branch of rose-cut diamonds. "I love watching the aerial performances of these birds and listening to their musical twittering. Thank you." She kissed his cheek. "I shall wear it every day while you are gone."

Then, with most exquisite misery and utter despondency, Darcy and Elizabeth bade one another farewell until they would meet at the altar in fifteen days.

⚜

As Darcy left the assembly room and entered his carriage, he hoped the six Bennet ladies had returned to Longbourn in good spirits.

Good humour was not the case at Netherfield.

"I still do not understand why you went to such bother, Mr Darcy, just to rectify a silly little remark you made to Eliza Bennet eight months ago."

"How would you feel, Miss Bingley, if I said within your hearing that you are not handsome enough to tempt me?"

She gave a ladylike little laugh and smiled beautifully at

him. "But you never would say that of me, sir." At the look on his face, her smile faltered. "Would you?"

When he did not answer, she sniffed. "And what could Eliza have meant by wearing the same dreary gown she wore eight months ago? And you! To have danced with her *twice*, sir! Why, you might as well have declared yourself to the entire assembly! I cannot imagine how you are going to resolve such a conundrum."

❄ 31 ❄

DEARLY BELOVED

On Friday the third of July, wandering along the chalk bourn, away from prying eyes, Elizabeth broke the seal on the first of her letters and opened it. The hint of juniper that wafted outwards and upwards all too soon dissipated in a gentle breeze that, together with the sun, began drying the earth after two days of rain.

Missing Mr Darcy and their daily conversations, which had become so very precious to her, she was a trifle disappointed to perceive only one sheet of letter paper, although it was written quite through, as was the envelope. A se'nnight had passed since their passionate farewell; so, with every expectation of pleasure, she read his words while her feet followed a well-worn path beside the stream.

Pemberley
June 29, 1812
My beloved Elizabeth,
I trust you and your loved ones are in good health. As I am blessed and fortunate enough to count myself

amongst those you love, I assure you I am well.

As must be evident by now, I have arrived home safe and sound. But, despite the bustle within these walls, my home is empty and dull without you. Home has become the place I find only in your company and, particularly, in your arms.

At times, I feel as though I have gone quite mad. What IS that enticing fragrance you wear? I think it must be violet—soft, tender, powdery, romantic. Then I walk through a meadow of clover, and I think of you. Honey and vanilla remind me of the sweet taste of your kiss. Good heavens, even salads of lettuce, apple, and fresh cucumber evoke your freshness. Dare I say that I hunger for you?

Perhaps it is for the best that I have responsibilities occupying much of my time, but thoughts of you—never intrusive, always welcome—frequently distract me from whatever task is at hand. You are with me not only throughout daylight hours but at night when my work is done and I am at leisure to imagine our life together here in this ancestral home. And when I eventually drift into slumber, you are there, too, in my dreams. I cannot escape you, it seems. Not that I want to, I assure you!

Nevertheless, estate matters are being addressed. Sadly, I arrived a day too late to say a last farewell to Mr Ward but not too late to be a pallbearer at my friend's funeral. His nephew is settling into the position for which his uncle trained him, and I am confident all will be well in that regard.

Mrs Reynolds, our housekeeper, is eager to welcome you to your new home. Our preparations are progressing nicely, and we pray that—upon completion—the improvements to Mrs Darcy's apartments will please you. I must admit, Elizabeth, that the very thought of you in those rooms thrills me.

Be forewarned, however, that there has been an unavoidable delay in the installation of a door to connect the master's bedchamber to the mistress's. Shall I ask Mrs Reynolds to prepare guest apartments for you, or would you consider sharing mine for the foreseeable future?

I imagine you now sport an attractive blush upon your cheeks, but I do not mean to make you uncomfortable. I may be reserved—or, as someone once put it, taciturn—but, much like you, I say as I like. Your maidenly modesty is expected, I suppose, but we are, very soon, to be husband and wife.

Helpmates, Elizabeth. You and I. Each of us speaking frankly and contributing to our marriage, to this home, this estate, and, God willing, to our children's well-being and future happiness.

I shall leave you now with those thoughts. Please send me yours in return and assure me all is well and that my candid words have not sent you running for the hills.

Yours for evermore,
Fitzwilliam

Having read Mr Darcy's words for a third time and having blushed only after the first two, Elizabeth placed the letter in her gown's hidden pocket and continued strolling along the stream, trying to imagine a home so far removed from Hertfordshire.

Longbourn

July 4, 1812

My dearest Fitzwilliam—Yes, Mr Darcy, of all my many Fitzwilliams, you are the dearest.

Oh bother! I should cross out that line. I forgot you have relations by the name Fitzwilliam and that I can claim an acquaintance with one of them. Be assured that, while I found Colonel Fitzwilliam quite charming in Kent, in no manner is your cousin dear to me. Strike that. He will become dear to me once we are married. I mean once you and I marry.

Wisely, I shall abandon the above awkward subject matter and mention my appreciation for your letter of the twenty-ninth. I appreciated it so very much that I slept with it beneath my pillow last night, and I have it in my pocket even now. I miss you terribly, Fitzwilliam (terribly as in very much, not terribly as in very badly done), and although the sun finally shines from a blue sky here at Longbourn, for me it is all glumness and gloom without you. How I long for your return and the commencement of our married life together.

Which reminds me...

Another letter arrived yesterday. The message therein, written in an unknown hand, congratulated me on my imminent marriage to such an illustrious personage as yourself. Can you possibly guess, dear sir, who has wished us joy? I shall provide you with several hints. She is a recent acquaintance of ours, and she learnt of our engagement from Mr Hadley. Oh, bother! I should have phrased all that as a charade, for we met the lady at Oakwood during the tournament. Yes, Miss Sophia Kensett, who soon will wed an admirable, worthy gentleman from Ipswich and leave behind her controlling father and brother in Maidenhead.

As glad as I was to learn that Miss Kensett is well pleased with her intended, I am rather delighted with mine. In fact, I am the happiest creature in the world!

I once told you that I desire a marriage with a balance between romance and reason, somewhere betwixt Jane's idealised view of it and Charlotte's more sensible perspective. A marriage founded on both love and good sense. But where, sir, was your good sense when you, the wealthy nephew of a nobleman, offered marriage to a young woman with nothing—neither love nor money nor peerage—to offer in return?

Do you see my dilemma? I cannot imagine life with a nonsensical man, nor can I imagine a life without you. You are too good. Too honourable, too forgiving, too generous. Too self-sacrificing. I do not deserve you. Nor do you deserve a young woman who had not the good sense to accept the aforementioned offer of marriage. So, what are two nonsensical people to do? Shall we abandon reason and good sense and embrace a life of love and romance? What a conundrum!

And what nonsense! See? This is what happens on a Saturday when I have nothing to do but pine for you.

As I write, Jane is with Mama choosing wedding clothes, food for the breakfast, and which flowers from the cutting garden she and I shall carry at our weddings—the weddings of two complying, easy, and generous souls and two nonsensical others.

Now, in all earnestness, sir, I assure you that my love is genuine. I love you for who you are. You are my friend and the love of my life. You know me. And you know I can be brazen. However, a lady must not be quite so brazen as to tell her gentleman how very much she longs for his embraces, kisses, and caresses, or how she cannot wait to become his wife.

And here I shall brazenly answer your question by saying that I have no objection to sharing your bedchamber for the foreseeable future. However, if you snore in a way resembling my father—who can be heard from a mile away—I cannot promise that 'foreseeable' will last beyond one sleepless night.

But, speaking of becoming your blushing bride, I should mention that there is another wedding taking place at St Mary's on the morning of the eleventh. Therefore, ours has been planned for eleven o'clock. I trust that meets with your approval.

Until we meet on that date and at that time, my dearest Fitzwilliam, I remain...

Your nonsensical, brazen, and lovesick,
Elizabeth

⚜

HAPPY WAS THE JULY MORNING THAT ELIZABETH REACHED THE age of majority and married Mr Darcy at St Mary's with Kitty and Georgiana as her attendants and Jane and Mr Bingley as witnesses.

She had not realised it at the time, for she was far too engaged in the business of getting married to glance at a timepiece; but, at the exact moment the vicar pronounced that they be man and wife together, the minute hand had ticked over to eleven past eleven. It had not been planned that way; however, as the elder sister, Jane thought her and Mr Bingley's marriage should be solemnised first.

In the churchyard afterwards, Sir William Lucas—who had, by coincidence, glanced at his watch during the ceremony—gleefully informed Mr and Mrs Darcy that eleven minutes past eleven o'clock was considered a significant moment in time for an event to occur.

Elizabeth thought her husband's expression mirrored her own scepticism, but what had occurred was, indeed, the most significant event of her life.

"I hope to encounter the two of you at St James's now and then," continued Sir William. "And, speaking of such, I was looking forward to seeing some of your noble relations today, Mr Darcy."

"I am afraid my sister was the only family member able to attend, Sir William. My parents, of course, are deceased. Colonel Fitzwilliam is on his way to Upper Canada due to the American war, and his parents, the Earl and Countess of Matlock, are at their estate in Derbyshire. And as you no doubt are aware, and unfortunately for them, Lady Catherine de Bourgh and Anne are unable to grace us with their presence."

Biting her lip, Elizabeth stifled a smile. With one's standing often uppermost on Sir William's mind, her husband had just flaunted his own noble heritage for the Knight Bachelor's benefit.

In a light drizzle, while congratulations and best wishes were extended to both happy couples, Elizabeth's memory captured images of her special day. Mr Darcy, so handsome in a blue coat. Her father and her husband smiling and shaking hands. The mother of the brides lording over everything and everyone. Lydia and Georgiana, arm in arm. Lydia in silk she referred to as her Midsummer gown. Miss Bingley's affectionate and insincere felicitations. Mr Hadley in their midst, no doubt due to Kitty's presence. Jane radiant; Bingley beaming.

All in all, it was a mostly happy group that returned to Longbourn for a lavish breakfast. During the feast, Elizabeth thought her husband bore her family's raucousness with decent composure and admirable forbearance, particularly when her aunt Philips took them aside and dispensed questionable and inappropriate advice about marital felicity. If Mr Darcy squared his shoulders and huffed at her vulgarity, he at least waited until the woman was out of sight and earshot. Doing all she could to shield him from her aunt and mother, Elizabeth directed her husband to those of her family with whom he might converse without mortification.

"I wish we were already at your town house," she whispered.

"*Our* town house, Mrs Darcy."

"Most of all, I look forward to removing from not only Longbourn but London. I hope you plan to take Georgiana and me to Pemberley soon. I long to see the place you so dearly love. Take me home, please, Mr Darcy."

They were gone in under an hour.

Overflowing with love, Elizabeth sat beside her husband on the forward-facing seat. Holding hands, they talked of the day and of those to come.

He truly is the best of men. Giving so much, expecting nothing in return but my love, which I freely give.

"Elizabeth," he whispered when she had grown quiet,

head upon his shoulder. "Are you sleeping? I have something to confess."

"Oh. *Now* you tell me. You keep a mistress, frequent gaming establishments, and have a penchant for spirits."

"No!" He looked aghast. "Nothing so sordid. It is just that... Were I the superstitious sort, eleven might once have been considered an unlucky number for me."

"The number *eleven*? The day of the month on which I was born and the day we wed? *That* eleven?"

"Yes, but I now believe it to be the luckiest of all numbers. Happy birthday, my love."

The morning's drizzle had not ceased; still Mr Darcy drew the curtains across the side-glass.

⚜

To Elizabeth's great relief, her husband did not snore in his sleep. In fact, she doubted he slept at all that first night. Nor had she. Of course, sleeping in an unfamiliar place often results in less sleep than that to which one is accustomed.

Their first excursion outside the town house occurred three days after they were wed, and it was to Pemberton & Monroe on Chancery Lane that they went.

There, Elizabeth's inheritance was discussed in meticulous detail, and ten-thousand-pound dowries were settled on Mary, Kitty, and Lydia. Next, she informed the attorneys that she wished to find someone reputable to lease Oakwood Manor until it might be needed by either a Bennet or a Darcy.

"I only ask that you find a worthy tenant who will appreciate it and care for the house and the gardens as lovingly as Miss Armstrong did."

"You are looking at such a person, Mrs Darcy," said Mr

Monroe. "Grace and I have been hoping to find a place in the countryside. We very much wish to leave the city, and I would like to set up a practice somewhere in or near a small town. Would you consider us?"

Thus, it was settled.

ACKNOWLEDGMENTS

Every time I'm fortunate enough to have a story polished and published by Quills & Quartos, I'm convinced that, along with mine, two other names should appear on the book. And those names are Amy D'Orazio and Jan Ashton. I can stress over storylines and characters and wrack my brain for which words to use; but, thanks to Amy and Jan, my flights of fancy are a reality rather than just abandoned files gathering dust on my computer. Thanks, you two, for believing in me and for being so caring, trustworthy, helpful, and professional. It's a privilege to be part of the Q&Q family.

And where would I be without pep talks—'You can do it, Momzie!'—from daughters Heather and Jessica? Then there's their father, who knows what is implied when I hold up a hand, fingers splayed, palm facing outwards. *Stop talking until I finish typing this thought!* I'm fortunate to have such an understanding husband.

ABOUT THE AUTHOR

Marie Croft (Joanne) is a life-long resident of Nova Scotia, Canada, but spends a lot of time in Regency England with Jane Austen's beloved characters. She has written eleven Austenesque stories. Joanne shares with her husband a love of their adult twin daughters, the great outdoors, and geocaching.

ALSO BY J MARIE CROFT

NOVELS BY J MARIE CROFT
A Golden Opportunity

Enduring Connexions

Whims & Inconsistencies: A Collection Containing Love at First Slight and Whimsical in His Civilities

MULTI-AUTHOR ANTHOLOGIES
Dangerous to Know: Jane Austen's Rakes & Gentlemen Rogues (The Quill Collective)

Elizabeth: Obstinate Headstrong Girl (The Quill Collective)

Mr Darcy's Second Chance

Rational Creatures: Stirrings of Feminism in the Hearts of Jane Austen's Fine Ladies (The Quill Collective)

Sun-Kissed: Effusions of Summer

The Darcy Monologues: A romance anthology of "Pride and Prejudice" short stories in Mr. Darcy's own words (The Quill Collective)

Yuletide: A Jane Austen Inspired Collection of Stories (The Quill Collective)

Printed in Great Britain
by Amazon

58911019R00169